Day of the
Women

and other stories

by

Niko Zinovii

Zinovii Art Studio

Santa Monica, California

chrysos
argyros
chalkos

Published by: Zinovii Art Studio
Santa Monica, California
www.zinoviiartstudio.com

ISBN: 978-0-9860685-0-8   (trade paperback)
ISBN: 978-0-9860685-1-5   (ebook: ePub)
ISBN: 978-0-9860685-2-2   (ebook: mobi)
LCCN: 2015917252

First Edition, 2015
Printed in the United States of America

Day of the Women

and other stories

Dedication

To those who imagine

Contents

Stories

Opening Note from the Author

Contained in this book are twelve tales of speculative fiction that this author wrote from July 2013 to August 2015. They are presented chronologically in the order in which they were written. They can be read in any order.

The title of this book, *Day of the Women*, is the title of one of the novelettes contained within. Of the stories of greatest length in this collection, "Day of the Women" has the strongest or most traditional science-fiction tone.

Niko Zinovii
Santa Monica, CA
15 August 2015

Niko Zinovii

Little Miracle

The future was not what everyone had expected. There were no flying cars, no mile-high skyscrapers. No undersea cities. There was no star travel. Fusion power remained elusive. Advances in computing and nanotechnology had slowed. Physics remained stalled. There had been modest progress in robotics and artificial intelligence, but there were no great new scientific discoveries. The Singularity and its hyper-acceleration of technology had not come. For the longest time, it was simply much of the same.

And so stood man and science, balanced in this spell of listless equilibrium, until the arrival of Little Miracle, which unveiled to all that it was to be an unanticipated change in man, rather than in technology, that would fundamentally transform the entire world. A biotech company had developed a treatment for temporal-lobe epilepsy in the form of a tiny white pill capable of polygene altering. This pill, nicknamed Little Miracle, cured temporal-lobe epilepsy. In addition, it had the beneficial side effects of dramatically improving memory and enhancing intelligence, boosting IQ scores by a minimum of twenty points. It also, unexpectedly, eliminated religiosity and the predisposition to believe in God.

The link between temporal-lobe epilepsy and religiosity had been well known. What became clear with the use of Little Miracle was that the proclivity for religious belief was purely a

3

genetic component of the mind—that is, that man had been programmed by evolution to believe in God. Little Miracle changed this. It subtly altered areas of the brain, including the so-called God-spot—part of the brain's left parietal lobe—after which the brain perceived reality freely, without superstitious interpretation. The psychological need for a God, or gods, was also no longer present. Reality and truth were suddenly seen more clearly.

The use of Little Miracle, despite the vociferous and often violent protests by organized religious groups, had become widespread in record time. People who sought an advantage over others chose enhanced IQ and memory over religiosity. Many took it as an experiment, especially the young, not bothering to consider that its effects were irreversible. Nontheist activists worldwide, after learning that Little Miracle could be dissolved in water without inhibiting its polygene-altering ability, tainted city and bottled water supplies, convinced that the end justified the means. The first target of such calculated subterfuge had been Vatican City State, the Holy See, the maneuver carried out by university students from Milan. And copycats followed, globally.

In short, Little Miracle had become a runaway snowball, a mad wave that swept the planet as the percentage of nonbelievers increased daily, rising in a short time to become the democratic majorities in the developed nations of the world. It was then that the United Nations and the World Health Organization elected to supply the developing world with Little Miracle, free of charge, in an ostensible effort to reduce poverty and decrease war—the first to be accomplished by increasing human capital via boosting IQ, the second by eliminating the tensions and hostilities between humankind's major religions.

Authoritative governments, soon afterward, required their citizenry to consume Little Miracle, in order to keep up with the global IQ race.

Within six short years, Little Miracle had dramatically altered humankind's perception and collective worldview. It had provided man with what was celebrated as a "Great Awakening." God had been vanquished from the Earth. The phenomenon of religion, one of the most dynamic and powerful forces of human history, had been wiped out. Almost. For there were still small, isolated pockets of unaltered religious minds scattered about the globe. The Kung Bushmen in Africa's Kalahari, for example, as well as indigenous tribes deep in the Amazon and in the remote highlands of New Guinea, pockets of Islamic fundamentalists in the mountains of Afghanistan, and isolated others. But these religious minds were but a tiny drop in the vast sea that was humanity—a new humanity that had been forever altered. And people everywhere suddenly felt themselves collectively ready to face a new human future, one without superstition: a future without the need to recognize a pantheon of gods, or the single God.

But humankind had so easily forgotten that in any situation involving man and nature there is always the quality of the unpredictable, due to elements unforeseen by our limited understanding. New humanity was instantly reminded of this when something utterly puzzling happened. God appeared. And it (God) was unlike anything imagined by man.

Recommendations

• This author recommends to readers who are interested in learning more about belief in the supernatural being explained as a phenomenon of the human mind to survey the growing body of literature on this matter, as it is intriguing.

A Note from the Author

"Little Miracle" is a vignette that this author teased out of the prologue of his 2012 science fiction novel, *The God Antenna*.

Niko Zinovii
Santa Monica, California
5 July 2013

Niko Zinovii

Just Add Water

They're going about it all wrong, thought the professor as he slowly walked away from Pan Cryonics Incorporated. "Nope," he said to himself, half making up his mind, but still not certain, "I'm not signing up with them. Or with any of the others."

Stepping off the electric sidewalk, he obstinately refused to use it. Despite his advanced age, he still enjoyed the exercise of walking, the sheer physicality of it. Besides, the lawn felt soft and good beneath his tired feet.

As he walked on, he looked about reflectively. How this city had changed, he thought. He had grown up here, played here as a boy in this very neighborhood. But that was a long, long time ago. Now he could barely recognize any of it, except for...

The professor blinked in the bright sunlight and slowly turned his gaze toward the old cemetery that lay across the street, green and inviting with its quiet gardens and serene ponds. *Only old cemeteries now,* his thoughts rambled. *Old graves. No new ones. No one's had themself buried now in what, well, it must be half a century now, I guess. Yes, it was just a little over fifty years ago, when man abandoned religion as a path to immortality, to place his hope in science instead...*

Walking into the cemetery, the professor sighed in relief as he sat his weary, old bones down upon a soft pine bench. He sat there in silence for a long moment, feeling as anachronistic as the grounds around him. For even in today's scientifically advanced world, where one could honeymoon on the moon or vacation to Mars, he knew that it was rare indeed for anyone to reach the ripe old age of 150, which he had turned yesterday.

The wet lick on his hand pulled his focus back to the here and now. Petting the lean stray dog, he looked into its gentle brown eyes and saw a kindred creature perhaps as old as he was—if one calculated in dog years, that was.

"Everyone's fooling themselves," the professor said to the old hound as he gently scratched the mutt behind its floppy ears. "Freezing their bodies like that. After they die. Banking on some yet-to-be-developed future technology to one day not only revive them but also repair all the cellular damage."

The old dog closed its eyes, enjoying the petting and the warm sunlight that settled upon them.

"You see," the professor continued in his even tone, "when water freezes, it expands. Everyone knows that. Ice crystals form. Cell walls burst. Remember, the human body is 75% water. Sure, they say they give you a choice. Pan Cryonics pumps you full of patented chemicals, to eliminate the ice damage, claiming that future science will solve the problems created by their toxic solutions. And the others, the bargain-rate ones, well, they just freeze you, claiming that future science will solve the problem created by the ice damage. Humph. What if the nanotechnology required is never developed? Or has limitations? No. No, freezing isn't the answer. It simply won't work. There's no difference between the millions and millions of bodies lying frozen stiff at Pan… and the bodies lying here in this cemetery."

And a longing sadness swelled up in his eyes. Rising, he walked deeper into the cemetery, the dog following. He turned left here, right there. He knew where he was going. Although he didn't visit there often.

Deep within the magnificent landscape of loneliness, he stood there, over his wife's grave. It felt odd to him, surreal. He *knew* she was there, but he *felt* that she wasn't there. Not at all. He couldn't sense her, not in any way. To him, she was only in the past. Entirely lost to him, except for his memories of her.

The hound's ears lifted slightly as the professor unexpectedly began to sing softly, pensively, to his departed wife, in loving memory of her. He had a nice voice, filled this moment with the truer emotions of the heart.

"Do you re-mem-ber, long time a-go?
I sneaked you kiss-es, when the lights went down low.
And I still won-der, nights all a-lone,
I sure do miss you, oh I wi-sh that I'd known.
I dream of the old gang, the plac-es we went.
Drink-in' and dan-cin', till the moon-light was spent.
Long times of laugh-ter, of love and of song,
I sure do miss you, all the ni-ghts seem so long.
Now we're gow-in' ol-der, the good times are gone.
We've on-ly our mem-ries, left to help us a-long.
I can't help feel sad-ness, as time speeds on by,
I sure do miss you, can't help this tear in my eye.
I sure do miss you, and I wi-ll till I die."

As the collage of memories swept through the professor's mind, he smiled in reverie, deciding finally to embrace his personal suspicion that all those memories, all those moments, must still exist somewhere in reality, locked within the fabric of time. That time itself was actually somehow akin to individual pages of a great book, a book without beginning or end, its pages continuing on forever into the past and off into the unknown future. He had not really lost her, not entirely. He was just presently separated from her. But rather than by spatial distance, it was by *time*. He was presently further down the timeline, in a future chapter of time's infinite book, a chapter that came after their pages spent together—after the pages that marked her upper *boundary* in time, which she could not pass beyond. But they were still together, right now, simultaneously alive in those prior pages of the past. Sharing all those moments, forever living them all simultaneously, although unknowingly, on those different pages of time. Pages turning but never being destroyed. Pages existing forever. His past self would always have those past pages. His past self, being locked in those past pages. But his present self... He must look to the pages ahead. To the future. Only to the future.

The professor crumpled up his Pan Cryonics brochure and dropped it upon the grass. And it felt good to do so. In fact, he felt rather triumphant, in a way. Suddenly, he couldn't wait to get back to his laboratory. To look down through his microscope, down at Rip Van Winkle, his tiny pet waterbear.

Leaving the cemetery with renewed vitality in his stride, he took no notice of the old hound following quietly at his heels.

~

"Oh," the professor said when he finally did notice the dog, after the two of them were already inside his laboratory, which was nested within the large greenhouse behind his home.

"I guess you're a bit lonely for company," the professor went on, scratching the dog behind its ears. "And maybe curious about me also. Maybe as curious as I've been about my waterbear."

And the professor sat himself and peered down through his binocular microscope. Down into a petri dish containing water, moss, lichen, and one miniscule waterbear aptly named Mr. Winkle.

"Mr. Winkle is 150 years old," said the professor, grinning at the irony of their identical ages. "I found him by accident, in a museum specimen of old, dried-up moss. He was essentially completely dehydrated. Dead, but not truly dead. More in a lifeless state of suspended animation. When I added water to the moss, he was... recalled to life.

"He swelled up. Rehydrating. His eight stubby legs paddling about. So cute, squishy. You'd never think he was virtually indestructible. The most extreme survivor on our planet. Kingdom: Animalia; phylum: Tardigrada... A micro-animal of an ancient group. Its lineage extending all the way back to the Cambrian."

The professor turned his attention back to the dog. "You see," he went on, "when things get too difficult for Mr. Winkle, too dry, or too hot, say above 300 °F, or too cold, say below minus 300 °F, he just lies down and loses nearly all the water from his body. And he stays that way. Until conditions improve."

The dog whined softly, and the professor reached out an arthritic hand, gently stroking the old hound. "There, there," the professor's words grew soft as he comforted the dog with his genuine and compassionate touch. And the dog slowly sat, and then lay down, tired, old. Yet content and comfortable.

It was at that moment, at that instant, that the professor suddenly knew that today would be the day. *Yes*, he thought, *why wait until an end by natural causes?* Some painful end. Possibly filled with agony, or worse, humiliation. Why not now? When he was reasonably comfortable, content. For he had lived out a long, good life. His pages in time composed a good book. Had not Plato's Socrates spoken of a good death being dying in comfort and control, with courage, in peace, at an old age?

Yes, the professor was now suddenly ready to surrender himself to his great experiment. And possibly to life's greatest mystery as well.

"They're all wrong. I'm sure of it," he whispered, reassuring himself one last time. "I'll show them."

With these final words, he stepped over to what resembled an oversized, futuristic casket. Crawling into its wide, comfortable interior, he lay down on his back. As he relaxed, preparing himself to surrender his consciousness... with a wonder of supreme mystery, he felt the old hound crawl up into the casket to join him, curling up at his feet. The professor didn't object. For some reason it seemed right. It felt right. It felt good.

And so he watched as the heavy glass lid gently and silently closed down atop them, pneumatically sealing the airtight casket with a reassuring hiss. As the invisible medical mist, of the professor's own invention, filled the chamber, the professor inhaled its secrets. The air grew rarified and he felt his skin slowly begin to tighten about his face, due to the commencement of the "Winkle Drying Process." It didn't hurt. There was no pain. Only a calm tiredness that descended upon him. A feeling of very slowly drifting off to sleep, thoughts wandering.

He thought of how he wanted to see more of life. Wondering what the world of a hundred years hence would be like. What wonders lay ahead? What marvels? A hopeful, relaxed smile rose on his lips. His final thought being: *If hope is truly the last thing to die in a man, then I should soon be like my tiny little waterbear: not truly dead. For I still have hope.*

Reaching down to pet the dog, he felt his hand grow still. Before closing his eyes, for perhaps the last time ever, he read the words printed on the casket's glass lid. From his inside perspective the letters were all reversed, but he knew what they said:

To resurrect me

Just add water

A Note from the Author

Preservation of the human body, to prepare it for *another* life, is an idea that extends all the way back to ancient Egypt. The impetus for this story was the thought of presenting, in fictional guise, an alternative idea to that of today's cryonics. Namely, dehydrating the body instead of freezing it, in order to circumvent the ravages of ice damage or toxicity. This author wanted to advocate taking the cue from nature's real-life waterbear instead of the natural precedent associated with cryonics, i.e., specific fish and frogs that can survive freezing. Thus, the foundation idea of "Just Add Water."

The ideas expressed in "Just Add Water" on time are those of the fictional professor alone, and are not shared by this author. If a reader is curious about time, this author recommends looking into the interesting and thought-provoking recent speculations of physicist Julian Barbour.

This author would like to thank his brother, Taylor, for suggesting the title "Just Add Water."

The song "I Sure Do Miss You" is one of a number of songs written by this author's father.

Incidentally, this story was written one quiet, sunny afternoon in Hotchkiss Park, Santa Monica, where this author, pen and paper in hand, shared an old park bench, for an hour or so, with a friendly and inquisitive squirrel.

Niko Zinovii
Santa Monica, California
24 December 2013

Niko Zinovii

The Transfer Mechanism

David had traveled tirelessly all night to reach Malta, hoping that the remote shores of this archaic isle would somehow bring to him a needed sense of calm. Yet now that he had arrived, he only felt the grip of his own cool, almost desperate sanity trying to ground him. He still believed that he had been followed since his departure from Moscow. He had absolutely no proof of this, yet he felt certain of it, and so he continued to fear for his life.

Silent and absorbed, David found his thoughts adrift, his mind continuing to fight against accepting the magnitude of the events of the past week. Events that had left him shaken, unsure, in doubt, wondering if anyone in their right mind would believe his remarkable story, take him seriously, he a mere tourist, an obscure thirty-eight-year-old psychiatrist, undistinguished within his profession, on an extended holiday from his dreary little practice in Upstate New York. Nevertheless, he clung to the hope of convincing one specific man.

~

It was midday by the time David finally reached the rural countryside where he knew he would find the villa of the man he sought. Peddling his rented bicycle across the scenic landscape, he periodically glanced backward, in fear, paying little attention to the corbelled stone huts and crumbling walls of rubble that decorated the ancient terraced fields and agrarian openness. Even the menacing dog that chased David halfway across the land's time-worn, sprawling cemetery failed to really distract him, although he imagined he continued to hear barking long after he had distanced himself from the animal.

~

When he finally reached the secluded villa that was his destination, he no longer felt a stripped-down man, not totally—the exercise had cleared his thoughts, focused his sense of purpose. But still, when he knocked, he did so softly, diffidently. After a time, the knotted pine door opened slowly, revealing an elderly housemaid garbed in traditional Maltese dress, dark in color and loosely draped.

"Hello, I'm Dr. Time," David introduced himself, his voice calmer than he was. "David Time. I'm here to see Dr. Azov. Dr. Mikhail Azov. I called two days ago."

The woman responded in Maltese, the Sicilian and Arabic origins of her native tongue seemingly rooting her language to the dry earth, the sound of her words and the cadence of her voice conjuring up mental images of old ruins, forgotten customs, and even myth.

Repeating herself, she pointed an arthritic finger to the worn stone path that unevenly wound its way toward the back of the villa, where it disappeared into the overgrown greenery of trees of ash and holm oak, Maltese pines, and a magnificent flowering Judas tree.

David stopped as he cleared the trees and stepped into the garden behind the villa. There, hunched over, his bare back to David, was Dr. Mikhail Azov, working an old hoe, tilling and chopping up the dark, root-filled soil of a stretch of newly exposed earth. The man was in his seventies, yet sinews of muscle still bunched up in his back, shoulders, and neck as he worked the ground, his arms extending down to strong, calloused hands.

So, David found himself thinking, *this is the amazing Mikhail Azov.* David then struggled to reconcile the strikingly different aspects of this man. Russia's long-ago but still-unforgotten, and in fact now legendary, Greco-Roman wrestling champion and strongman. "The man with the iron grip." "The Russian Hercules." "The Russian Lion." And then, later in life, a celebrated Nobel laureate for his brilliant work in particle physics…

David remained silent as the Russian physicist slowly turned to him, as if having somehow sensed his presence. David could not help his curious stare, for although the Russian was well past his prime, his physique still displayed strong echoes of his old athletic prowess. Out of modesty, the man retrieved his shirt, which rested nearby.

He then smiled a lopsided, generous smile and strode toward David with a calm, friendly sway in his walk. His countenance was humble, earthy, with no trace of egotism. His thinning, flowing hair had long since turned silvery white. His eyebrows were bushy, his ears cauliflowered, his expression sentimental, congenial.

"To live far from men," the Russian said as he approached, his accent thick, his voice warm, genuine, "and not to need them. But to still love them."

David found himself being quietly appraised by the Russian's unusual steady gaze. Baltic blue eyes seemed to tell David: *It's okay. I'm benign. I won't hurt you. You're safe with me.* And David felt himself relax for the first time in days. It was only then that David noticed how peaceful and surreal the garden setting was. The cooling shade of the oaks, the susurration of the wind gently blowing through the surrounding trees, and how the sound lingered there, invisibly, accenting the soothing ripples that flowed continuously across the garden's pond. The old chapel mirroring its reflection off the water. The distant view of seaside cliffs and open sea. The heavy scent from the wildflowers and fruit trees. The butterflies flapping about lazily in the hazy beams of sunlight.

"Something about this place…" David heard himself comment aloud, his voice low, almost reverent. "It's so peaceful. Sheltered. Hidden away from the turmoil of the rest of the world. I feel that I should whisper here."

"A good place to garden," Mikhail answered, still smiling, pleased to have a visitor. "To work the earth, to think. To be alone with memories. Even to hide from memories."

David just looked at him.

"It's true," the Russian explained, soberly, "I have the stars above, the land to my left, the sea to my right. But I am not living in a fairy tale."

And David perceived in this man the sense of loss, of a sadness that sometimes comes after bright accomplishments fade into the past and are overtaken by later failures, regrets, and an existence of the mundane, of isolation and loneliness.

David extended a hand. "Dr. David Time; please call me David. Thank you for agreeing to my visit."

"And you can call me Mikhail," the Russian reciprocated, shaking hands. "But I still do not know what I can do for you. What you want of me. You said very little on the phone."

"Your son," David answered. "He is the Russian prime minister."

"Yes," Mikhail acknowledged, his smile dropping.

"There's something he needs to know," David explained. "Something I need to tell him."

"So why not go to him?" Mikhail answered, his mood altering further—an old wound opened.

"I tried to," David responded carefully. "But I couldn't get past the gatekeepers."

Mikhail just looked at David for a long moment, and then: "I have not spoken to my son in over ten years. I am no longer political."

David felt his own unease, his sense of hopelessness, returning full force. He opened his mouth but failed to speak.

"It's hot," Mikhail finally said, sympathetically, recovering his genuine congeniality. "Let us go inside. Besides, it looks like it might thunder." And the old man placed a fatherly hand on David and led him into the villa.

Inside, Mikhail walked straight to his liquor cabinet. "You drink with me?" he asked, smiling his amiable lopsided smile. "This is the nicest vodka in the world. Distilled by me, from potatoes in my garden."

David smiled, nodded, and Mikhail poured vodka, straight, warm, and they downed the drinks together in silence. Motioning for David to sit, the old-time strongman-turned-scientist sat across from him.

David noticed the Russian guitar on the wall. "Do you play?" he asked.

Mikhail's eyes sparkled with an endearing quality. "I do little else these days."

"Would you play," David asked, "for me?"

Mikhail appraised David again, with his charming, unwavering gaze. He then smiled warmly and poured two more drinks. "Remember," he playfully warned David, "you asked me to do this."

And the old Russian Lion, the man with the legendary iron grip, sat and began to play, his strong hands and calloused fingers remarkably adroit. "You are American?"

David nodded, thinking about his host, wondering if everything came easy to this man who had long ago been an extraordinary athlete, one of the strongest of all men, and then later rose to become a preeminent scientist of the world, one of the smartest of all men, and now, a man who displayed unexpected and impressive musical talent as well.

"I think you are old enough to remember what happened," Mikhail said. "So there is no need for an introduction. It happened in your state of Texas. In Waco."

Mikhail closed his eyes for a moment and then began to play something in particular. Strumming strings, songlike, he unexpectedly began to sing. His voice was surprisingly melodious. As he sang, his warm voice deepened, filling with the stronger emotions of the heart that his music conveyed: love, regret, loss.

"There's a la – dy I know,
I – n old Mex – i – co,
Who's been wait-ing and wait-ing to hear.
From her sen-ior in Wa – co,
Who makes her heart glow,
She waits sur – roun-ded by fear.
She looks up to the Hea- vens,
And prays to the An-gels,
Then she lights can- dles and cries.
Well there's one thing I know,
Lo-ve just won't let go,
She re- members the happ- i- er years.
Then the Gov-ern-ment played games,
They all went up in flames,
All she's got left are some tears.
May the Hea- vens ac-cept them,
And for – give the may-hem,
And pardon those a – gents some day."

Mikhail went on playing for a few moments more, until the instrumental of the song ended.

"I thought you said you weren't political," David commented, surprised and also touched by the lyrics.

"Not in action," Mikhail answered. "No more. Now, only in art. The result of confinement. Of my exile. And disappointment."

David just watched this intriguing, charming man as he poured them another drink. He thought of Mikhail's fall from politics. Of his forced exile, of his quasi-imprisonment here on Malta after the revolution that he had led failed.

No, thought David, *not everything has come easy to this man. Not acceptance of his banishment, of the circumstances of his defeat. But did he really believe that scientists could replace politicians? That Russia could endure another great social experiment and transform itself into some utopia ruled by its scientists?*

"And now," Mikhail said as he returned and sat back down, "I think it is time for us to talk."

"Yes," David responded, unable to resist Mikhail's inquisitive smile, accepting that the moment had come, that he could delay no further. So he came right out with it: "Could reincarnation be a real phenomenon, one that has been poorly observed and left unexplained?"

Mikhail sat there stonily silent for a moment, for a third time casting his steady, appraising gaze on David. Finally: "But what could serve as the storage facility? And the transfer mechanism?"

"I thought you would just say I was crazy and walk away," David confessed, breathing a sigh of relief.

"Is it necessary for me to say that I do not believe in reincarnation?" Mikhail responded, good-natured. "That I believe everything has a rational explanation?"

"But..." David thought out loud, "there are many who do believe in reincarnation."

"The fact that a belief is widely held is not evidence that it is true. In fact, most widespread beliefs are more foolish than rational."

"What about case studies?" David asked. "Convincing cases of past-life experiences? Cases studied by psychiatrists, using hypnosis?"

Mikhail leaned forward. "Careful not to make the mistake of making things so simple. Look under the hood and you will find uncertainties, falsehoods, absurdities, unknowns, unfounded speculations. Even outright lies."

"And truth?" David asked. "Where is it?"

"To find the truth, you must doubt," Mikhail answered. "It is the only way. Doubting is essential to science. Far more important than believing. You must doubt. You must doubt what others tell you. What you read. The results of your experiments. Even what your own reasoning tells you to believe."

David felt the rushing return of the uncertainty and doubt that had shaken his intellect so. "But what happens after death? Could we ever come back?"

Mikhail's reply, when it finally came, was very gentle, yet firm and final. "David, all ideas must be tested by experiment and observation. We then build on only those ideas that pass the tests. We must reject those that do not. If we do this, and follow the evidence, doubting and questioning everything, only then can the 'truth' be won. Only science can properly lead us forward. Only science."

And David sat there in silence, nodding in agreement, yet disturbed.

"Each year," Mikhail went on, "a scientist must appraise many new ideas. Treating each with doubt. Using his education, his experience to evaluate the idea. In this appraisal, a scientist must also consider the source…"

And David looked up. The moment that he had feared had arrived. Why would anyone believe him, what he had to say?

"There is more," Mikhail determined. "More that you are not telling me. Is that not right? You should tell me."

David suddenly felt that perhaps he should instead remain silent. He wondered to himself, *Have I really come all this way to now elect to keep secret that which I sought to divulge?*

Mikhail slowly leaned back in his seat, giving David space. "In the early 1900s," the Russian then said genially, "the German geophysicist Alfred Wegener proposed a new idea. Continental drift. The world refused to accept it. No mechanism was then known that could account for the movement of entire continents. Plate tectonics was unknown. Science had to wait, to discover the mechanism that would later explain Wegener's observations.

"David, we do not know everything today. And we live in a strange universe. So, although I am a great skeptic, I have long ago learnt to use the word 'impossible' with great caution. I try to have an open mind."

David found himself surrendering to his host's friendly and coaxing smile, and so he began his story. He described how he had met a Russian psychotherapist, Anton Solovev, at a seminar in Moscow, last year. How Anton had visited him and his wife in New York on several subsequent occasions. How he became close friends with Anton.

"The nature of Anton's work," David went on, "was past-life investigation. He worked in a hypnosis center, in Moscow. We had only spoken about his work briefly, on a few occasions. I think he sensed my skepticism, my disinterest in the subject. I hadn't heard from him in a month or so, and then I got the call. He didn't sound quite himself. It was as if he was under some great stress. He asked me to fly to Moscow, said that he needed someone whom he could trust. A psychiatrist. A skeptic. He needed an unbiased, psychiatric-based opinion from a neutral observer.

"Tourism still seemed reasonably safe in Russia, despite the politics. And my wife, she told me that I looked like I could use a vacation. And she reminded me that the baby wasn't due for another month. And that after the baby was born, well, that she would want me around. So I flew off to Moscow.

"Anton showed me a file on a young woman who was undergoing hypnotherapy. The hypnosis sessions revealed evidence of a past-life incarnation. Meticulous research verified details from the sessions with real-life records. Everything matched perfectly. The woman could only recall her past life when under hypnosis. When recalled from her trance, she remembered nothing. It didn't appear that she was pulling a hoax. She seemed quite normal, although distressed by a recurrent nightmare, which she couldn't remember upon waking. Anton had hoped to find and examine the experience that he believed formed the root of her current suffering. He believed this experience lay in a past life.

"Anton had me sit in on her last session," David continued, his voice starting to show signs of stress. "I had never experienced anything like this. It was so convincing. When under, she would actually speak as the person of her past life. Answering any question correctly. She gave names, dates, she described places, events, people… It was uncanny. Later, all the details were verified.

"During that final session, Anton revealed to me the source of her recurrent nightmares. It was her memory of her murder, in her past life. The memory of her execution."

"Execution?" Mikhail asked.

"Yes." David nodded, steadying himself as he revealed the unbelievable. "This young woman's past-life regression revealed her to be... She claimed to be..."

Mikhail simply waited for it, his attention focused entirely on David.

And so David just came out with it: "Anastasia Nikolaevna Romanova. The daughter of Tsar Nicholas II, last tsar of Imperial Russia. Anastasia, her father, her mother, her sisters, they were all shot dead by the Cheka, the Bolshevik secret police, on July 17, 1918."

"I know the history," Mikhail responded, disappointed.

And Mikhail stood and poured them another drink. "David"—he made sure that his guest saw his smile as he went on—"my time is still reasonably valuable. I must tell you honestly, I do not consider your story to have any chance of validity. None. What is it you really want? Why have you come here?"

"This young woman," David explained, "she's your son's daughter. Your granddaughter. Polina."

"My Polya?" Mikhail slowly sat back down.

David nodded silently, allowing Mikhail time to absorb this.

"She is ill?" Mikhail asked, deeply concerned. "Mentally?"

David shook his head.

"The human mind," Mikhail mumbled slowly, thinking it out aloud, "it can sometimes work in strange and labyrinthine ways—"

"There's more," David interrupted. "Anton was killed. Murdered."

David stood, wrapped his arms about himself, an attempt at self-comfort, and began to pace. "I—I witnessed the murder," he continued. "It was late. I was at the center, waiting for Anton to return. He rushed in, frightened. Couldn't catch his breath. He had been running. He led me to a back office, pushed me into a closet. Went to a desk, retrieved a gun. But it was too late. This man grabbed him. A tall, bony man, but so strong. Brutal. Vicious. He, um, he beat Anton to death."

"And you watched this happen?" Mikhail asked gently.

David nodded.

"... You didn't help your friend?"

"No, I, um"—David dropped back down into his seat, exhausted—"I couldn't move. I was... too afraid. Too afraid. I'm not a strong man."

Mikhail placed a fatherly hand on David's knee. "I had always hoped for a son," he said, "who would have been more like you."

David looked up at Mikhail, shocked.

"It takes strength," Mikhail explained, sympathetically, "to admit such weakness. Rather than hide it behind actions and words that are not truly your own..."

Mikhail stood back up, shook off something from the past, paced, and then turned back to David. "Why?" he asked. "Why did this man kill your friend?"

"From what I was able to piece together," David replied, still a bit weak, "the Russian president, President Kulikov, his re-election is coming up. The opposition, the new communist party, it's very strong. I understand their candidate has a very good chance of winning the presidency. Kulikov, anything that might come out that the press could spin negatively... A prime minister's daughter who thinks she's a living Romanov. Kulikov's people, somehow they found out about the hypnotherapy. And they had Anton killed. I barely got out alive. Your granddaughter—I believe her life's in danger."

"Oh no..." Mikhail sat back down, his face etched by the deepest concern, torn by ragged helplessness, and distorted by a weary, haunting disappointment in humanity. "And they wonder why I led a revolt. With the virtue of science to be the instrument of change. No more criminal politicking, no more state crimes, no more deceptions, only truth would have been embraced."

It became all too clear to David that Mikhail had found no peace in his garden, its beauty serving only to keep the man's painful memories and brooding frustrations at bay. His disappointments and passions, they had never died; they had only been bottled, laid dormant by the crushing weight of his forced exile to Malta.

"Only science," Mikhail asserted wearily, almost dazed, as if declaring it again despite having been beaten into near submission, "can lead man toward a better future. Never politicking. Science does not attempt to ignore, distort, hide, or spin the truth. No... It brings truth into the light. To attain transparency. To clarify what are the real issues. To attain the deeper understanding necessary to offer real solutions; to solve real problems..."

David thought of what it must have been like for Mikhail, to have been toppled, dragged before a court, tried for sedition, insurrection—treason against the state. The death sentence only stayed because of a plea for clemency coming from a rising brutal political figure on the side of the neo-fascist presiding powers. With what mixed emotions did Mikhail greet his sentencing of life in exile until death, knowing that the plea had come from his own son, the soon-to-be prime minister of the very fascist establishment that he had revolted against?

Mikhail's speech slowed and he steadied himself as reality tugged him back, and he realized all too well his inescapable situation, his hopeless exile and solitude. His imprisonment on Malta.

"Political issues are complex," Mikhail appealed his old case resignedly, solemnly, solely to David, "but rarely as deep as the problems science continually faces and conquers. Science is far better equipped than politicking to make public policy. To solve political problems. Societal problems. I offered my country rational order. And they cast me out…"

David just looked at him, caught up in the powerful intimacy of the moment.

"As I grow still older," Mikhail slowly added, "it becomes more and more obvious to me. It is not starvation, not microbes, not cancer—but man himself who is mankind's greatest danger. Reason does not help man. Man has no adequate psychic protection against the emotions and needs behind politics.

"Perhaps it is a hopeless cause. Man's irrationality… His criminal politicking, perhaps this is engrained into the very dynamics of the universe itself. Physical laws gave rise to chemistry. Allowed biology to arise. Which gave rise to populations. Then economics. And then politics. Man, the political animal. Man, the irrational…"

Mikhail rose, steadying himself. "I must warn my son," he mumbled. "For Polina's sake."

David placed a hand on Mikhail, stopping him from leaving. "Wait," he said. "Mikhail, if Polina was reincarnated, if it is somehow true, the repercussions are staggering. If people reincarnate after death, endlessly. If I am born again and again… Is there any way that this could be true?"

David shrank as he felt Mikhail's wise eyes scrutinize him. He wondered if Mikhail could guess at the reasons behind his distressed insistence on obtaining some answer to this question.

"If science had to guess," David pleaded, weakening under Mikhail's searching look, realizing the transparency of his desperate need for an answer, a speculation, something.

It was startling how the housemaid, at that moment, then stepped into the room before them, tottered, and dropped dead, her head turned completely around, her neck twisted, broken like a rag doll.

As they stood there, frozen in shock, Anton's tall, bony assassin appeared, slowly stepping up beside the corpse, pistol in hand, his presence confirming David's suspicions of having been followed.

David felt a shiver run through him as he saw this man in the light for the first time. The man's head and face were eerily distorted by acromegalic features—thickenings and elongations that made him appear thuggish and cruel in a surreal manner. His hands were likewise abnormally large, bony, brutish. Like his prominent skeleton, accentuated by his thinness. He was a gaunt, inhuman, demi-giant out of some dark, forgotten nightmare.

"It's the man… who killed Anton…" David murmured.

The brute pointed his weapon at David and appeared to grin, but it was difficult to tell for sure.

Mikhail stepped in front of David, shielding David with his body.

"You enter my home," Mikhail said slowly, steadily, with a fixed stare, "take my servant's life. Threaten the life of my guest. And what next, my granddaughter too?"

The dead housemaid's arm twitched. In the ensuing moment of distraction, Mikhail slapped the assassin's gun from his hand. It bounced once and then disappeared under a heavy armoire.

The killer slowly and silently stepped back and then moved stalkingly around the dead woman. His droopy eyes flicking to the armoire.

Mikhail stepped between the armoire and the intruder.

31

"No," Mikhail said, his voice defiant, steadfast.

But the man shoved Mikhail back into David and rushed to recover the gun.

David found himself knocked backward and to the floor, rolling upon the carpet. It was out of his peripheral vision that he saw Mikhail grabbing and locking up one of the assassin's long arms in some improvised Greco-Roman hold, preventing the man from reaching the armoire.

The thug clawed at Mikhail's face in retaliation and then grabbed Mikhail by the neck, digging in huge bony fingers, choking, strangling. Mikhail released his hold, but then surprisingly took the man's wrists, pulling them in close, locking up his adversary's arms. Shifting, Mikhail next grabbed the man above an elbow and yanked, toppling the killer off balance, bringing him crashing to the floor, trapping him in a Greco-Roman headlock, straining to somehow maintain the hold.

"The gun," Mikhail called out to David. "The... gun..."

David's eyes looked for the gun. Was it retrievable? There, deep beneath the armoire, against the wall. Yes, perhaps he could reach it. But then David heard Mikhail groan out in pain. He looked back to the fight and witnessed the gaunt giant sending knee after knee smashing into Mikhail's torso. The attack was horrific, followed by a rain of relentless bony fists pummeling Mikhail's back and sides, beating ferociously down upon his ribs, liver, spleen, and kidneys. But Mikhail somehow held the headlock.

David tried to turn his eyes away, but found that he could not. And he shivered as he once again felt himself hidden away in Anton's closet, just watching, watching and doing nothing to help his friend, too afraid to even move. *And now I must watch this great man die too?* David heard his inner voice cry out.

"David?" Mikhail strained as his grip weakened.

Mikhail then noticed David's frozen state. There would be no help from his guest. No gun. Mikhail thought for a long moment, as if struggling with what he must do next. But there was really no choice.

"This is what you force... me to do," Mikhail said to the assassin, plain faced, emotionally detached. "To stop you." And Mikhail released his hold on the man's elongated head, securing the grip again after shifting downward to apply the necessary choke hold. And Mikhail began to squeeze.

The intruder must have understood what was coming, as he flailed wildly, in a mad panic, swinging desperate fists into Mikhail's head and back, struggling to push the old Russian strongman off him, to break the death hold. But Mikhail's legendary iron grip did not fail, and his embrace only constricted—like a python's.

It took less than a minute before the bony giant could no longer inhale, no longer breath. Mikhail continued to hold the choke until he felt the pulse in the man's neck stop. He then released the dead, limp brute and rose, wobbling on his feet.

"David?" Mikhail trembled from the exertion as he made his way over to his guest. "Are you all right?"

David nodded as he rose, ashamed, speechless.

Mikhail placed a fatherly hand upon David's shoulder, and then staggered and collapsed against the grandfather clock behind him. David tried to keep him upright, but the old Russian was too heavy for him to support, and so David slowly collapsed down with him until they both sat on the floor.

"Warn my Polya," Mikhail breathed slowly, wincing in pain.

"I will," David answered. "I swear it, I will."

"Thank you."

"I'm sorry," David apologized, "I'm so sorry."

"No," Mikhail responded with a gentle smile. "Do not think less of yourself."

And for a few moments Mikhail just lay there, his breathing labored, looking at David.

"Virtue…" Mikhail finally said, "… I hope virtue… has a place in the future…"

The grandfather clock started to chime. By the third and final bell, Mikhail's blue eyes went lifeless.

~

It was not until after the Maltese police had safely escorted David to the airport and placed him upon his outbound flight that he found he could think clearly. It was deeply satisfying for him to know that Mikhail's son, accompanied by his daughter Polina, was en route to Malta, and that the island's authorities had told the Russian prime minister everything. And that the prime minister had taken measures to ensure Polina's safety.

But as the jet lifted off, David thought of Anton, and of Mikhail, and his insides churned at the self-admittance of his own cowardliness. This admittance was hardly cathartic, however; it only deepened the disturbance still working havoc in his mind. For he had withheld from telling Mikhail what had really shaken him, disturbed him, down to the very core of his being. Anton had discovered that all cases of reincarnation that displayed convincing validity appeared to have one factor in common: the reincarnated person had meet death valiantly.

If reincarnation was a reality—and David had become convinced that it was—and if only the valiant lived again, David knew that he would not be coming back. He knew he lacked the required bravery. It would be only darkness for him.

What could serve as the storage facility? And the transfer mechanism? Mikhail's initial questions echoed in David's consciousness, and a passing thought came to him. He knew it was sheer nonsense, and that he should dismiss it at once, but his mind held on to it and the idea lingered. Could the transfer mechanism be something intangible? Something that a rational man, a scientific man would never consider? Could it be a quality, a state of mind? Could it be courage? As unreasonable as it sounded, could it somehow be true? But, even if possible, what could then serve as the storage facility?

David's head spun. Exhausted, he fell into a slumber, his unconscious mind seeing images of Anton, Polina, and Mikhail. Plummeting into deeper sleep, he dreamed fitfully of the gaunt assassin, and then of distorted images of Plato's allegory where people lived shackled in a cave, forced to face a blank wall, seeing only the shadows flickering on this wall, cast by a fire behind them, a fire whose existence they were unaware of. David's unconscious mind twisted these shadows into every shape imaginable, and confusion and disorder reigned. These shadows were as close as one would ever get to witnessing reality. Yet these shadows were but only a reflection of the smallest portion of reality.

~

Although it was late, David took a cab directly from the airport to the hospital.

At the hospital, by the time he finally found the correct ward, he felt himself physically weak and mentally fatigued due to the strain of recent events. He was not a strong man. Twice he walked into the wrong room, and he may have done so again if a nurse had not physically taken him by the arm and escorted him to his wife's private room.

He found his wife asleep, so he quietly walked past her, navigating his way through the semidarkness of the room, moving over toward their newborn, who had arrived early while he had been away. The fact that the baby was being kept in the same room was a good sign, for although premature, obviously their baby was healthy and not in need of special care.

As David grew nearer and he could begin to make out the baby in the dimness, he suddenly felt his weary consciousness jolted, and he staggered on his feet. There, in the shadows, his son appeared to be quietly appraising him, casting an unusual steady gaze at him. Light blue eyes seemed to tell David: *It's okay. I'm benign. I won't hurt you. You're safe with me.*

David felt the spreading pinpricks of panic sinking into him as if they were weighted daggers, and he felt what it was like to face insanity.

As David collapsed into the nearby chair, clutching its arms so as not to topple it, he watched as the baby's unusual gaze seemed to fade with the shifting of the room's shadows, vanishing completely within seconds, replaced by normal blue eyes casting a baby's typical unfocused stare.

Slumping into the chair, David immediately questioned if he had really seen what he thought he had. The room was dark, the shadows changing as he walked, he was so drained, exhausted. Possibly suffering from psychological trauma. Could the blue color of the baby's eyes have triggered some guilt-born illusion? Was it because of his cowardliness that Mikhail had died? Or was he now trying to use reason and logic to brace his sanity, to avoid confronting unsettling mysteries of the unknown?

It was then that he noticed his baby's chart, hanging there, and the noted date and time of birth. David could hear in his mind Mikhail's grandfather clock sounding as he did the necessary mental time-zone calculation to determine that his son had been born at the exact time that Mikhail had died...

What could serve as the storage facility? David heard Mikhail's voice in his head. And David wondered, did there need to be one?

Could Polina have possibly had other past lives, undiscovered by Anton? Past lives that would bridge any gaps in time, so that there would be a continuum of existence residing within Polina? The date of death of one life being the date of birth of the next life?

David knew that these speculations were not something that could be tested by science, proved or disapproved, and that he should doubt. Yet it all seemed to make sense to him, intuitively. And this, oddly, gave his tired mind a sense of peace. And as he sat there, looking at his child, he thought about the future. About how one day in the far future—a future that he himself would not see by way of reincarnation—perhaps there would arrive a day when man would have learned to tame his emotional proclivities. Perhaps there may one day be a utopia, ruled by science, by logic and virtue. And everywhere would then be like Mikhail's garden. Where the wind sings to you as it passes through the pine trees.

And David smiled at this vision of the future, even though he knew and accepted that he could not possibly be part of it, his mind toying with the thought that perhaps reincarnation was but a part of some unknown built-in process of selection that guaranteed that the future would be better, that it would be instilled with greater and greater "virtue."

David found himself believing, although he had absolutely no proof of it, that his son, the essence that was now his son, would in some incarnation be part of that future. Yes, he was certain of it.

And he laughed softly, openly embracing the belief that the universe was far stranger than man could ever possibly imagine.

Acknowledgements and Identifying Notations

• In the beginning of "The Transfer Mechanism," when Dr. Mikhail Azov states "But I am not living in a fairy tale," he is paying homage to lines from Greek writer Nikos Kazantzakis' *Zorba the Greek*:

"To live far from men, not to need them and yet to love them. To have the stars above, the land to your left and the sea to your right and to realize all of a sudden in your heart, life has accomplished its final miracle: it has become a fairy tale."

• In the story, Dr. Mikhail Azov paraphrases in his dialogue a quote by German rocket engineer Werner von Braun, who once stated:

"I have learnt to use the word 'impossible' with the greatest of caution."— Werner von Braun

• The thoughts expressed by Dr. Mikhail Azov on science being a desirable substitute for politicking are the ideas of Hungarian American physicist Leó Szilárd, as expressed originally in his 1961 book of short science fiction stories titled *The Voice of the Dolphins*.

• Dr. Mikhail Azov expresses: "Physical laws gave rise to chemistry. Allowed biology to arise. Which gave rise to populations. Then economics. And then politics."

This is derived from the works of Belgian physical chemist and Nobel laureate Ilya Prigogine, who extended concepts of non-equilibrium chemical systems to complex social and economic systems.

• The character Dr. Mikhail Azov also utilizes in dialogue some wording loosely borrowed from Swiss psychiatrist and psychotherapist Carl Gustar Jung, who wrote on psychic epidemics in his book *Modern Man in Search of a Soul*.

• David's dream on the plane references Greek philosopher Plato's "The Allegory of the Cave," presented in Plato's *The Republic*.

• The song "Waco," sung in the story by Dr. Mikhail Azov, concerns the Waco Massacre, also referred to as the Waco Siege, where in 1993 the FBI put under siege a compound in Waco, Texas, belonging to a religious group led by David Koresh. Seventy-six men, women, and children, including David Koresh, died in a fire that broke out in the compound when under siege.

The song "Waco" is one of a number of songs written by this author's father.

A Note from the Author

The inspiration for crafting this story, "The Transfer Mechanism," arose solely from this author's appreciation of a response given by the late science and science fiction writer Arthur C. Clarke to a question once posed to him by Venezuelan futurist José Cordeiro:

Question: Do you believe in reincarnation?

Arthur C. Clarke: No, I don't see any mechanism that would make it possible. However, I'm always paraphrasing J. B. S. Haldane: "The universe is not only stranger than we imagine, it's stranger than we can imagine."

This author hopes that the spirit of Clarke's answer was captured in "The Transfer Mechanism."

It is recommended by this author that readers consider obtaining the April 1961 issue of *The Magazine of Fantasy and Science Fiction*, to appreciate the article by the late author and professor of biochemistry Isaac Asimov titled "My Built-In Doubter," as the core of the ideas expressed therein by Asimov on why scientists should be skeptical are reflected in brief in "The Transfer Mechanism."

In regard to "The Transfer Mechanism," this author would like to add that if Dr. Mikhail Azov had the time in the story to respond to David's pleading question, regarding if science had to guess at explaining the evidence for reincarnation, Mikhail would have guessed thusly:

"If it was not fraud, or the ravings of an ill mind, or purely some natural mental phenomenon of the brain, then possibly the construction of past information somehow received by the present subconscious."

Mikhail would have answered in this manner because, if a perfectly normal explanation, one that fit comfortably within the known structure of the universe as presently determined by science, would not suffice, then before leaping to a supernatural belief, he would first propose a possibility that might have a better chance of fitting in with some possible unknown quality of our universe.

Leaving the ending of "The Transfer Mechanism" open to the reader's interpretation was a device employed by this author purely for entertainment purposes. The intended underlying subtle message is that coincidences—such as David's son being born at the precise time of Mikhail's death—are a troubling thing to science, as they can lead to incorrect thoughts and conclusions.

In summation, it should be pointed out that the speculations expressed in "The Transfer Mechanism" on reincarnation are purely for entertainment purposes and are not beliefs held by this author. Reincarnation was simply a tool used by this author to pay homage to the J. B. S. Haldane quote:

"Now my own suspicion is that the Universe is not only queerer than we suppose, but queerer than we can suppose."
— J. B. S. Haldane

Niko Zinovii
Santa Monica, California
10 June 2014

Niko Zinovii

The Mind of Juda

The night was humid, the air hot and heavy with the smell of thunder. The odor of the city, of its seedy pavement and old cobbled stone, continued to waft aloft, rising up to the rooftops, where it lingered languidly in the still air.

Juda stepped out onto his high balcony, his deep-set black eyes focusing on the lightning flashing feebly, miles out over the Ligurian Sea. The unhealthy pallor of his face, his sallow complexion, strangely mirrored the weakening, departing storm and the surrounding deep gray sky.

It's dangerous to think back to your past, Juda reminded himself, turning his gaze out over the rich and time-worn architecture of Genoa. But his eyes grew sullen, and pain crept up to the corners of his mouth. Slowly, he reached a hand up to his bandaged head, and with boney fingers, he lightly touched his bald, stitched skull. *Black hair,* his mind rumbled. *Before this all began, I had black hair.*

His thoughts jerked him backward in time, and he felt the sudden panic of the hunted as he remembered how he had awakened in that alley in Zurich, a year and a half ago, lying there, cold, numb, sprawled out in the rain, his head swollen and bloody—apparently he had been clubbed senseless by the pipe lying there beside him. He could still clearly see in his mind's eye the two dead men at his feet. He could still feel the weight of the gun, still clutched tightly in his right hand.

But most of all, he remembered the panic in his mind and the question he mumbled aloud, dumbfounded, as he staggered to his feet: "Who am I?"

Juda shook the past away, and his eyes dropped down to the old harbor below, searching for that damn boat, the one haunting his dreams and his waking thoughts. He could barely make it out down there in the darkness. Later, he knew he would descend into the city, walk its streets, slowly making his way over to the port, to stare at that boat. But it was hot. He would first go up to the roof for the next few hours, as usual, lie there naked with the fat Genoese woman whom he paid to stay with him, to submit to his carnal needs. He spoke to her very little. He felt no need to. She was only flesh to him, just like any other woman. When she spoke to him, she did so in her Genoese dialect, of which he comprehended little. He welcomed this, as it stopped him from having to tell her to shut up, for he had so much on his mind.

For over a year now, he had locked himself up in this apartment, alternating between sleeping, fornicating, drinking copious amounts of liquor, and taking nightly walks. He bothered very little with eating and only did so to build up his strength, for the next operation.

A clap of thunder and his mind jerked back again to that alley in Zurich, where he had stood in the rain, noticing the letters J-u-d-a tattooed, dark and bold, across his left inner wrist. His name? It sounded right. It felt right, for he was lean, dark, thick black eyebrows, a hooked nose. So he accepted it, adopted it, Juda.

He sensed, there in that alley, that it had been his profession to kill others. The sight of the shot, dead men bothered him not at all. They were nothing to him. There was only a disconnect within him, a disconnect from humanity.

Robbery, too, seemed to be his profession. At least that was how he explained the briefcase full of blocks of SNC-coin, the world's new digital currency that offered complete and guaranteed anonymity. He was suddenly rich beyond the dreams of avarice. But without a memory, and with a head wound that was bleeding profusely and beginning to blur his vision and his consciousness. He had to get away, get rid of the gun, hide the briefcase, before he passed out.

As Juda's focus returned to the present, he heard himself, in Italian, order his fat concubine to pour him a drink. Later, as they lay there together on the roof, their naked bodies pressed against one another, Juda once again gingerly touched his stitched, bald head. *Only one more operation*, his inner thoughts mumbled. Somewhere, down in the city, the distant sound of an ambulance reached his ears. And when he slowly closed his eyes, he was back in Zurich, staggering into a hospital. It was explained to him that he had suffered serious injury to his left temporal and parietal lobes, the areas of the brain responsible for the processing of sensory information.

As he recovered, he surprisingly discovered that he now experienced an emotional association to numbers, that he could visualize numbers in an infinite landscape within his mind. That he could solve any mathematical problem without having to think, without having to calculate consciously. He would simply see the answers in his head, as if his brain now somehow worked magically. He also noticed mathematical patterns now, everywhere, in leaves, in the bark of a tree... He could read pages of a book in eight to ten seconds. And he could recall everything he read. His memory was photographic.

The doctors partially explained these incredible new abilities by what appeared to be a forced cross-linkage between the different damaged areas of his brain, due to the tremendous blow that he received to the head. Synesthesia, they called it. Whatever it was, he felt himself a super genius. And without having suffered any mental disability from the injury, unlike the handful of severely mentally handicapped savants in the world. He was now one of the extraordinary, but without handicap. He was in a league of his own. It gave him a sense of self-importance that he knew he had never had before. He came to see himself as important, as worth preserving. And his new wealth granted him a power over his life, an agency over his future. Even, perhaps, over death.

It was long after midnight when Juda descended from the roof to walk the Genoese streets, slowly making his way toward the harbor, as he knew he would. This city, it looked as if it had not changed in hundreds of years. And yet the world was now changing, dramatically, although most were completely unaware of it, for Transhumanism was a small, nascent, private religion, open only to the super-wealthy elite.

The air at the port was rich with salt and the smell of fish, motor oil, and fresh paint. Juda saw the boat. *There it is…* And he recalled that one Sunday afternoon, months ago, when he had first ventured down to the port and discovered the boat, as it was tonight, blocked up, elevated off the ground so that repairs to its hull could be carried out. Planks infested by boring shipworms replaced. Planks worn by time replaced. Over the ensuing weeks, Juda watched as plank by plank, seemingly each and every piece of the boat's wooden hull was marked to be replaced. Once, he arrived to find the owner surveying the progress. He asked the man, "Will you rename the boat?" The owner only grinned, and replied that he did not have to. And Juda's fixation was augmented to mental obsession and torment. And now, here he stood tonight, again staring at the boat. There were now only a few planks left to be replaced.

The work would be completed tomorrow. Just like him. Tomorrow he would undergo his twelfth and final surgery. The irony made him snarl.

Juda decided to walk along the shore before returning home. He knew he would not sleep, not tonight. And he knew he could not stomach having to endure listening to any idle chattering from his fat harlot. Not tonight.

As he walked across the sand, he stopped here and there, from time to time, to watch the waves slowly roll in behind him, swallowing up and washing away his transient footprints. His past life was unknown to him. But he was certain that before Zurich he had been a nobody. No one of any consequence. Footprints across a landscape, cities built to stand, time would wipe them all away, like ancient Jericho, with only remnants of its walls remaining today to remind mankind of its long-forgotten settlers. And time, eventually, would claim those walls as well.

Standing there, alone in the darkness, Juda recited aloud from memory something he had read while convalescing:

"High up in the north, in the land called Svithjod, there stands a rock.

It is a hundred miles high and a hundred miles wide.

Once every thousand years, a little bird comes to this rock to sharpen its beak.

When the rock has thus been worn away, then a single day of eternity will have gone by."

The little bird of Svithjod had become Juda's mantra. It was his motivation to have undergone the past eleven operations. The promise of eternity. That was what money could now buy. No need to cling to, to placate oneself with, religion. Besides, he had been a bad man. He was surely condemned to burn in hell... But science now offered an escape from such a fate. The rich and sinful had once paid the church, bribed the church, in order to secure the salvation of their souls. Science now offered itself as a substitute means to achieve immorality. For those who were rich enough, and desperate enough… to go underground and pay for such illegal salvation.

Juda drank heavily upon returning, and he lay in bed, motionless, staring at the ceiling through the entire afternoon of the next day. Until the surgeon arrived.

Upon regaining consciousness, Juda felt different, again, just as he had felt noticeably different after each preceding surgery. But this time it was more. The doctor reassured him that there had been no unexpected complications and that everything had gone according to plan.

This time, however, the difference was dramatic, akin to Juda's experience of discovering his extraordinary newfound abilities when recovering from his bludgeoning in Switzerland. His perception of space and time now seemed heightened. Time was different now, the future was clearer, like a chessboard on which he could foresee all possible moves. The future felt like one reduced to likely outcomes and probabilities, a predictable playground. He could simulate and see all possible futures in his mind. He felt himself to be a massive genius, able to outwit and outmaneuver anyone. He felt beyond human, not human…

Juda swung his thin legs off the makeshift operating table and steadied himself. Rising, he swung his black eyes to the nearby surgical tray, staring at the 120-cubic-centimeter lump of brain tissue that lay upon it, soft, pink, wet, and glistening. It was the final biological piece of his mortal brain to be replaced by hardware. One operation a month over the past year. Finally, it was over. His mind, his new brain, could last forever. He was eternal.

One thing is for certain, he heard himself thinking as he stared down at the last, discarded piece of what had contained him, *I'll now never remember who I was.*

And Juda weakly pushed the surgeon aside and feebly made his way out onto the balcony, where he stood looking out at the old port and to the sea beyond. That damn boat, the planking of its hull completely replaced, had been launched and was now sailing out to sea.

Juda reached a hand up to his freshly bandaged head, and with trembling fingers, he lightly touched his bald, stitched skull, his new mind contemplating the paradox. Was it the same boat as the boat dry docked a year ago? If it was not, when did it change? When did it become a different boat? At what point? Which plank being replaced made the difference?

Am I the same man? Juda's disturbed thoughts rumbled. *Is it still really me? Or did the last piece of me die... in there... and I don't even realize it?*

Like back in Zurich, Juda once again felt panic sweep through his mind, and he mumbled aloud, "Who am I... now?"

This time, however, he had an answer. It was the name of that damn boat, the name that its owner had said he would not have to change. Brain tissue or wooden planks, it mattered not, he was Theseus, and he had just set sail toward a new horizon.

Acknowledgements and Identifying Notations

• The story of the little bird of Svithjod is from the opening of *The Story of Mankind*, a 1921 book on the prehistory and history of Western civilization, by Hendrik Willem van Loon. (When a young boy, the author of "The Mind of Juda" was gifted an edition of *The Story of Mankind* by his father. The author never forgot the wonderful opening prelude or his father's habit of often quoting it.)

• The mathematical abilities gained by the character Juda in "The Mind of Juda" are based on the real-life mathematical abilities of Daniel Tammet, of the United Kingdom, who can calculate to 100 decimal places in his head. Daniel experienced severe seizures as a very young child, and it has been hypothesized that these seizures changed something in his brain that provided him his extraordinary abilities. There are cases of others with similar abilities also apparently gained from suffering brain injuries in their youth. To readers who would like to learn more about this phenomenon, the 2005 British documentary *The Boy with the Incredible Brain* is recommended.

• The speculations offered on Juda's new ability to forecast the future as a result of his final brain operation are based on the thoughts of theoretical physicist Michio Kaku, who proposed that extraterrestrials with a higher intelligence than humans may possess such abilities.

A Note from the Author

"The Mind of Juda" touches upon the philosophical question of identity, and how this question may deepen in a future of sufficiently advanced technology.

Ancient philosophers addressed a similar question with the "Ship of Theseus" paradox. The mythical Greek hero Theseus, after slaying the Minotaur in the Labyrinth on Crete, returned to Athens. Legend has it that the ship that Theseus returned in was kept seaworthy by restoration over time, old and decaying planks being continuously replaced by new timber. Ancient philosophers questioned if the restored ship should be considered the same ship or not. The question was never resolved.

This author asks the reader: is Juda, after his operations, the same man, in regard to his identity?

Niko Zinovii
Santa Monica, California
25 June 2014

Niko Zinovii

Wonderland

It began with the cry of sea gulls and a beached dolphin. But Simon did not notice the dolphin, not immediately. As he tied his small boat to the dock, he did glance up at the birds, and then down at their flapping shadows, but his mind was elsewhere, his thoughts entirely back on the main island of Thira's tiny, circular archipelago, on its small picturesque village of Oia, from where he had just come.

Turning, he gazed back out across the huge, sea-drowned caldera, out across the indigo-blue expanse that now separated him from the main island. Instantly, Thira, as always, cast its magical spell on him. The untamed nature of the island was stunning almost beyond description, its multicolored cliffs of orange, red, and brown, towering to nearly one thousand feet in height, where, dramatically perched high above, lining the volcanic cliff's rim, clung the island's pastel villages, houses shining dazzling white and brilliant blue. The stark, breathtaking landscape, contrasting with the colorful Aegean architecture, appeared otherworldly, radiating a beauty that projected itself from the depths of the Mediterranean's past.

And yet Simon's heart sank still deeper, filled with disappointment, weighted by concern. He had just learned that his private benefactor was leaving Thira. There would be no more funding for his project. These past few years, Thira had come to mean so many different things to him—words, sounds, scents… the caldera, his research… all of it, it was what had sustained him after the accident, after the tragic death of his beloved wife and young daughter.

And his research—he was so very close to the final deciphering. His curiosity, his scientific drive had not been blunted by sorrow. He still heard the siren call of discovery. His eyes were still those of a dreamer. The wonder always grew.

As Simon stared across the submerged caldera, he noticed the three hundred steps leading from distant Oia down to the shore. He thought of how he had just descended those steps, one by one, with each step the weight of the heavens above seeming to settle heavier and heavier upon his shoulders. When he had finally reached the bottom, he felt only the awful, terrible weariness that settles upon troubled men.

It was then that he looked back up at Oia, and in his mind's eye he imagined its dazzling-white houses, its blue-domed churches, its arches, its terraces, but most of all, its disturbingly deserted cobbled streets… All the village's inhabitants now uncharacteristically indoors, out of sight, inactive, plugged into Wonderland. Every one of them with hardware in their heads… Spending nearly all their time in the new, global electronic ether.

For the first time, Simon began to really wonder about where humankind was now heading. About what Wonderland was doing to man. He slowly came to the sobering conclusion that Wonderland was dangerous. And more, he suddenly wanted to see more clearly. He found himself wanting to know why he was where he was. Where he was heading. What new purpose he might find, to sustain himself.

The wind blew, and it was then that Simon saw the dolphin, lying there helpless on the black-pebbled, stony shore.

Simon felt an immediate urge to rush to the dolphin, to help it, but not wanting to frighten the gentle being, he forced himself to approach slowly, with equanimity.

"It's okay." Simon spoke kindly, with genuine compassion, his voice steady, comforting. "I won't hurt you. I only want to help you."

Simon kneeled beside the dolphin. It was a beautiful striped dolphin, the most common cetacean of the eastern Mediterranean. "You look young, strong...." Simon remarked, bewildered, and he wet his hands in the nearby sea and gently ran them over the dolphin, following the dark, bluish stripe that decorated the entire length of its beautiful light-gray body.

"Are you ill?" Simon wondered.

Then Simon's eyes met with the dolphin's sentient gaze, and he sensed its deep loneliness. And more, he saw a reflection of himself.

"You're alone. Lost." Simon understood, soothingly stroking and wetting the dolphin again. "But you're a castaway on a good beach. You're with me now. In my care. Here you will find purpose. And Thira... will sustain you."

And Simon looked out at the sea-flooded caldera and considered the irony of life. He had been a successful neuroscientist up until the plane crash that took from him what he loved most. Afterward, he had wandered, alone, until he somehow found himself here, alive but unable to move forward. One afternoon, when swimming in the caldera, legs cramping, he had begun to sink, to drown. And he would have, if it had not been for the amazing striped dolphin that saved him, retrieving him from below, pushing him up to the surface, where the dolphin stayed with him, keeping him afloat. As he floated, the surreal, looming volcanic cliffs of Thira encircling his view, it was as if nature had reached out to him, embraced him, as if the caldera itself had accepted him. It was at that moment that Simon suddenly knew, beyond any doubt, that this was where he would live, and one day die.

The time he spent floating with that large, beautiful dolphin touched his mind, his heart, and his soul. He would never forget the sadness he felt when the dolphin suddenly splashed away and he found the hand of a stranger reaching down to help him from a passing sailboat. It was the hand of his benefactor-to-be. And his life changed completely that day. He was soon engaging in research that he had never in his wildest dreams anticipated pursuing. Things had just fallen into place. It just happened.

But where was he now heading? He could not help but ask himself this again, feeling that this beached dolphin was an auspicious sign, a herald of something new in the offing.

~

Five days after rescuing the dolphin, Simon stumbled to and seated himself at his desk, elated, yet in a state of stunned shock. Finding himself slowly smiling, trepidatiously, he thought of how the wonders of the universe were truly without end. For he had just been delivered the means to deal with the threat of Wonderland, with a way to attain a much-needed personal triumph over life, and simultaneously with a way to give his dolphin, whom he had named Hope, true purpose, by achieving something truly positive and remarkably important for humankind.

Across the large, open room came the happy squeal of Hope, the dolphin. Simon's communication laboratory and residence, built into the cliffside on the islet opposite Oia, were open to the sea, and the bright blue water of Thira's caldera sloshed in the wide channel and pool that u-shaped its way in and out of his abode. The pool was the new home of

Simon's dolphin, who was not a captive but could come and go as she pleased, which she took advantage of at this moment, jetting out into the deep caldera to make a series of high-arcing leaps in the waning yet resplendent light of the setting sun, rotating rapidly before splashing back into the darkening sea.

Watching Hope roto-tailing, Simon smiled at the unexpected appropriateness of the name that he had selected for her. In myth, after Pandora had opened her infamous box out of curiosity, releasing its countless evils upon humanity, she noticed one thing remaining within, Hope. Hope had chosen to remain, to be with mankind, as promise of a mitigating force, as a reminder that although we are hopelessly human, life is not without hope. A mixed blessing, for hope often lures men to their destruction...

"I have to tell Thomas," Simon mumbled to himself. "Yes, Thomas, I'll need his help with this."

Simon opened a drawer and pulled out what looked like a small key. "Wonderland..." Simon remarked, disturbed. "Can't even make a call without it. Damn." And he inserted the key into the back of his head. He thought of Thomas's unique identification number and he waited, hoping that his friend was plugged in. He was.

"Simon," spoke Thomas's voice inside Simon's head. "I've been trying to get in touch with you. I was beginning to worry about you."

Simon closed his eyes, and his mind filled with a lifelike, three-dimensional, living visual image of Thomas, indistinguishable from reality. The thick red beard, the dense eyebrows, the life in his eyes—Simon felt convinced that he was actually looking at his friend, even though he knew he was not, that in reality it was only imagery in his mind.

"You need to come here, right away." Simon thought the words and instantly heard them spoken aloud in his mind.

"Really?" Thomas responded. "Why?"

"I need your help," Simon answered slowly, growing serious, rigid. "To set a trap. To capture a mermaid."

Utter silence. Even the image of Thomas momentarily froze, motionless.

"Thomas?"

"… And how do you catch a *mermaid*, Simon?"

"You have a dolphin call for help," Simon responded sincerely. "In Dolphinese."

"—You've deciphered their language? The dolphin language?"

Simon nodded. "And I learned something undreamed of. Mermaids actually exist."

"… I'll be right there…"

~

It was not long afterward that Thomas unabashedly barged into Simon's home. "You're serious?" he bellowed. "Mermaids?"

"The trap is set." Simon smiled. "But first, I need to introduce you to Hope."

Simon led his friend to the pool where swam his dolphin. He then handed Thomas a very small and delicate key. He took one himself, inserting it into the back of his own head.

"The translation key," he explained. "For Dolphinese."

Entering the pool, Simon inserted an identical key into a barely noticeable slot, located between two short strips of white medical tape near the posterior of Hope's skull.

Thomas inserted the key given to him, pushing aside his thick, bushy mop of hair to do so.

"And now," Simon stated, "Hope, tell our visitor about your friends, the mermaids."

Hope's eyes filled with the joy of life and she opened up her world to Thomas. Simon smiled as he heard Hope's translated voice in his mind. She was so innately curious. Rather than launching directly into a monologue, she instead questioned and conversed with their visitor. And Thomas learned firsthand that talking with a dolphin was a lot like speaking with a conversational prankster. Communication was playful, witty, abounding with verbal maneuverings that lured one into an unexpected joke or an amusing linguistic trick or a mischievous antic of word play—but always pleasant, imbued with the palpable emotions of Hope's pure and noble heart. A number of times Thomas laughed out loud, heartedly, fully expressive, as was his nature. It was exhilarating and fun, like mental dancing. It made one feel very much alive, even young again.

As Simon listened, he recalled his own first conversation with Hope and how it had become quite obvious to him that the IQ of dolphins, if Hope was a representative example, surpassed that of man. For it was simply not possible to verbally outmaneuver a dolphin.

"Hope," Simon interjected, "please, the mermaids."

And Hope calmed and became quite serious, telling Thomas about the fish people who long ago fell from a distant star. They colonized the Aegean during man's early prehistory. They befriended the dolphins but chose to remain hidden from man, as best they could, relegating themselves to the nebulous depths of the sea, where they lived in comfort and security. They knew all the knowledge of man millennia ago. And today, they were as technologically far above man as man was above the beasts of the fields.

"They're our only hope," Simon interrupted.

"Hope for what?" Thomas asked.

"Wonderland," Simon answered, his tone rather severe.

"Wonderland?" Thomas did not understand.

"Thomas," Simon said, calm and steady, "these past years, I've felt the rain, embraced the smell of Thira's wildflowers, the spray of the sea, the touch of life. Felt the power of the caldera... But not the thrill of a battle won. This is what I desperately need, what my heart yearns for. In order to complete my life's journey, through time. Do you understand?"

Thomas thought for a moment and then shook his head.

"Hope understands," Simon went on, climbing up out of the pool. "And she agrees. Humanity must unplug. To save itself. That's why we set the trap. I need to trap one, to ask for their help. I don't believe they'd listen otherwise, without being forced to. They witnessed the rise and fall of Atlantis, and did nothing. They're great spectators. I need to convince them."

Simon pointed to the channel that ran into the pool and to the large fishing net that hung above it. "A simple net," he continued. "They're surprisingly unsuspecting, perhaps naïve, and rather weak, physically. They probably came from a lower-gravity world, possibly an ice-encrusted moon, containing a global ocean underneath, like Jupiter's Europa or Callisto. At least that's what dolphin lore seems to indicate. The heavy gravity here, it inhibits them. Even after all this time. You see, they don't die like you or I, they're eternal."

Silence.

"Hope," Simon finally said, "could you please call for a mermaid?"

And Simon's dolphin swam out into the immense caldera. Facing the open Aegean, she called out in her language, a language that the mermaids understood.

"They live right out there," Simon remarked. "Not far from where Thira drops off. Still, it may take a while for one to respond. We should make ourselves comfortable."

~

It was long after midnight when Simon heard Hope slowly entering the channel. If things were going as planned, she was baiting the trap, luring in a mermaid.

Simon looked for Thomas and found him there in the dark, by the net, his unkempt, wild hair casting a monstrous shadow on the far wall. All was set.

Then the unexpected happened. Hope's graceful head rose up out of the water, and she looked directly at Simon.

"They are waiting." Simon heard Hope's translated words echo in his mind.

"Waiting?" Simon whispered, stunned. "For what?"

"To listen to you…" came Hope's response.

And Hope turned about and swam back out into the sea-flooded caldera.

Simon rose, unsteady on his feet, and silently moved over to Thomas, anemically waving him out of concealment, no need for either of them to continue hiding there in the dark like two children. He suddenly felt the flush of embarrassment, feeling as if he had a stone-aged brain and had been caught pretending that he could control things he could not.

The sea swirled in front of them, and slowly, ever so slowly, something colorful and majestic rose up out of the depths. It was a large transparent pod, with giant membranous wings, glasslike, like those of a tremendous flying fish, glowing with unreal alien light. Out of the pod swam three strange beings.

Simon trembled as he laid eyes on these approaching "mermaids," for it was as if their presence was a clarion trumpeting that life, that the universe, was one of absolute wonder.

Unlike the mermaids of legend, these aliens were not beautiful women with the tailed bodies of fish. True, they were composite-looking creatures, their torsos and heads vaguely humanlike in form, distinctly feminine and fragile in look, and their lower bodies were giant tails, but overall, they appeared very fishlike, true finned, aquatic denizens of the deep sea. Their bodies were pearly white with a silvery sheen and covered by larger-than-expected overlapping scales. Their two large eyes were almost perfectly round, cold and distinctly fishlike, yet unmistakably intelligent. They had nothing like noses, and the lips of their mouths were thick, barbed, and rubbery, like those of bottom-dwelling fish.

"Mermaids..." Simon heard himself announcing their presence.

One of the mermaids unexpectedly spoke to them, in a voice that was feminine yet fishlike, its words delivered with considerable effort outside its normal aqueous environment, the gills within its reddish-pink throat quivering. It spoke, of course, in Dolphinese.

"I don't believe this..." Thomas mumbled as he and Simon heard the translation in their minds. The mermaid told them that Hope had informed them of the sad truth of human science and technology progressing faster than human wisdom, and of the sad result.

With this, the mermaid turned and looked across the caldera at the dim lights of far-off Oia. Simon surmised that she—if it was a she—must have thought, at that moment, how although the lights were on in the houses, the lights were off in the lives of the town's addicted inhabitants.

"It's not a wonderland," Simon offered. "It's a limbo. Purgatory. It's not real. It's not life."

And the mermaid looked at Simon. She really looked at him, so deeply that Simon felt her thoughts, her question: *But how can we help?*

Simon stepped closer to them, preparing himself for something to come. "I need to plug into Wonderland," he explained. "And then I need you to use your godlike technology to put me above all the chaos, all the noise, so that every mind on the planet is focused on me, for a few moments, so that I can explain to them, ask them all to unplug."

The mermaid, she stared at Simon in silence for the longest time.

"Please," Simon pleaded. "Life and death... Death is simple, you simply cease to exist. But life, it's meant to be lived. Truly lived."

The mermaid slowly blinked twice and then said something in an alien tongue to her companions. They all swam away from their craft, entering the channel flowing into Simon's residence. Hope followed.

Floating together, the alien trio gathered in a circle, holding webbed hands, concentrating. Soon afterward, their craft began to glow intensely, emitting power unseen. The lead mermaid turned to Simon and blinked twice.

Simon looked out over Thira's dark flooded caldera and drew strength from its raw, untamed, natural beauty, which had sustained him these past years. He then gently removed the Dolphinese translation key from the back of his head. Opening a long box, he next pulled out a Wonderland key. It dwarfed the translation key, as well as the simple phone key he had used earlier to call Thomas. It was huge, abominable, obscene.

With trembling hands, Simon closed his eyes and inserted the Wonderland key into the back of his skull. —*Thooom!* He was in another world. He was in Wonderland. Where nothing was real but anything was possible. He was alone, on his pebbled beach, standing before Thira's mighty caldera. It was midday, the sun shining brilliantly. The sky filled with unheard-of ethereal colors, clouds shifting as if being sculpted by the invisible hand of God.

Simon could see people floating and flying along the shoreline, across the expanse of sea. And over Oia, people likewise defying gravity frolicked in the sky. So many of them beautiful or strong, or whatever they wanted to be, anything but themselves, anything but a true reflection of reality. The one exception, the one constant, was the caldera and its majestic cliffs. It remained the same, spectacular and breathtaking. It could not be improved, not even by Wonderland.

Simon felt his heart ache, knowing that more than half of the visible people were not real. They were nothing. Only convincing simulacra. Some of ideal lovers, imagined by someone and brought to life by Wonderland, but most were imposters of the dead... Lost loved ones, remembered, idealized, recalled from the past to sit with and talk to, to touch again, to love again. Simon knew that all he had to do was wish it and Wonderland would conjure up for him his lost wife and daughter. Stand them right there beside him on the sand. Make it seem so real that he would never want to unplug.

Simon growled out in grief, shook his head, and waited; he waited for the godlike technology of the mermaids. And it came, he felt a surge of power unlike anything he had ever experienced, real or unreal, and he began to float aloft on golden, membranous wings. Higher and higher he climbed, soaring above the caldera, which seemed to hold him steady in its center, anchoring him, physically and spiritually. As he rose still higher, the sky suddenly changed and filled with nine billion faces, all looking at him in puzzlement. This was his moment.

Simon passionately pleaded with this sea of humanity to unplug from Wonderland. But the billions of faces only stared at him in bafflement. He desperately attempted reasoning with them, telling them about life and love, real life, real love, and how Wonderland was depriving them of these greatest of all gifts. But one by one the faces began to turn away, one by one the population of the Earth stopped listening, and their faces began to fade.

"No!" Simon yelled out in despair. "No!" And he felt himself begin to slowly sink from the sky, his power ebbing, the winds, picking up about him, buffeting him about.

"Thomas," Simon shouted out in desperation. "If you can hear me, tell the mermaids, tell them they must elevate my presence still higher. They must make me godlike. Godlike! Turn me into their virtual god. The god of Wonderland! So that I can command them. Command them to unplug. And to never plug in again. And they must obey!"

Simon's golden wings elongated, thickened, and broadened, and he felt himself glowing, his entire body glowing, as he rose up toward the sun at zenith. The sky once again filled with all the faces of humanity, all staring at him, only this time their faces were filled with the fear of God.

Higher and higher Simon rose, until he touched the sun. It was then, as he felt his power peak upon his contact with the unbearable heat of a star, that he commanded every human being on the planet to unplug. And they did so, at once. Suddenly, he was totally alone, the only human mind left in Wonderland. No one to see him fall.

His wings, melted, he plummeted toward the sea, Thira's majestic volcanic cliffs embracing him from a distance, cradling him, the island's mighty flooded caldera waiting to receive him, to take him back. As he fell, he thought of his wife, of his daughter, of the scent of Thira's wild cliffside flowers, of the salty spray of the sea, of the coolness of the depths of the sea-flooded caldera, and he accepted its embrace.

Simon collapsed in front of Thomas and the others. For Icarus, burnt by the sun, had fallen into the sea on broken wings and drowned on dry land.

And that night, a friend wept, a dolphin cried, and three alien beings felt a sorrow deeper than they had ever known, loving with an empathy that only an eternal could fathom when embracing the loss of a singular, sentient life.

And humankind awoke, set free.

A Note from the Author

This author hopes you enjoyed this tale, which sprung from a feeling as opposed to an idea. Around this feeling, I then tinkered together the story, drawing upon the majestic Greek island of Thira (also known as Santorini), my appreciation for Greek mythology, and my love of dolphins while borrowing a description of a mermaid that I had written for a feature-length screenplay back in 1990, titled *Things that Never Were*.

The feeling came from my appreciation of "The Song of Seikilos," the only complete musical composition from ancient Greece, composed by Seikilos circa 200 BC in loving memory of his deceased wife. The song:

> As long as you live, shine.
> Let nothing grieve you beyond measure,
> For your life is short, and time will claim its toll.

An ending thought to ponder: Does dolphin vocalization actual represent language utilized by dolphins? Or is the study of dolphin vocalization just a blind alley?

This author has offered this story as science fiction. If, however, it is one day determined that dolphins do not have a complex language, then this story should be regarded as a fantasy.

Niko Zinovii
Santa Monica, California
1 August 2014

Niko Zinovii

Box of the Supermen

J osef, aloof, handsome, blond, stood alone over his large, comatose Samoan friend, who lay interned at the Moto'otua National Hospital in Apia, Samoa. He crossed his arms awkwardly as he sat in the nearby chair, solemn, remote, eyeing the tubes connected to his friend with distrust and near surrender. As he sat there, steadying himself with his crossed arms, he felt the mortality of the hospital room settle upon his weary intellect, and he momentarily closed his wide-set blue eyes. When they opened, they were dull, and filled with grief and despair.

"Patu," Josef whispered intimately to his dear friend, "we were supposed to make tomorrow ours. You and me, together, taking on the world. To make it sane. I'm no longer the idealist, but I still hold some of our dreams. But don't worry. I'm patient…"

Rather morose, he flashed a disapproving look to the nurse out in the hall, who continued to present as far too solicitous, almost as if she were eavesdropping on his private one-way conversation with his helpless, still friend, Dr. Patu T'eo, esteemed historian and political scientist.

~

The seaplane's twin propeller engines droned as the craft lifted off from Samoa's Vailele Bay and turned in a wide arc heading east out over the South Pacific, into the glow of the rising sun.

On board, Josef turned his tired eyes from the window to find that he was indeed the sole passenger, the other five seats empty. Perhaps it was the early-morning hour of the flight? Whatever the reason, he smiled, changed seats, and stretched out. Leaning his head against the hull, he allowed the humming of the engines to lull his eyes closed.

My fortieth birthday, he thought, and here I go, off alone again. Ever since childhood he had felt the instinctive need for private contemplation, for intellectual expansion, for growth. Almost as if it were a solemn duty, to sincerely develop his potential. He accepted that minds were born, but he also believed that minds were partially self-created. He had long ago become convinced that his mind was something that he himself had contributed to the making of. That thoughts, actions, experiences—that expressive and creative forces became ingrained in the mind of a person. And that for the mind to grow, it needed to renew itself in order to continue to develop its potentialities. He was convinced that this process of self-renewal should never end.

Although he was formally an evolutionary biologist, he was also a self-taught amateur philologist, anthropologist, and geologist. Presently indulging his interest in geology, he was flying off to the island of Mangaia—of the Cook Islands group—the oldest island of the Pacific Ocean. The small island was over 18 million years old, and more, its geology was rather intriguing, as it was completely surrounded by an incredible wall of fossil coral cliffs, *makatea*, that rose over 200 feet high from the beach.

As Josef dozed off, he found himself looking forward to the solitude that he would find on lonely Mangaia, to the peace of mind that his planned independent hiking and surveying would offer him—to having undisturbed time alone with his thoughts. For in addition to self-renewal, he very much needed to seriously contemplate his stalled future direction.

~

When Josef awoke, shaken conscious by a jolt of air turbulence, he felt rather refreshed, and he wondered how long he had been asleep. It was at that moment that he noticed something peculiar—the position of the sun was wrong. The plane was heading directly south, and his destination lay far to the east, to the southeast.

Josef rose and moved forward, past the few empty seats that separated him from the cockpit and its pilot. "Is there a problem?" Josef asked.

The pilot, a young Samoan, explained that he was diverting to Tonga, in order to land and make a minor repair on a fuel pump that was acting up again, not functioning properly. That he would put down in a calm lagoon that he knew of, make the repair, and that they would be off again without mishap.

"You'll like Fonoifua," the pilot named the Tongan atoll where they would be landing. "It's the only place in all of Tonga where the sand is green, red, and even silver."

"Sounds interesting," Josef commented as he returned to his seat, briefly wondering why the pilot had not simply diverted to Tonga's northern Vava'u islands, instead of flying so much farther south to the remote Ha'apai atolls… But the thought of the idyllic Ha'apai isles, with their untouched palm-fringed beaches and languid lagoons, seduced him immediately, and he found himself welcoming this unanticipated South Seas experience. Also, it would give him time to clear his head a bit, to get a better hold on the feelings that tore at him, haunted him, of his friend stranded in Samoa's Moto'otua Hospital, before flying on to the coral-walled island of Mangaia.

71

And so he sat back and waited, pensively, to land in the lagoon of Fonoifua, in the Kingdom of Tonga.

~

The pilot estimated two hours for the repair of the fuel pump. He also suggested that Josef wade ashore, stretch his legs, enjoy the island before they flew off again. The old Tongan village on Fonoifua was to the east, so they had this cove all to themselves.

Once ashore, Josef found himself slowly walking off, strolling barefoot down the silvery-white sand, moving aimlessly alongside the water's edge. Lost in thought, he was oblivious to the spectacularly translucent lagoon and to the vibrant and dazzling colors of its submerged coral heads.

Spying a large, flat rock, he walked over to it and sat beneath a stand of towering palms, which leaned sleepily out toward the sea. He then heard his mind silently asking the ocean a number of questions, although he did not bother to listen for any answers. Instead, he peered off to the distant horizon, where he could see where the world *ended*, and his unconscious mind drew security from this comfortable visual limitation set by the Earth's curvature.

It was then that Josef noticed the incredible woman walking up the beach, toward him. Clad in a golden-brown bikini, she was visually stunning, radiating a smoldering-yet-aloof presence. She seemed the most attractive and desirable woman Josef had ever seen—or even imagined. Dripping wet, she had obviously just been swimming. She walked up to Josef, smiled ever so slightly, and calmly sat beside him.

"A man," she said slowly, in a sultry Swiss German accent, "who travels to where it's most isolated to simply think, is really waiting for someone to listen to his silence."

And she sat there, poised, listening.

Josef felt a stunned smile lift and drop upon his face. But she just sat there, in silence, ready to listen to him, her eyes genuinely searching his, looking into his soul. Surrendering to her gaze, his staid silence evaporated, and as he spoke, he felt a near-cathartic relief from the long-overdue unburdening of the mind and heart.

"… Science," he started, unsurely, thinking it out aloud, explaining himself, "has such power—or perhaps I should say man's mind reaching out into wonder, it has the power to shape the lives of billions of people, to dramatically alter the course of human history. I've always felt the need to be part of that. In order to be fulfilled. I'll never stop wanting it. It's something I've always reached out for. Otherwise I wouldn't be true, to myself."

Josef paused as he thought he perceived a hint of a sensitive, approving smile rise momentarily upon her lips and then vanish, although it seemed to linger on within her lovely eyes.

"It's been something I've pursued above all else," he continued, feeling drawn to her in a way that he had never experienced before. "Working for goals larger than myself, goals beyond my own lifetime. Even my own self-interest. Such things are paid for with the cost of great sacrifice. But the spirit of science—I've always worshipped it. Because of this, I recently followed a man, a great man, who preached organizing our society, our culture, our politics by intelligent planning, by science. Together, we challenged the status quo. And we lost. We were crushed. He more than I…

"And the sacrifices paid…" he continued, his voice fading. "The loss of a great man, a man who was to me the older brother that I never had, the brother of my soul, an anchor for my… restlessness. And other sacrifices too, no wife, no children. There have been women, lovemaking. But nothing real or lasting… And now, here I am alone, and momentarily lost."

Standing, he walked up to the water's edge. She followed. They stood there together, for a time, in silence.

Finally, Josef turned to the mystery woman, still lost but emotionally somewhat unburdened. "What's your name?"

"Ayesha," she answered.

"Ayesha…" Josef repeated it, recognizing it immediately as also being the name of the mysterious white queen of H. Rider Haggard's novel *She*, the all-powerful sorceress who possessed the secret of immortality, whose beauty was so great that it enchanted any man who beheld her. Ayesha, 'She-Who-Must-Be-Obeyed.'

And Josef half smiled, wondering if perhaps he was still asleep, in that seaplane, flying high above the Pacific, maybe even by now approaching Mangaia and its fossil coral cliffs. But as he felt the power of love fill his heart and unbridled lust aching in his loins, he knew beyond the shadow of any doubt that he was awake and that this South Seas interlude was real.

Standing there with her in the sunlight, Josef saw something that he had not noticed beneath the shade of the palms. On each side of Ayesha's neck there were three faint, parallel horizontal lines, with a half-inch space between them. The lines looked almost like subtle tattooing, but not quite, as they did not appear to be artwork. In a way, they reminded Josef of the three horizontal strips that a midshipman lieutenant wore on his shoulder. Joseph wondered if they were scars. Possibly the remnants of tattoo removal? The marks perhaps having been some initiation practice of some abandoned Polynesian cult? Tattooing was prevalent in Tonga, Samoa, Fiji, Tahiti—throughout the South Pacific.

Ayesha's alluring eyes found a blue jellyfish trapped within a shallow of the lagoon, near where they stood. She recited poetically, in her soft, feminine voice:
"The short morning ending—
close to the water's edge
a jellyfish."
Josef smiled. She motioned to the lagoon directly before them but kept her eyes focused on him, reciting aloud again:
"On the water
the reflection
of a wanderer."
"Haiku," Josef nodded, pleasantly surprised, acknowledging his recognition of the haiku style of Japanese short poetry, with its characteristic paused, dramatic delivery.
Her eyes flicked upward very briefly, her long eyelashes fluttering seductively before she regained intimate eye contact with him, reciting another:
"A bird floats
at the place in the sky
where it floated yesterday."
Josef took the lure this time, realizing her subtle inference to his temporarily stalled life, and so he recited philosophically in response:
"I must step on fallen leaves
to take a new path..."
And there again was that hint of a sensitive, approving smile rising on her lips, mirrored within her lovely eyes.
Taking her hand, he guided her back to the rock, and they sat. Thinking briefly, he smiled and recited:
"Rain clouds—
the frog
puffs his belly out!"

Ayesha laughed, and Josef felt the thrill of entertaining a beautiful woman.

Ayesha's turn:

"In an old pond
a frog ages
while leaves fall."

Josef:

"Summer rain—
it drums on the heads
of the carp."

Ayesha:

"The little fish
carried backward
in the clear water."

Beneath the shade of the leaning palms, they were like two musical sitars, responding to and answering one other, each matching the emotional and intellectual content of the other.

Josef:

"Buckling in the heat
where the A-bomb burst…
a marathon."

Ayesha:

"Even in Kyoto
when I hear the cuckoo
I long for Kyoto…"

And Josef remained silent, just looking at her, still feeling her smoldering physical presence yet now also appreciating the presence of a stimulating intellect, of a like mind.

"I could tell you," Ayesha said, her sultry voice calm and low, "that I understand your grief, your frustrations. But would you believe me, Josef Bschließmayer?"

"… Now I'm entirely confused," Josef responded.

"Come," she said, taking his hand. "My father would like to meet you."

"But—"

"The pilot won't leave without you," came her response.

And Josef followed her off into the jungle, the intrigue totally captivating him.

~

As Josef stepped into the short valley, he was at once overwhelmed by the idyllic ambiance of a South Seas culture standing apart from modern man, a place completely isolated from the outside world, a secluded land, an earthy utopian paradise of tribal Tongans working in harmony, guided by the seemingly wise hand of a small group of fair-skinned Europeans... It all appeared so surreal, as the old colonial aspect of the white man was visually present yet palpably absent; here the relationship was symbiotic, ideal, welcomed. Paradoxically, there was also a fervor of purposeful activity here—the opposite of what one would have expected to find in a lost corner of the sleepy South Pacific, on a serene, blissfully isolated atoll.

Agriculture and the domestication of livestock dominated the scene, but there were also unexpected surprises, such as futuristic greenhouses, a hi-tech solar power installation, utilitarian vehicles powered by compressed air, inspiring geometric infrastructure, and dramatic buildings constructed from huge blocks of coral and decorated with carved totems of chimerical animals, Tongan spirit beings, and Pacific gods.

As Josef followed Ayesha, he caught glimpses of men, European men, whom he thought he recognized. Prominent scientists from various fields—all men who had recently vanished without a trace from the face of the Earth in the past few years...

Ayesha led Josef into the largest of the coral buildings, one that resembled a sprawling lamasery, located idyllically at the end of the valley, where the valley opened to meet the sea. Within, she guided him into a high-ceilinged chamber that made one feel small and sense the presence of some imagined power greater than man.

"Please remain here," Ayesha instructed him, turning to walk off.

"Wait," Josef said, taking hold of her wrist, turning her back toward him. "How do you know my name? My surname, Bschließmayer, it's very Austrian, very Viennese, unpronounceable for most..."

She looked at him lovingly yet aloofly. "Patu T'eo and you," she answered softly, "although the world of modernity rejected you, you did not go unnoticed."

And she left him there alone.

Josef watched her leave, and then he began to slowly pace forward as he noticed a series of Tongan woodcarvings hung along a wall. The series artistically depicted the development of the human fetus at its various stages. As an evolutionary biologist, this was, of course, intimately familiar to him, but he had never before seen the metamorphoses captured in such artistic celebration. It was almost religious, an artistic honoring of the developmental pattern humans inherited from their remote and common ancestors. Josef stared at these woodcarvings in awe as he moved from one to the next, beginning with the earliest segmented stage of the embryo, and next, after the development of vertebrae and muscles, the fish stage, where the embryo displayed gill slits, then to an amphibianish state with the embryo possessing paddle-like hands and feet, onward to the mammalian stage, featuring the presence of a well-defined embryonic tail...

"Dr. Bschließmayer," interrupted a richly textured voice with a velvety resonance, one that strangely sounded to Josef like the trickling of critical tears… It came from a man who entered the chamber in a purposeful manner, a rather plain-looking man who paradoxically displayed a commanding personality, one tinged with cynicism and touched by arrogance.

"Josef, please," Josef requested as he shook hands with Ayesha's father, seeing the family resemblance in the eyes.

"Alun," the man reciprocated, "Alun Last."

"Dr. Last?" Josef replied, surprised, knowing full well, by name, who this eminent scientist was. "But I thought you were living in the Galapagos, studying the marine iguana. What are you doing here?"

"On Fonoifua?" Dr. Last answered, his velvety voice bringing his words to life in a manner most captivating. "Oh, it's a place I visited in my youth, where I laughed, and cried. A place of wonderful memories."

Josef half smiled but then grew serious. "Forgive me, but given this situation…"

Josef watched silently as Dr. Last considered him, staring into his eyes, visually evaluating him, taking his time in doing so.

"I appreciate your directness," Dr. Last finally responded, eyeing Josef approvingly. "So, I'll respond in kind. I'm here on Fonoifua because where you are an admirable but hopeless idealist, I'm a very pragmatic man. Society is self-organizing; it's always been so. Those in power will only relinquish it for something they value more. Never for utopian ideology, or for what's logical or right, unless of course it happens by chance to exactly align with their greed or opportunistic ambitions.

"I rely on individuals and groups selfishly pursuing their own petty self-interests. Tonga is the sixth-most-corrupt nation in the world. The concentration of power is fully vested in the hands of its king and a small group of hereditary nobles—all of whom can be bought to look the other way."

Josef considered the response, the truth behind the cynicism, and then asked, "What's happening here? Outside? This new settlement? The men I recognized?"

Dr. Last nodded, digested the question, and then paced off, responding in a rather arcane manner: "Back in the 1930s and '40s, the German people… deep in their subconscious collective mind lay Wotan, their god of storm and war. This unexpressed fundamental attribute of the German people, it was released by Hitler—and an entire people was sent marching off in an out-of-control state of frenzy. Wotan was behind that uncontrolled downpour, like a transient desert rain that found its old riverbed, regardless of its long absence."

Josef just stared at him, in silence, his mind working on the scientist's abstruse response.

"Under the right conditions," Dr. Last continued, after a purposeful pause, "the proper guidance, a people can be awakened to its collective unconscious—unleashed, so to speak. To be swept along in the grip of something latent, or even something new…"

"You're *awakening* these Tongan people?" Josef asked, skeptically.

"The Tongans are a proud and unconquered seagoing people," Dr. Last responded.

Josef stood silent, waiting for more, beginning to wonder in the depths of his mind if perhaps Dr. Last's cause could somehow fill the present void in his life.

"A set of ideas," Dr. Last went on, "promoted by an influential and empowered proportion of a population, this can promote a distinctive group psyche, a distinctive culture, a distinctive style of behavior, a new way of responding to stimuli. A new way of seeing the world. The pursuit of new objectives. Of a new purpose."

"I don't understand," Josef responded.

"Don't you?"

"A revolution?" Josef guessed.

"A revolution," Dr. Last confirmed.

"And so I was brought here why?" Josef struggled with the obscure conversation, with the references to Wotan, Hitler, and the German people. "Because I'm some physical embodiment of the Aryan type?"

"Oh Josef," Dr. Last shook his head, his rich voice vibrating silkily, "such shallow thinking disappoints me. Especially coming from you. You'll find no racists here. Only men like yourself, seekers of truth and discovery. Only the next men, the men of tomorrow."

"Go on," Josef responded, wanting to make sense of it.

"Man has inherited the Earth," Dr. Last expounded. "He has risen up from several million years of subhuman evolution to see into the invisible atom, and produce genocidal bombs... But the power behind the ability for such insight, it doesn't need to be focused destructively. It can equally be employed creatively."

Josef nodded, following the line of thought.

"Man has recently peered down into our genes," Dr. Last went on, "and acquired new insights. We have plucked a new fruit from the great tree of knowledge, and nothing will ever be the same again."

"And?" Josef asked, although he guessed where this was leading.

"In this new age of man," Dr. Last answered, "this new knowledge, it can be applied to manipulate a human society.

Not only to improve how its members now exist, but in terms of the shape of things to come..."

"Pandora's box." Josef summed it up.

"Needs to be opened," Dr. Last added.

Josef stood there, silent, critical, digesting the thought, his emotions wanting—needing—to grab onto a new cause, but his intellect, his Western inculcation, warning him, cautioning him.

"Josef," Dr. Last appealed to him, "both evolutionary and revolutionary change come only from the actions and interactions of individuals. Thoughts not pursued into action are ephemeral."

"Why was I brought here?" Josef asked.

"Controlling such a thing," Dr. Last explained, "the shaping of a new culture, the power to intensify certain human traits, eliminate others, to awaken certain latent genes—success will ultimately depend on wisdom. Here, cultural mores are different than in the West, which rejected you... And here, the means and the will presently exist to produce a race of supermen. Here, a new society is being birthed, one which will soon experience all of the agonies and pain that growth and change necessitate."

"You have a tiger by the tail," Josef said dispassionately, secretly struggling to remain objective, oddly feeling hope in his heart that he would be extended an offer to join them—and Ayesha—yet simultaneously believing in his mind that it would be an offer that he would have to decline.

Dr. Last placed his hands on Josef's shoulders. "Josef, men are all born unequal, and each sees the world in a somewhat different way than any who has seen it before him. I need you to see what we're doing here with open, unbiased eyes, with an open mind."

Josef watched Dr. Last pace off a bit, as if considering how to frame what he was to say next.

"When visual regions of the mind attain new heights," Dr. Last continued philosophically, "a Michelangelo arises, gifting humanity with unparalleled artistry of shape and form. When these regions combine with a heightened sense of dynamic action, a Leonardo da Vinci is birthed."

"Uncommon giants," Josef remarked. "Men who arose from the common populace."

"Yes," Dr. Last responded with a hint of a smile, "from the common man. And so they stand as *the* symbol. Of what can come. They show us the path that lies ahead, if we can only see our way clear to take it. If indeed our intelligence is a positive attribute, and I think that it is, we must be unafraid to use our minds, to increase our capacities, to improve life."

And Dr. Last stepped up quite close to Josef, face to face. "Josef, will you commit to being part of opening my box of supermen?"

Josef found Dr. Last searching his eyes, through and through, as he found himself suddenly at war between the dictates of his heart and mind.

"To make tomorrow ours," Dr. Last added, speaking it as a quote, which Josef immediately recognized as his own words, his expressed sentiment to his comatose friend, Dr. Patu T'eo, at the Moto'otua National Hospital—where he had apparently been under surveillance. And Josef's mind reeled, jerked back to his past ambitions alongside T'eo and how utterly different they were in scope and concept than what was now unexpectedly being offered him here on lonely Fonoifua.

"Revolutions..." Josef finally said, plaintively. "I think the reality is... revolutions are a place to hide from oneself.

They only leave you empty. They're an illusion, that you're doing something worthwhile, something important with your life, while you're really only suffering, sacrificing... ignoring your own life..."

"No, Josef," Dr. Last gently and compassionately corrected his guest. "Revolutions change things. And sometimes for the better..."

Josef maintained eye contact with Dr. Last, wanting to believe, but disappointedly he found that he could not...

"You're staying the night," Dr. Last informed Josef, his eyes still searching Josef's. "Your room has been prepared. You have much to consider. Ayesha has made sure the pilot won't leave without you."

And Dr. Last walked off.

~

Josef sat motionless on the edge of his bed in his prepared room, his hands cradling his head, his mind lost in labyrinthine thought, when he heard a light rapping knock on the door.

"Come in," he responded.

Ayesha entered, clothed in a sheer nightgown, one that displayed rather powerfully her impressive and seductive physical attributes. She stood there, framed by the open door, hope in her eyes. Her voice was soft when she spoke, reciting aloud, with appropriate pauses:

"Late evening—
a single chair waiting
for someone to stay..."

Josef felt his troubled thoughts temporarily slip away, his heart, body, and intellect all suddenly yearning for this mysterious woman, on this mysterious island. And so he reached out for her with his heart, poetically, romantically.

Josef:
> "The thief
> left it behind—
> the moon at the window."

Ayesha:
> "I've seen the moon
> I sign my letters
> lovingly yours."

And her eyes expressed more than words could convey. Closing the door, she sat beside Josef, as they had sat earlier, at the beach. Josef looked at her, sitting there bathed in the moonlight, which cast a light-bluish hue over her soft skin.

Josef:
> "Moonlight...
> When a woman's skin
> is revealed..."

And he took her in his arms and together they slowly sank into the bed.

~

Later, as they lay there in each other's arms, in the dark, Josef found his troubled thoughts returning.

"Ayesha?" Josef asked.

"Yes?"

"Eugenics..." he whispered.

After several moments of silence, she answered, thoughtfully. "If an individual could improve himself," came her soft answer, "without harming others, shouldn't he strive to do so?

Josef felt his emotions jerk, answering yes, but he remained silent.

"If a people," she added, "could improve themselves, positively change themselves, their society, without harming anyone, shouldn't they do so?"

"I don't know..." Josef answered, as disturbed with himself as with the topic. "I don't believe it's as simple as that."

"... Those who might oppose this," she responded, "it's only because they feel threatened in some way. But when all benefit, there can be no tenable objection."

Ayesha sat up, making eye contact. "Utopia is not an end result, Josef. It's merely the act of striving for something worthy, for something better. And doing so bravely, with your heart. And when an entire people strives for Utopia, it becomes a reality."

"'A map of the world,'" Josef stated slowly, aloud, reciting it from memory, "'that does not include Utopia is not worth even glancing at...' Oscar Wilde."

And they both relaxed, closing their eyes, Josef allowing her spoken words to repeat over and over again within his mind, allowing the words to lull him to sleep.

~

In fitful slumber, Josef's unconscious mind took him to the fictional land of Shangri-La, of James Hilton's utopian novel *Lost Horizon*. There, beside Conway and Perrault, he found the deepest contentment, and a complete acceptance of and belief in their patient, pacifist cause. But day then faded to blackest night and all shapes changed, they changed into night shapes, and Josef found himself on H. G. Wells's *The Island of Doctor Moreau*, with Dr. Last playing the island's doctor and his own reflection in the mirror being that of a man-beast...

~

Josef jerked awake to the morning sunlight, finding himself alone in bed, Ayesha apparently having departed sometime during the night.

Rising shakily, he moved to the window for a breath of fresh air, feeling a bit feverish, still caught up in the emotions of his dreams. Down below, at the edge of the sea, Josef noticed Ayesha, in her bikini, slowly walking into the languid lagoon. The tide was high and the water soon rose to her neck. She continued walking straight ahead and gently disappeared beneath the calm surface.

~

Down on the beach, Josef looked for but could see no sign of Ayesha, only her footprints leading into the sea.

Looking back toward the settlement's coral buildings, decorated with their austere totems of Tongan land and sea gods looking out over the Pacific, he noticed Dr. Last, standing there against the early dawn sky, his image a formidable silhouette, as if it commanded the rising sun itself and owned the horizon and the limitless possibilities it represented.

"Josef," Dr. Last greeted him as he walked down and joined him at the lagoon's edge.

He stepped up to Josef, close again, face to face. "So?" he asked.

"I don't know," Josef answered, torn.

"My daughter was not enough to convince you to remain here, with us?" Dr. Last snapped.

"Is that what she is?" Josef's voice trembled. "An enticement?"

Dr. Last retreated, pacing away and then back. "Forgive me. No, on the contrary, it was her idea to have you brought here."

Josef found that he could breathe again. Dr. Last stepped back up to him, cautiously this time. "So?"

Josef looked back at the small but promising, expanding utopian settlement behind them, and then out across the ocean, toward the horizon, where lay the rest of the massively populated world. Where lay the modernity that had rejected him and struck down the man he had followed.

"Is this what mankind's hope for sanity is reduced to?" he then asked.

"It's a question of practicality," Dr. Last answered sedately. "It's a choice between what is possible and what is not. Between quantity and quality. But keep in mind, time can do so much; from the smallest seed can grow the mightiest tree."

There was silence between the men for some time before Dr. Last spoke again. "I must ask you again. Are you joining us willingly?"

But Josef could not find the answer, and he did not know why.

"Loyalty?" Dr. Last guessed it, identified the reason. "Is that what's holding you back? Loyalty, and guilt?"

And Josef realized it himself, for the first time, and he nodded, tired, feverish, feeling as though he were burning up inside. In his mind's eye he relived in an instant those horrible, awful moments when his great and dear friend Dr. Patu T'eo willingly stepped in front of him, taking the assassin's bullet that was meant for him...

Dr. Last took Josef by the arm, steadying him. "Josef," he said in a strong, reassuring voice, "we've already arranged to have Dr. T'eo transported here. We have methods that can help him. Awaken him."

"Methods?" Josef responded, startled. "What methods?"

Dr. Last motioned with his eyes to the lagoon. Ayesha had broken the surface and was calmly walking toward them, leaving the lagoon as she had entered it, in a tranquil straight-ahead walk. As she neared them, salt water flushed out of the gill slits on the sides of her neck as she switched to breathing air. The slits closed tightly against her skin, almost unseen, except as faint horizontal lines, one above the other.

"My first superman," Dr. Last announced. "Can you imagine an ocean populated by a people capable of breathing underwater

like fish? Amphibian men? And women. Drawn to the sea as much
as they are to the land, like the marine iguana. Living on atolls and
in the sea, free and content, exploiting the vast richness of the oceans.
A new society where there is neither rich nor poor, only plenty."

And suddenly, in a flash of insight, Josef saw it all and
understood the full picture, the scope of the project expanding
tremendously beyond his earlier lack of understanding and
imagining. The vast Pacific waiting out there... The
surrounding sixty-plus Ha'apai atolls, sprinkled across the
central waters of the Kingdom of Tonga, most of them
uninhabited. The nearby sparsely inhabited northern Cook
atolls... And still farther east, the nearly one hundred atolls of
the Tuamotu Archipelago, mostly uninhabited... A frontier
larger than the whole of Europe.

"When can we start...?" was all Josef could utter, his throat
unusually dry. Yes, his future would be here, on Fonoifua, on
this remote, idyllic atoll completely open to the sea, at one with
the sea, ironically the complete opposite of his original
destination, the coral-walled island of Mangaia.

"We already have," Dr. Last answered ever so slowly, his richly
textured voice sounding like dripping tears. "Last night. A virus,
passed on to you by Ayesha. A much more pleasurable method
of delivery than a painful injection, I'm sure you would agree.

"You see, it will take supermen to direct such a project as
this wisely. And the world had no supermen. Until now. But
now it has two. The first two."

Josef suddenly felt a pleasant aching in his throat, a tingling
along the sides of his neck, and an inclination that drew him
irresistibly to the sea.

"The box of the supermen has been opened," Dr. Last
continued. "And from now until the end of time, man must live
with what has been released."

Acknowledgements and Identifying Notations

• A number of the sentiments expressed by this story's Dr. Last, in regard to genetically improving man, were the views of English marine biologist and professor of zoology N. J. Berrill, as presented in his nonfiction book *Inherit the Earth*, first published in 1966.

• When Dr. Last talks about the pre-WWII German psyche being influenced by Wotan, these are the opinions expressed by Swiss psychiatrist and psychotherapist Carl Gustav Jung in his essay on Wotan, published in 1946 in his book *Aufsätze Zur Zeitgeschichte* (*Essays on Contemporary Events*).

• Tonga was named the sixth-most-corrupt country in the world by *Forbes* magazine in 2008.

• The haiku poems utilized in this story were sometimes slightly modified from the original poems, all of which follow the author's note in their unadulterated form with author identifications (in the order that they appeared in "Box of the Supermen").

A Note from the Author

This author hopes the reader appreciated this modest South Seas utopian tale. It was inspired by:

1) The opening chapter of N. J. Berrill's book *Inherit the Earth*. The chapter was titled "Pandora's Box."

2) The 1971 episode of Jacques Cousteau's *Undersea World of Jacques Cousteau*, titled "The Dragons of Galapagos," in which Cousteau advocated science studying the marine iguana further in the future in order to possibly physically alter future human divers, making man better adapted to the sea.

3) James Hilton's novel *Lost Horizon*.

Niko Zinovii
Santa Monica, California
31 October 2014

The original Haiku poems and their authors

The short night ending—
close to the water's edge
a jellyfish.
Author—Yosa Buson

On the water
the reflection
of a wanderer.
Author—Santōka

A kite floats
At the place in the sky
Where it floated yesterday
Author—Yosa Buson

I must step on fallen leaves
to take this path
Author—Suzuki Masajo

Rain clouds—
the frog
puffs his belly out!
Author—Chiyo-ni

In an old pond
A frog ages
While leaves fall
Author—Yosa Buson

Summer rain—
it drums on the heads
of the carp
Author—Shiki

The little fish
carried backward
in the clear water
Author—Kitō

Buckling in the heat
where the A-bomb burst
a marathon
Author—Kaneko Tōta

Even in Kyoto
when I hear the cuckoo
I long for Kyoto
Author—Bashō

Late autumn—
a single chair waiting
for someone yet to come
Author—Arima Akito

The thief
left it behind—
the moon at the window
Author—Ryōkan Taigu

I've seen the moon
I sign my letter to the world
—respectfully yours—
Author—Kaga no Chiyo

Moon flowers!
When a woman's skin
is revealed…
Author—Kaga no Chiyo

Niko Zinovii

Day of the Women

~ 1 ~

Twenty-three-year-old Yoshi stood on the coarse sand of John Man Beach, his slim, sandaled feet submerged in the crystal-clear water of a tidal pool. The tide was out and a multitude of stranded fish darted about beneath him, evading the subtle movements of his slender shadow, seeking refuge amongst sedentary starfish, colorful coral, and craggy underwater rocks.

As the island of Okinawa lay along the easternmost border of the East China Sea, Yoshi found his eyes lift and wander first westward toward rising China, which loomed there invisibly beyond the distant horizon, and then eastward, out over the vast and lonely Pacific. The sun felt warm on his face, and he closed his eyes for a moment to enjoy the pleasantness. During this moment of stolen pleasure, he became aware of the soothing effect of the subtropical sea on his sore and tired feet—for he had just walked the eight circuitous miles from his old family home near the high sea cliffs of the fishing port of Itoman. He always journeyed to the old home whenever he had news to share. Even though the place was now vacant, boarded up... Still, he could not stop himself from visiting it at a time such as this, so deep was his love for his grandfather. So plentiful and fond were his memories.

Freshest in his mind, he remembered racing down to Itoman just last summer, after he had received international recognition and official confirmation of his successful decipherment of Linear A, the pre-Hellenic language of ancient Minoan Crete, from the second millennium BC. As a philologist, as a young scientist, he had pursued the deciphering to open up a lost world of the past, to enrich man's understanding of his early history. But as a human being, he knew that he had pursued the deciphering above all else simply to please his grandfather, to gain favor in the eyes of the one man whose opinion meant so very much to him.

Yoshi smiled as he next recalled one of his earliest memories, one of himself as a small boy, standing on this very beach alongside his grandfather, who was about to adopt and raise him after the tragic accidental death of both his parents.

"How long will you live?" Yoshi remembered timidly asking his grandfather, who already looked most ancient.

"At eighty," his grandfather had answered, "you are still a child. And if at ninety heaven calls, say 'Go away and come back when I am a hundred.'"

"How old are you now, *Tanmee?*"

"One hundred and three." Yoshi's grandfather had smiled warmly. "But the air is nice. I want to stay healthy and live longer than anyone else."

A melodious sound from a nearby *ojii* (an elderly man) playing a three-stringed *sanshin* gently gained Yoshi's attention, pulling him back to the here and now. The old man was leaning against a bent wooden fence post. He paused in his playing to take a sip of homemade beer before continuing. The traditional music, *min'yō*, was plucked with precision and beauty. The man did not sing to the music, as was typical; rather, he allowed the sounds of the rustic, natural world about him to accompany his gentle melody: the sea birds, the calm waves, the soft breeze, even the rhythm of the tide.

Yoshi felt inside himself his Okinawan heritage being stirred—a heritage which was distinctly different from being Japanese. Okinawans had their own culture, their own language, and their own history. They also lived longer than anyone else on the planet.

"Grandfather," Yoshi heard himself whisper out to the sea as he allowed the melody to engulf him completely, "I've been summoned by the Vatican. No explanation given. They're sending a private jet for me, tomorrow."

~ 2 ~

Yoshi felt slightly ill, a bit feverish, by the time he reached the Vatican, although he kept this fact to himself, not wanting to risk missing this unique opportunity due to the possibility of having a contagious flu. After courteous introductions with the secretariat of state, Yoshi was guided through Clementine Hall, of the Apostolic Palace. The mix of people gathered—religious and laity—and the wealth of art, the palpable sense of religion, of history, of time—everything seeming ancient and ageless yet still intimately part of the modern Western world—the mix was overwhelming. Yoshi suddenly felt himself wishing to be standing back in the quiescent safety and dullness of his small tidal puddle, back on Okinawa. He felt himself that inadequate to his surroundings.

True, he was eminently accomplished in his chosen field, in the study of languages, their origins and meanings; in fact, he was often described as a genius by his peers. But looking over the gathered personages, the magnificent Renaissance frescoes and other valuable works of art, he felt himself to be nothing more than a naïve little boy from Okinawa, so unfamiliar was he with the world, with life. He had brilliance, but not yet the necessary life experience to provide him with the confidence born from wisdom.

Yoshi's private audience with His Holiness Pope Adrian VII, in the Papal Library, was surprisingly succinct, a mere formality, much too short to form any impression of the monarch, yet Yoshi sensed an odd anticipation in the man's eyes. A sense of hope?

Leaving the library, Yoshi tried to imagine all of the foreign heads of state and dignitaries that had visited this room in the past, but he found he could not focus his thoughts clearly, his growing fever interfering with his imagination. His mind spun a bit as he took one last glance back at the library's glorious adornments, at its priceless works of art.

Yoshi remembered little of the walk to the Holy See's central repository, to the Vatican Secret Archives, where he was taken next. Upon arriving, he was greeted rather enthusiastically by the cardinal archivist, who at once escorted him to a private chamber, one curiously guarded by the microstate's colorfully and flamboyantly garbed Pontifical Swiss Guard.

After signing and dating a multitude of nondisclosure agreements and other contractual documents in the presence of a Vatican attorney and notary, Yoshi was finally allowed to enter the room. Within it, there was a simple, long wooden table with a single chair. Yoshi sat himself with relief, feeling hot, his head beginning to ache, flu-like. When he finally gathered himself and lifted his eyes, he saw lying before him a dozen or so tile-sized sheets composed of an exotic, silvery material.

"Go on," the archivist said, "touch one."

Yoshi picked up one of the sheets. It was extremely light and extraordinarily thin, like tinfoil, but thinner, lighter... Overcome with curiosity, Yoshi gently crumbled up one corner in his hand and then let it go, only to watch the material straighten itself back out, wrinkle free, as if by magic.

"They're indestructible," the archivist commented.

Yoshi focused on the hieroglyphic-like symbols that seemed printed upon the sheets. The symbols were very small and a shiny purple in color. Here and there on the sheets, large portions of these symbols were missing, effaced, faded, or blurred beyond recognition...

"This *metal paper*," the archivist explained somberly, "it's not of this Earth. It's extraterrestrial. It came into the Church's possession back in the eighth century... Found in a debris field, scattered amongst the wreckage of a small hexagonal disc, in a farmer's field, outside of Rome. We're hoping *you* can tell us what it says."

~ 3 ~

The cardinal archivist saw to it that a hot meal was brought down to Yoshi, but Yoshi did not eat, so focused and intent was he on the bizarre extraterrestrial script, on the alien alphabet—if it was an alphabet. Perhaps it was nonalphabetic?

Yoshi had been informed sotto voce by the cardinal archivist that over the years the world's best and brightest philologists had all attempted to decipher what now lay before him. But all had failed, completely, making no progress whatsoever.

The only positive outcome came from the one sheet not provided to Yoshi. It contained extraterrestrial mathematical symbols. It had been deciphered some years ago. It provided the location of the alien planet from which the wrecked disc had originated, affirming the alienness of the ancient materials. This knowledge, like the fact that the Holy See was in possession of the alien writings, remained private to the Vatican. When Yoshi had asked about the wreckage of the alien craft, the cardinal had merely shaken his head and mumbled, "Buried and reburied down through the ages. Lost... It had been feared to be a thing of evil... sent by Satan..."

Hours later, the cardinal himself brought down a plate of raw chopped garlic and a bottle of dark brandy before leaving Yoshi again. "To remedy your flu," the cardinal winked, "cleanse your body. Sharpen your mind."

At 9:00 p.m., Yoshi refused to retreat to the bedroom the Vatican was providing him. He asked the Swiss Guard if instead a small cot could possibly be brought down to him, explaining that he needed to rest but wanted to keep working, off and on, throughout the night. That he didn't want to leave his effort just yet. He had become utterly intrigued, fixated, obsessed. A cot, blanket, and pillow were brought down.

Around midnight, utter frustration set in as Yoshi's fever heightened. It was then that the long night of garlic, brandy, and fevered delirium began. Yoshi normally abstained from alcohol, but he was desperate to remedy his fever.

Symbols blurred, separated, and merged, hallucinatory. The small purple hieroglyphics swam about in Yoshi's mind, forming into an enigmatic labyrinth of unknown meaning. Yet the order of the symbols, their arrangements, it was all eerily beautiful, in an arcane, alien, yet strangely familiar manner. Sinking deeper into delirium, Yoshi panicked and wished that he was back home, on Okinawa. He heard in his thoughts the music played by the elderly man on his *sanshin* on John Man Beach. There was a beauty to it... The musical interrelationships, its scale, rhythm, structure, beat and metre, repetition, melodic range... harmony... *My God*, Yoshi realized, *the alien language is like music. But where does this clue lead?*

Yoshi's thoughts swept back and forth through his mind, rising, falling, twisting, turning—searching restlessly, madly, for a solution.

"*Stay strong*," Yoshi heard his grandfather's words from time past echo in his mind. "*Smart, thoughtful. Unbreakable. With hope and faith, you will break it down…*"

Sometime around 3:00 a.m. Yoshi awoke, still suffering from fever—the brandy had not reduced it—to find all his mad scribblings sprawled out over the table before him. He had, sometime during the night, translated the alien text, having somehow deciphered it during his fever-born and alcohol-enhanced delirium. Somehow, his mind, employing intuition, learned technical skills, leaps of logic, and fever-induced imaginative mental wanderings, had granted him a string of singular insights. He had found the *key* that melted away the mystery of the extraterrestrial script. For the script was meant to be read. It had been designed to be decipherable. But it had been designed by an alien mind, one that thought differently than a man's. It had thus taken a unique human mind, in an unconventional state, to recognize the key, which fortunately had survived unadulterated, complete, intact within the script.

But as much of the script had been damaged, effaced, the alien message was incomplete, fragmented, and thus tantalizingly enigmatic. It seemed to promise the offering of a 'revelation' of knowledge and wisdom, referencing the disclosure of some important universal 'discovery.' And yet the message also seemed to contain a warning to all 'aware' civilizations. There was a continued reference to 'dark nature,' and to something untranslatable, the closest human word for it being 'evil.' And something linked to this, something rather frightening, something like: 'Save your world.' There was much more, but the pieces of the message that had survived provided little coherent meaning. Thus, the fragmented message was open to being interpreted in different ways…

~ 4 ~

Yoshi was still at the Vatican, recovering in its infirmary, when Pope Adrian VII, the successor of Saint Peter, the Bishop of Rome, the Vicar of Jesus Christ, the leader of the worldwide Catholic Church, the Sovereign of the Vatican City State, made his startling announcement to the world proclaiming papal infallibility in exercising the absolute temporal powers granted him.

Pope Adrian revealed that the Church would send an expedition to a far-off planet, one that had issued to humanity what he interpreted as a warning. That the Church would pay the Russians to build a spacecraft capable of such interstellar flight. That the Church would strip itself down to absolute poverty if necessary to pay for this spacecraft, selling off all its holdings in land and property, all its priceless art... That the Church was doing this to learn new revelations from God and to save the world from evil.

~ 5 ~

To build the Pope's starship, the pragmatic Russians simply modified a design first conceived and developed back in the 1950s, an Orion ship: a spacecraft mounted with shock absorbers upon a huge armored pusher plate. In essence, a firecracker under a tin can. Only the explosions in this case would be nuclear...

With the injection of antimatter into the nuclear fuel, the Orion ship would be capable of attaining a velocity of a respectable percentage of the speed of light. This was needed, for although biological science had recently made incredible breakthroughs that allowed man to dampen time by means of nearly unlimited suspended animation, even at its great speed it would take this Orion ship approximately two hundred years to reach the star system from which the alien message had originated, and then that same amount of time to return. Nearly four centuries would have gone by on Earth before the expedition's reappearance.

The crew would, of course, send a message back to Earth, at the speed of light, shortly after they arrived at their destination, but even this would still not be received for well over two hundred years.

Pope Adrian believed the wait of several centuries was a small price to pay to save humanity. He expressed to the Roman Curia his unalterable belief that the Catholic Church had endured the past two millennia in preparation for this very moment. That God was guiding his decisions.

The crew selected for the Vatican's expedition was named in the Holy See's official newspaper, *L'Osservatore Romano:*

Cardinal Antonio Marini — Vatican emissary

Major Sergei Leonov — Cosmonaut

Dr. Isa Leone —MD

Yoshi Yamashiro — Philologist

Yoshi had not expected to be honored with such an invitation, and without hesitation he accepted, unable to say no to this historic opportunity. Being young, and having spent his life so far devoted entirely to his studies, he had no wife, no family—no close friends or loved ones to leave behind. He believed that his grandfather would have been very proud, also that the expedition would importantly expand the frontiers of science, as a body of knowledge, by leaps and bounds. Little did he suspect that the venture would also dramatically challenge and alter his own perceptions and sentiments.

~ 6 ~

Yoshi completed his training course outside of Moscow, spending time in the microgravity of Star City's giant underwater pool to learn to space walk, experiencing zero-G simulations aboard plummeting Ilyushin military aircrafts, enduring centrifuge high-G training—and a barrage of other tests—before blasting off in a Soyuz rocket from the Baikonur Cosmodrome, out on the remote and lonely Kazakh Steppe, to rendezvous with the new Russian Mir-4 space station.

From the station, Yoshi was transported directly to the Vatican's Orion ship, the *Blessed Trinity*, assembled in orbit by the Russian Federation. As he floated aboard, he felt himself tremble inside. Physically, he felt up to the challenge, but mentally, spiritually, emotionally, he felt inadequately prepared for the unknown trials and possible tribulations that lay ahead.

As he pulled himself past a series of austere and utilitarian viewing portholes, he looked down at Earth, at its magnificent blue oceans, at its familiar landmasses, at its heavenly clouds. The planet glowed resplendently in the sunlight, beckoning like a jewel, Earth, the pearl of this solar system. And Yoshi suddenly understood intimately and humbly how humankind was tied to Earth, for he felt it in his heart. And an unexpected insecurity crept over him, being so disconnected from Earth, as he was. He felt his innermost emotions rising, longing to return to the pleasant gentleness of his home in Okinawa. To hear the calm coastal waves waking him at dawn, the distant voices of his neighbors. The sensation of the sunlight warming his face as he opened his eyes, feeling the island's sweet, subtropical breeze. Like a child, his heart secretly called out to Mother Earth and its comforting, living cradle; he suddenly ached to touch the ground, the sea, in respectful appreciation.

And so, Yoshi physically and mentally steadied himself as he forced his eyes to turn away from Earth, to peer out the opposite portholes, out into the sterile, vacuous blackness of deep space. Glimpsing the infinite, he felt its utter loneliness momentarily still his young heart, its sheer immensity trouble and diminish his inexperienced intellect, its imagined desolation and coldness chill his soul… and he suddenly found himself questioning whether or not time and space were meant to be conquered by men.

Yoshi felt a feminine hand come to rest upon his shoulder. It was the mission's attractive Italian doctor, Isa. She floated up beside him. Yoshi wondered how much older she was than he—possibly only seven years?

"Are you afraid?" she asked him in Italian. "Of the Long Sleep?"

"No," Yoshi answered her honestly, in her language. (A polyglot, he spoke seven languages, among them Italian and Russian.) "I trust you. I'm not afraid of your part. …Only of everything else."

She smiled.

"What do you think they will be like?" Yoshi asked.

She thought for a moment and then answered, reciting something aloud, something she had recently read and committed to memory:

"Nowhere in all space or on a thousand worlds will there be men to share our loneliness.

"There may be wisdom; there may be power: somewhere across space, great instruments… may stare vainly at our floating cloud rack, their owners yearning as we yearn.

"Nevertheless, in the nature of life and in the principles of evolution we have our answer. Of men elsewhere, and beyond, there will be none forever…"

"Yes…" Yoshi commented, understanding and appreciating the words, allowing the penetrating insight to expand his fledgling perception of reality. "They will be different."

And he fell silent, finding the depth of the poignant thought awe-inspiring.

~ 7 ~

The Long Sleep beds were within the shielded flight-crew station, occupying the tip of the crew module. This station was positioned behind an immense windshield that offered a staggering panoramic vista of deep, dark space. As Yoshi entered, he again felt his instincts call out for Mother Earth. But the umbilical had been cut; he was now on his own. Not even his grandfather could rescue him... And so he struggled to calm the waves of primitive and unexpected emotions that undulated through him.

The Vatican's official emissary, Cardinal Antonio Marini, priest and scientist, was already lying within his Long Sleep bed, which looked rather like a metallic coffin. In his mid-sixties, Marini appeared on the other end of time from Yoshi. Lean, angular-faced, he spoke with a mature confidence and an appealing emotional openness.

"Yoshi." The cardinal reached out affectionately to Yoshi, stopping the young Okinawan. "This is our time."

Yoshi nodded.

And then Yoshi could see Marini reading his thoughts, as if the cardinal had walked in Yoshi's shoes decades ago. As if Yoshi could hide nothing from him.

"How do we dare attempt such an insolent challenge to nature?" Marini smiled calmly to Yoshi. "Arrogant foolishness or magnificent madness, Yoshi, we're part of this brief, audacious moment in the age of man. Whether the mission is fated to be tragic or triumphant, embrace it. We rebelled against confinement."

He then looked fatherly into Yoshi's concerned eyes. "We'll be fine."

Yoshi, proceeding toward his bed, next encountered the mission's commander and pilot, Major Sergei Leonov, the Russian cosmonaut, a bearded bear of a man.

"God-awful fission bombs," Sergei mumbled and cursed to himself in Russian. "Antimatter madness..."

Isa floated up beside Yoshi and escorted him to his personal Long Sleep bed. This comforted Yoshi somewhat, although he found himself unconsciously glancing aft, imagining in his mind's eye the ship's gigantic propellant magazines, its huge nuclear pulse propulsion unit, and its heavily armored pusher plate, suddenly doubting if any spacecraft could survive, for propulsion purposes, the detonation of a stream of "God-awful fission bombs."

Yoshi knew that he would need something on this journey, something in his mind, to steady himself, to ground himself. As Isa silently strapped him in for the Long Sleep, he found his eyes looking past her, peering out the craft's immense windshield, out to Earth below. Through the cloud cover, he hoped to see the Pacific and the outline of the islands of Japan, knowing that Okinawa, although it would be impossible to see, lay a mere four hundred miles south of Kyushu.

But instead of the Pacific, it was the familiar outline of the African continent that lay below. And Yoshi smiled an unexpected smile. It was quite easy for him to visually trace his way up the continent's east coast, to Tanzania, and then to find the majestic, dormant-volcanic Mount Kilimanjaro, the highest mountain in all of Africa—the highest freestanding mountain in all the world. Yes, it would be lofty Kilimanjaro, Earth's mountain of greatness, that would stabilize him. Yes, it would be Kilimanjaro.

As Yoshi felt the cold salt water begin to circulate through his body, dropping his temperature and slowing his cellular activity, as he felt himself slowly slipping into a hypothermic state of torpor, his thoughts focused solely and intently on ice-capped Kilimanjaro.

"Will I dream... in Long Sleep?" Yoshi found it difficult to even whisper the words.

Isa shook her head "no" as Yoshi's eyes slowly closed.

... *6,500 feet in altitude*: A spider's web broke across Yoshi's face as his mind placed him back in the mud of the humid rain forest at the foot of Kilimanjaro. The smell of the recently fallen rain, the towering ferns, the moss-draped landscape... he found himself vividly reliving, in his imagination, his climb of Kilimanjaro last year.

Looking through the mist, Yoshi stared up in awe at the solitary mount that loomed above the clouds, at the giant, snow-capped volcano that rose up from the equator. And he suddenly felt himself to be such a tiny, insignificant part of the mountain. So odd how this feeling comforted him, pulling his drifting psyche away from the coldness of outer space and back to Earth's bosom. Nature engulfed him with its raw beauty, and he felt in his place.

Yoshi carried a whispering vestige of his grandfather with him on this journey, and he imagined the man's voice in his mind, talking to him:

"The mountain will change, Yoshi. Like life. Show awareness of the change. Allow it to happen. Do not struggle against it."

Yoshi felt his mind drift further, his thoughts becoming disconnected as the Long Sleep pulled him in deeper, slowly stilling his heart.

... *9,000 feet in altitude*: Unusual trees... a kingdom of shrubs... splashes of color—wild flowers. A magnificent rainbow... Ever so slowly, the mountain was revealing itself to him...

His grandfather again:

"Yoshi, allow the change to unfold. Accept it. Try to understand what is changing and why—"

And the Long Sleep stopped Yoshi's mind.

~ 8 ~

Next, an eternity of nothingness... or but a single timeless moment?

~ 9 ~

And then, dim thoughts reassembling, forming a conscious mind... His mind.

... 10,500 feet in altitude: The morning mist hung silently above the melting snow. Kilimanjaro had transformed into a lonely and mysterious landscape, its rough slopes dotted by odd, ancient plants and giant heather reaching over thirty feet in height. It was like an alien planet...

Yoshi's grandfather's voice:

"Yoshi, accept change and it becomes your teacher. And you learn from it."

Waking, Yoshi felt his dry eyes flutter and open.

"Yoshi," Isa whispered to him, leaning over him, reviving him, "we've arrived. The system of the double suns."

~ 10 ~

Yoshi found it quite surprising that down on the planet's surface he did not see two suns hanging dramatically in the sky, or one sun rising while another of a different color set, casting uncanny double shadows amongst the ruins. Rather, one ordinary sun hung there gloomily in the dull red sky, the second being far too distant to be seen during the day. Even at night, it would have appeared merely as a very bright but distant planet, moving slowly against the backdrop of stars.

Yoshi walked up to Isa and Cardinal Marini, leaving Sergei behind to guard their shuttle—where they had ceremonially planted the gold-and-white flag of the Vatican City State, complete with its crossed keys of Saint Peter and papal tiara.

As Yoshi took his place beside Isa and Marini, he felt a comforting solidarity, perhaps generated by their matching ultra-lightweight flight suits, which ironically made him feel more like an impossible time traveler from the Renaissance than one of the modern star travelers they actually were. Modeled after the simple duty uniform of the Pontifical Swiss Guardsman, their functional blue uniforms sported fashionable high white collars, simple brown belts, white gloves, black boots, and rather stylish black berets.

They wore no space helmets, the atmosphere being quite breathable, the climate surprisingly suitable, even salubrious. Yoshi was glad for this, as their helmets were unnecessarily heavy and cumbersome, comb morion in style, like that of the ancient Spanish conquistadors. The beret by itself felt infinitely more comfortable.

Yoshi could not help but think about how he was a Vatican astronaut, sent forward in time and across dark light-years by a pope who was now long since dead. With a certain pride in the Vatican, in humankind, in himself, he stepped forward with his shipmates and walked to the foot of the alien city lying before them.

Cardinal Marini looked up at the high, elegant archways, at the height of the entrances leading into the ineffable, ruined alien structures that stretched to the horizon of this near-dead, lonely, wind-swept world.

"Giants..." Marini whispered. "They were giants. From another sun."

They all stood there motionless for several moments, taking in the arrestingly exotic, silent city. The sight was awe-inspiring yet paradoxically haunting, desolate, palpably forlorn.

"Oh..." Marini speculated aloud. "Here there was once power. Here there was wisdom. Poised resolve. Magnificence. They must have ventured into the highest realms of heavenly thought and discovery... Surely they were nearer the angel than the ape. And yet... what happened to them?"

One wondrous alien structure stood far taller than any other, a lovely pearly tower soaring up high above the clouds, its nacreous exterior refulgent in the bright sunlight. The Vatican astronauts made their way toward its shining glory.

~ 11 ~

Later, back onboard the *Blessed Trinity*:

Yoshi had already told the others. They all knew the essence of his translation of the new alien writings and audio recordings that they had found on display in the wondrous tower. And they had handled it in different ways. Sergei got drunk, alone. Isa went to sleep. Cardinal Marini prayed.

Now it was time for Yoshi to tell the Vatican, to tell Earth—to transmit to Earth an encapsulation of his translation of their findings. As he prepared himself to do so, he felt himself to be a terrible young man, to transmit such a message. He felt like crying. So he delayed. And sought out Cardinal Marini.

As Yoshi slowly circled the craft's inner structural spine, working his way down toward the crew module, he felt himself mentally maturing, painfully, due to his tacit and diffident acceptance of the sobering revelations of the alien writings— for he had become convinced of part of its message.

Yoshi found Cardinal Marini on his knees, in prayer, his back turned to Yoshi.

"Cardinal Marini," Yoshi whispered. But there was no reply—so intent and focused was Marini on his ethereal communication.

Wrestling with his mental and emotional restlessness, Yoshi ascended back to the communication board, from which he would transmit his message, alone. As he wound his way back up to the crew station, he imagined his grandfather's thoughts in his mind:

"*Nature speaks to those who care to listen,*" his grandfather's voice said. "*Man is still wild, as the Earth is wild. Nature—it reminds us of the wilderness that is still in our hearts.*"

Seating himself at the Orion ship's communication station, Yoshi manipulated the controls in preparation for sending his communication. He only wanted to get it over with. A red light flashed on the panel, signaling Yoshi to begin, and he did:

"Your Holiness," Yoshi began, "my transcription is completed, of the sacred writings of this extinct alien civilization. Of the revelation of knowledge that was sought. These giants, in their language I believe they called themselves what would have sounded like the 'Man.'"

Yoshi pictured in his mind's eye the images of the many-armed, many-eyed, many-headed giants that they had found within the tower, in the form of sculptures and paintings, all preserved to last indefinitely. It was ironic indeed that these most inhuman creatures had taken the name *Man*.

Yoshi felt his voice tremble a little as he continued. "The Man, they had abandoned religion, and philosophy. I'm sorry to say. To focus on a purely scientific examination of *evil*. The Man believed evil to be something real; it terrified them. They became obsessed with it.

"Bravely, they objectively determined that life was programmed for evil by the instructions of heredity. No matter what the species. Evil was, in their minds, a force of nature. They saw life as being preset for aggression.

"This led the Man to scientifically examine the manifestations of aggression. The phenomena of rape, murder, war. Terrors all too familiar to us... The Man found that aggression was inherent to sentient existence, manifest in the male of the species. That it was the male who savagely raped, brutally beat, violently killed, offensively raided, mass slaughtered… territorially invaded, and waged war…"

Yoshi could not help but think of Earth's last World War, and of the eighty-two-day-long Battle of Okinawa—*Tetsu ne Ame*, "Rain of Steel"… the bloodiest battle of the Pacific, fought two months before the atomic bombings of Hiroshima and Nagasaki. The battle claimed over 77,000 Imperial Japanese soldiers, over 14,000 American lives. And as many as 150,000 Okinawan civilians, who were either murdered or experienced death at their own desperate hands, ending their lives by suicide to escape the terrifying carnage and horror…

"This led the Man to scientifically study maleness," Yoshi continued. "They determined that the savagely violent nature of males could not be controlled. That evil could not be evolved away from…

"Furthermore, the Man speculated that the *demonic male* would be prevalent throughout the universe. And that the demonic male would always, eventually, bring about the extinction of its own kind…

"The Man came to believe that there was only one hope: the eradication of the demonic male. A philosophy grew out of this. Then a religion, dedicated to this cause. The religious claimed that the infallibility of the female mind was guiding their actions…"

Yoshi paused, shrugging his shoulders before continuing, considering the madness of it all.

"The Man eliminated their own male population… dooming themselves to extinction. Before their demise, they sent spacecraft out into the galaxy, to warn other sentient civilizations of the evil that they had discovered… but also to carry within them the means for the mass destruction of the demonic males existing on nearby planets…"

And Yoshi fell silent, sinking into thought. A bit bewildered, he looked back up at the small, still camera.

"Please tell Cardinal Archivist Leo Capponi that he was right—the alien craft the Church recovered, it was a thing of evil, to be buried and forgotten." And Yoshi caught himself, realizing the time difference. "Even though Cardinal Capponi has been dead for over two centuries…"

And Yoshi wondered if anyone at all would actually be listening to his message, after these centuries gone by…

~ 12 ~

All Yoshi wanted to do was to fall into Long Sleep, to take a time-out from thinking, from the apparent harshness of reality, to just experience nothingness for a while. He closed his eyes before Isa even gave him the initial injection. He was that ready. Yet he wondered, just for a moment, if he could dream, if it was possible to do so, would he dream of all the new technological wonders awaiting him upon his return, four hundred years into Earth's future? Or… would there even be such wonders? He suddenly worried, could Earth's demonic males have already obliterated the human race?

Then, as before, Yoshi found himself reaching back into his memory for Kilimanjaro, to ground himself.

… *15,000 feet in altitude*: How enormous the mountain still was before him, and how small it made him feel. Once again, this stabilized Yoshi's troubled psyche, putting him in a place of comfort, for he was again a child of the Earth, safe in his cradle.

… The air was now tenuous… and growing colder. Ice crystals were everywhere. He had reached the cold barrier zone. *Go slow… must go slow, to acclimate, to avoid altitude sickness.*

A three-hundred-foot lava tower… Rocks and swirling mist… The skeleton of an elephant! Also: the remains of an antelope. And a leopard. Why?

114

Still carrying that vestige of his grandfather with him, Yoshi continued to hear his voice:

"Yoshi, accept and learn from change and you will grow. You will become strong. Do not be afraid of the unexpected. Embrace it."

And the Long Sleep claimed Yoshi, separating him from a true state of life by a vast stretch of nothingness…

~ 13 ~

Unlike his first gentle, slow awakening from Long Sleep, this time Yoshi felt himself jerked from nonexistence to full alertness. He lurched upright in his bed, his muscles spasming in acute pain, his hands contracting uncontrollably.

The pain suddenly ended, and his fists unclenched. His eyelids fluttered and opened, and his mind—in a state of chaos, struggling to reassemble itself—was assaulted with utter astonishment and bewilderment.

There in the flight crew station, facing him, was an enormous starfish with a huge, single eye—staring at him. The creature reminded Yoshi of the red-and-orange-dappled starfish in the tidal pools at John Man Beach, only this starfish was over six feet in height, standing there on end like a star-shaped sheriff's badge. Its naked skin was rich in color, and granular white pores spotted it here and there, like a random sprinkling of dots. Its single huge eye—over two feet across—centered upon its wide, heavy body, appeared a reservoir of strange alien thought and deep alien intellect.

As this starfish scrutinized Yoshi, Yoshi noticed the other two starfish. They had taken Isa from her Long Sleep bed. They stepped into a blur in the fabric of space and time and disappeared with Isa, as if they could step across light-years in the throb of a single heartbeat.

Yoshi turned his scattered focus back to the enormous starfish standing there before him, against the star-speckled blackness of the immense viewing portal behind it.

Oddly, Yoshi felt absolutely no fear; he sensed no threat, only the most wondrous feeling of utter fascination—emanating from both himself and the starfish.

The starfish stared at Yoshi for the longest time, scrutinizing him with that one huge, alien eye. The gathered passing moments collected themselves into what seemed like an eternity. Yoshi began to wonder if the creature was reading his mind, his memories.

Then, slowly, Yoshi slumped back down into his bed. Slowly, his eyes closed. Slowly, his mind stopped, and he fell back into the timeless nothingness of the Long Sleep.

~ 14 ~

Nothingness…

~ 15 ~

Thoughts slowly, gracefully reassembling, Yoshi's mind calmly started up again.

… Over 16,000 feet in altitude: Cloudy mist everywhere… Frozen, wind-swept rock…

Climbing above the clouds now… The air bitter cold, difficult to breathe… *Will I die here? Can I make it? Can I fulfill my promise?*

Yoshi's grandfather's voice:

"Yoshi, embracing change, it allows you to understand. It brings you wisdom."

~ 16 ~

Waking, Yoshi struggled to open his eyes. It was difficult to do so this time, painful. When his blurred vision finally focused, he found Cardinal Marini and Major Leonov leaning over him, reviving him.

"We thought we lost you," Marini said, his face etched with fatherly concern. "You didn't awaken with us, earlier, as programed."

Yoshi sat up, his head aching, half his thoughts still swimming in limbo. He noticed Earth's familiar moon looming large outside. "... We're back?"

The cardinal and Sergei exchanged uneasy glances.

Marini then nodded, yet a disturbed grimness palled his features. "But there have been a few unexpected incidents, and an unfortunate... sinful reaction."

"Sinful reaction?" Sergei growled the words under his breath, cursed in Russian, and backed off, heatedly.

"First," Cardinal Marini went on, expressing absolute bafflement, "Dr. Leone is gone. Vanished."

Yoshi jolted, feeling as if he remembered something vitally important, but then he found only echoes of a dream there, lingering somewhere in his mind, impossible images tantalizing him, something about Isa. For a desperate moment, he tore at his memory, struggling to pull something forth, to make sense of what seemed a nearly forgotten, illusionary dream, but he could not.

"Second," Marini continued, his words pulling back Yoshi's focus, "yes, we are back. We're in orbit about Earth. But we've been warned away."

Marini helped Yoshi swing his legs out of the Long Sleep bed, sitting the young Okinawan upright. The cardinal was silent while doing so. Yoshi wondered if the priest was delaying, providing him a few extra moments to prepare his mind for what was to come next.

The cardinal, his confident voice stern, his face etched by deep and troubled emotion, next told Yoshi how the Vatican had a very old satellite still in orbit. And how this satellite had broadcasted to them, upon their arrival, informing them of how shortly after the *Blessed Trinity* had left Earth, the Vatican had mounted a secret search for the wreckage of the alien spacecraft that had crashed outside Rome back in the eighth century.

"They found it." Marini informed Yoshi. "Buried right beneath St. Peter's Square, beneath the Vaticano, the Vatican Obelisk.

"In the excavated pit, amongst the wreckage, they also found a sealed container, something like a giant egg. They cut it open, and a metal thing crawled out of it, robotic, artificially intelligent. This egg had been the Man's Trojan horse...

"This robot attacked and killed all those present, taking tissue samples. Studying human biology, discovering DNA. Afterward, in hiding, it manufactured in its internal machinery a self-replicating virus and unleashed it upon the world. The virus spread to every corner of the globe. It was in the air, in the water, impossible to escape. It soon killed every human male on the planet... leaving Earth solely to the female of the species."

The cardinal told Yoshi how unlike the Man, a small population of the women of Earth did manage to survive. For four centuries, the women of Singapore, Japan, Korea, Taiwan, Hong Kong, and Macau practiced reproductive cloning, asexual reproduction. Producing women from women. Humanity, its women, survived by parthenogenesis.

"Like our Blessed Virgin Mary," Marini emphasized, "giving birth miraculously, as a virgin."

Yoshi could not help but consider the unspoken irony that it was only the world's hi-tech areas strongly influenced by Confucianism whose women had survived. Nations that over four hundred years ago had refused to become signatory to the international laws initiated and passed by the Christian West banning cloning and other *morally objectionable* areas of emerging biological research. Confucianism promoted that birth marked the beginning of life—that an embryo did not have a separate existence. Yoshi wondered how Cardinal Marini was dealing with the future's chance affront to Catholicism.

Marini's gaze dropped rather weakly, and his troubled voice trembled ever so slightly as he ran out of words.

"We three, we three *demonic males*, we're the only human males left in existence. And one of us, one of us has already restarted the age-old male curse."

"No!" Sergei protested angrily. "Is it a curse to survive?"

Yoshi looked to Cardinal Marini for an explanation. Marini slumped up against the nearby wall, looking spiritually exhausted. "Look out the viewing port, Yoshi," he said. "We're in a geosynchronous orbit, facing the moon. The *Blessed Trinity* is facing the moon. Our propulsion module, our *nuclear pulse engine*, it's pointed backward, at Earth."

"*God-awful fission bombs*." Yoshi imagined Sergei's words spoken just before their launch; they echoed in his mind. And Yoshi turned to Sergei, their bearded bear of a commander and pilot. In Sergei's face, Yoshi saw only unbridled manly confidence, a leonine maleness, a male will not to be tested or denied.

"Earth's virgin women," Marini continued, "apparently they subscribed to the Man's philosophy, after receiving your communication two centuries ago. That it's the demonic male of the species that brings about the terror of violence, of war. Our women, they've been at peace now for nearly four hundred years. They warned us away.

"Technologically they've stagnated, they've made no advances—in fact, their level of technology has greatly regressed. They, um, they shot up an old air-to-space missile at us. A warning shot across our bow? Our ship's automated meteoroid defenses destroyed it. We weren't harmed.

"But our commander here, he went and turned the ship about... ejected two of our fissionable propulsion units—two nuclear bombs! The points of detonation set for the most destructive altitude possible. He obliterated Earth's two largest remaining cities in retaliation, killing millions of innocent women..."

"We were attacked!" Sergei defended his actions. "They needed to be warned. Not to attempt offensive actions again."

"Why two bombs?" Yoshi heard himself ask, his mind still reeling from the intake of all this startling information. "Why the second bomb?"

"They needed to be told," Sergei puffed out his chest, "that *man* is back."

Yoshi just stared at the large Russian in shock.

"That *man* is back to take his rightful place," Sergei then added forcefully. "At the head of the table. We are only three. Three! They are thirty million! We needed to immediately put them in their place. Punish them for their action. So they do not think of ever trying anything again. And also, to let them know that things will be different now. That *man* is back."

Yoshi remembered how Sergei had gotten drunk back in orbit around the Man's desolate planet. At the time, Yoshi had thought it quite peculiar how Sergei had taken what had happened to the Man so deeply personally. Allowed it to upset him as terribly as it did. Yoshi had understood the cardinal's religious reaction, and Isa's emotionally sensitive withdrawn state as well. But not Sergei's reaction.

Now, in retrospect, Yoshi realized that Sergei's response was simply a male one. That psychologically Sergei stood on the side of the males of the Man species, and he grieved for their elimination, and for the implications as to what it might mean if the Man philosophy ever found its way to Earth. And here, confronting Sergei presently, was this Russian's worst nightmare—and he was now reacting to it the only way he knew how, like a cornered animal. A cornered male animal.

"No virus," Sergei mumbled to himself, "can remain alive for two hundred years without a host, can it?

"I don't know," Marini replied, wondering where Sergei was going with this question. "Isa was our doctor…"

"We're going back down to our world," Sergei announced it to them—a decision made. "With our ship up here in orbit guaranteeing our safety. By remote control, from anywhere on Earth, we can launch down more bombs if they should try to harm us."

"My God," Marini protested, "so you'll turn the *Blessed Trinity* into a Sword of Damocles?"

"Why?" Yoshi heard himself ask Sergei.

"Why what?" Sergei asked.

"Why should we go down to Earth?" Yoshi made his question clear. He thought it a valid one.

"Why should we go down to Earth?" Sergei was mildly stumped, but only for a moment, before he experienced a sudden spark of insight. "To repopulate the planet. To start up progress again. Only the male drives progress. Through competition, conflict. War. The Man didn't understand that! Our women have sacrificed that. Soon they'll retrograde to the Stone Age. In the end, rejoin the apes in the forest!"

Sergei swung toward the cardinal, attempting to gain a convert. "Is that what your God wants? To reduce his creation back to an animal state?"

"No…" Marini said, slowly, developing his own line of reasoning. "Always to uplift us away from the ape, and toward the angel. Perhaps now toward the mother of Jesus. To mirror our Blessed Virgin Mary. God must want us to evolve, as a species, within the reality of the natural world. So that we can better follow the teachings of his son, of Jesus.

"Otherwise why would God have allowed the Man to send out those spacecraft to the far corners of our galaxy?

Why would God have allowed the Man to sacrifice themselves to extinction as they did—?"

And suddenly Cardinal Marini had his own moment of insight, realizing what ultimately made sense to him, individually. "… My God, the Man, they were a Jesus moment. Through their death came our resurrection as an immortal species—their extinction offered humanity salvation, the promise of eternal life as a species. With no demonic male to cause our extinction... 'Blessed are the meek, for they shall inherit the earth.'"

"No." Sergei shook his head, brusquely dismissing Marini's religious interpretation. "That's against all of nature."

Yoshi looked at the two men bewildered, unconvinced by either. They both turned to him.

"Are you with me?" Sergei asked most bluntly. "Or him?"

"Yoshi," Marini took his turn, repeating words that he had spoken to the young Okinawan at the beginning of their voyage but words that now held greater meaning. "This is our time. Our mission, it's led us to this moment. To this crucial decision."

Yoshi noticed how the cardinal saw the doubt in his mind, how the cardinal read his thoughts.

"Remove the religion, Yoshi," Marini continued calming, speaking again with his characteristic mature confidence. "Look only at the natural universe, if you wish.

"And ask yourself, dare we as a species attempt such a brazen challenge to nature? To change it so? By removing the male from our species in order to end violence, war, and suffering, to ensure the continued survival of our kind. Is it arrogant foolishness or magnificent madness, Yoshi? This single audacious moment will decide the future of humankind. It'll decide whether our mission is to be tragic or triumphant.

We need to be daring enough to embrace the decision we know in our intellects and feel in our hearts. We can rebel against nature. Yoshi, sometimes, to build a better world... we need to tear down the one that exists..."

Yoshi remained silent as he witnessed Sergei raise and point a formidable weapon at the two of them.

"Into the escape pod," Sergei commanded them. "Both of you."

"Escape pod?" Marini asked, utterly perplexed.

"Yes," Sergei explained. "I'm ejecting you both."

Marini reached for the firearm. In an instinctive reaction, Sergei shot the cardinal square in the stomach. The priest collapsed backward into Yoshi's arms.

"The fool!" Sergei barked. "Take him! Both of you, into the pod."

"Where will you eject us to?" Yoshi asked, in numb distress. "To Earth?"

"No," Sergei muttered, violently upset, for he had not intended to shoot the cardinal. "I'm ejecting you to the moon."

~ 17 ~

Yoshi sat on the floor of the cramped escape pod, cradling the bleeding, semiconscious Cardinal Marini in his slender arms. Out the porthole before him, Yoshi watched the *Blessed Trinity* growing smaller and smaller. As the distance increased, he felt the memory of the mission fading in his wake, but not entirely, for he was still holding a dying fellow astronaut of the Vatican City State. A man with whom he had walked upon a distant alien world and witnessed the spectacular ruins of its long-dead civilization of giants; a man with whom he had uncovered a most disquieting alien philosophy and religion.

Yoshi's inner psyche suddenly wanted to simply run off, barefoot, down John Man Beach. To distance himself from everyone and everything. To just be by himself, alone and safe with quiet nature. Someplace where he could ignore completely the outside world and simply be a boy forever, never having to experience any challenging or painful transitions in thought or perception.

But then he thought of the Man. Such bizarre beings. Now, in silent retrospect, they seemed much more mythic than extraterrestrial. Creatures that somehow stood outside evolution. Yet the Man had evolved—they had obviously risen up to solve the societal problems of pollution, of overpopulation, and... of war... But their solution only led to their demise.

With their many heads, thought Yoshi, *were they not thinking correctly? With my single head, my single mind, how can I hope to correctly understand all of this?*

Yoshi heard a soft thud as the escape pod automatically docked at Earth's long-since-abandoned lunar station. He trembled as he used all his strength to manually crank open the entry hatch. The air within the station was bitter cold and rarefied, but at least there was air to breathe. Fortunately, the station lay in full sunlight, and he had light because of this and likely enough heat to survive, at least for the present.

Yoshi heard Major Sergei Leonov's voice crackle over the escape pod's communication panel. Sergei was broadcasting to the women of Earth.

"Man is back," Sergei boasted. "And a man is coming down. Make any attempt to stop me and I will rain nuclear bombs down upon you!"

Yoshi looked out the large viewing port lying before him and saw sunlight glint off the *Blessed Trinity's* shuttle, which was speeding toward Earth, carrying inside it a burly Russian on a mission of male dominance. Perhaps carrying out some primordial male fantasy of individual male dominance of an entire planet of women?

"The evil on Earth," Cardinal Marini said weakly, "it has always been the male human being... I see it clearly... I accept it fully... The Man were right. For our kind to survive, potentially immortal, as a species... the male must remain absent. Sergei must be made absent."

Yoshi heard the pod's communication device crackle again, and he listened to Sergei laugh boldly, singing in Russian, manly, like some fearless cosmonaut Cossack, as he approached Earth's outer atmosphere.

"Yoshi," Marini whispered, his strength ebbing. "You can order the escape pod... to intercept the shuttle... at full speed... like a missile."

To kill Sergei, Yoshi's thoughts raced, *so that a race of human females can go on eternally?*

The cardinal went lifeless in Yoshi's young arms, and the steam of his last exhaled breath jerked Yoshi's mind back to Kilimanjaro.

... 19,340 feet. Ascending to the summit... Gloved, frozen fingertips pausing to touch an icy glacier sculpted by freezing winds into wild, fantastic shapes...

Climbing above the clouds, Yoshi reached the crowning ice cap of Kilimanjaro.

Yoshi's grandfather's voice:

"Yoshi, choosing to make a different choice is embracing change itself."

Yoshi typed something into the control console of the escape pod and laboriously cranked the entry hatch closed. There was a *whoomph!* as the escape pod flashed off, lifting up off the moon and jetting away.

Yoshi could no longer hear Sergei singing, but he imagined it as he wrapped his arms around himself, due to the intense cold, and stepped up to the nearby viewing port. He watched the escape pod sparkle, reflecting sunlight as it continued away from the moon. He also watched Sergei's shining shuttle as it reached Earth's atmosphere.

Yoshi then stepped back and instinctively covered his eyes as he witnessed the escape pod missile into the nuclear-propulsion module of the *Blessed Trinity*. After a silent second, there was a soundless series of incredible explosions as the ship's fissionable fuel went off in a succession of rapidly growing, terrible, awful, blinding, white-hot nuclear explosions.

When the brightness finally faded, Yoshi dared to look again. What remained of the *Blessed Trinity* was swiftly plummeting earthward, where Sergei's shuttle had just disappeared into the atmosphere.

Yoshi wondered what fate awaited Sergei at the hands of the peaceful women of Earth. And if the Man's male-killing virus might somehow still exist on Earth. If so, would it find Sergei before Earth's women? If not, how resourceful was Sergei? Most of the planet was undoubtedly empty now, must have been for the past four centuries. Nothing but abandoned, crumbling cities, sprawling forest. Was Sergei resourceful enough to evade capture and somehow survive, as the only man on Earth? As the last man on Earth?

Yoshi also wondered how he had arrived at his decision, to destroy the threat presented by the *Blessed Trinity*. He wondered if it was because he still felt so naïve. If he was able to make such a decision so quickly and easily due to naiveté. He never thought that perhaps it was because, in the end, only one who had developed the beginnings of wisdom by way of recognizing and accepting changes to his perception of life, of the world, of the cosmos, and possibly of the grand scheme of things, could ultimately decide so simply and wisely.

As Yoshi stood there in the cold, he watched the debris of the Orion ship fall into Earth's atmosphere, burning up upon entry, sprinkling down to the clouds below. Yoshi's vision blurred, and in his mind's eye he once again stood atop the summit of mighty Kilimanjaro.

... *19,340 feet:* Having carried his grandfather's ashes to the summit, to the top of Africa, Yoshi opened the canvas pouch and shook it vigorously, allowing the winds to carry off and scatter the whispering vestiges of his dear grandfather, sweeping the ashes down toward the clouds that covered the warm forest so far below. Clouds that Yoshi felt he could watch forever.

Yoshi's grandfather's voice:

"Yoshi, do not be concerned about forever. Simply choose to shape a future, instead of allowing a future to shape you. Goodbye, my son..."

Yoshi's grandfather had lived to be 129 years old—the longest-lived human. It was his final wish that he be cremated and that his ashes be scatted from atop the highest mountain on the continent that had given birth to the human species.

The young Okinawan, so utterly far from home in both time and distance, and so utterly alone, collapsed beside the viewing port. He wondered if now he too was at the end of his life's journey. Or could he possibly survive for some time here on the moon, within this abandoned lunar base? Scrounging the station for preserved nutrition packets, for water... Spending his remaining days trapped there on the moon, perhaps acting as a silent observer and chronicler of New Earth?

Rising, Yoshi looked over at Cardinal Marini, who lay there dead, a respected man who had spent a lifetime trying to reconcile the diametrically opposing views of religion and science. His lifelong struggle now over. Had he found peace? Was he now in a better place? Or was all that he had ever been still right there, lying prostrate on the cold floor?

And Yoshi thought again of Major Sergei Leonov, ex–air force combat pilot, failed political candidate, and then disgruntled cosmonaut, relegated to taking a one-way, doomed space voyage to an unknown planet. Was it the Russian's last desperate grab for greatness? Was his descent to land upon the new Earth his final battle cry?

And Yoshi thought again of himself. There he stood, a 423-plus-year-old, without a clue as to how to make his continued life meaningful. Perhaps, for now, he would just stand there and wait until it was night over the eastern Pacific and he, up high above on the full moon, could look down upon New Earth and see the lights of the surviving cities of the women. Knowing that there, under the cloak of darkness, a mere four hundred miles south of Japan, still lay his tiny Okinawa, and John Man Beach.

Despite his desperate, even hopeless situation, he felt himself a good boy—a good young man. A man. One who had done the right thing. He would not struggle against whatever was to come, but instead be open to recognizing and embracing some forward path. Even if that path meant a Long Sleep from which he would never awaken... Confucianism had saved the human race, the women of Earth. Perhaps Buddhism could save him from unnecessary panic. Perhaps it would provide him some needed mental and spiritual comfort.

Yoshi shuddered. It felt colder. The air, it seemed thinner now... His coordination, it seemed a bit off. He felt drowsy, somewhat confused. Hypothermia must have been slowly setting in.

It was then that the huge red starfish stepped out of nowhere. A second one then appeared beside the first, stepping out of the same blur of a hole, the same temporary opening in the miraculous fabric of space and time. Just as these strange beings had entered and left the *Blessed Trinity*, they now stepped back into Yoshi's world.

The mysterious starfish had for some inexplicable reason followed Yoshi to Earth's moon. But why had they come? Somehow Yoshi knew it was to take him. He would be alone amongst aliens...

Yoshi trembled as he made the decision to go with the starfish willingly. As the aliens took him, they gently communicated to him telepathically, calming him, informing him that they were great and far-ranging explorers of the universe. That they were also collectors, observers, and occasionally benevolent experimenters in cases of different possible paths that other sentient races might take. As the starfish communicated with the young Okinawan, Yoshi sensed that these benign alien beings were neither male nor female... Only then did he fully remember Isa and what had happened. Only then did he realize he was not truly alone, for these unusual creatures also had Isa.

But would Isa now be over two hundred years older? Incredibly wizened by time but somehow still alive? No, telepathically Yoshi received assurance that while he had slept through the past two centuries, the *Blessed Trinity* transporting him across distant light years, these enigmatic aliens had somehow stepped over that stretch of time. Mere moments had passed for them since they had taken Isa from the *Blessed Trinity*.

Yoshi thought of how the third starfish must even now be waiting for them, somewhere unseen, yet as close as one's next heart beat. Yes, somewhere outside of time the alien waited, with Isa—who would still be exactly as Yoshi had last seen her. Young. Beautiful. Suddenly there was hope. Hope for himself.

But also, it would seem, hope for perhaps a second path for humanity to take, elsewhere. One that would see where the Man's demonic male, Sergei's driver of progress, might take it.

He playing the role of Adam, and Isa of Eve. All while not jeopardizing Cardinal Marini's perceived sanctity of the virgin women of Earth. Allowing them to have their day in the sun. *Let it be a long day,* Yoshi wished.

The Day of the Women.

~ 18 ~

Sergei flew a flat and low trajectory for quite some time, hoping that he came in under the radar, if the women of Earth still possessed and monitored such devices. He landed smoothly on the flat Atacama Desert, in what had once been northern Chile.

The destruction of the Blessed Trinity had been quite a shock to him. It had disintegrated his confidence and jingoistic bravado altogether. And his most ambitious plans.

Fortunately, he had prepared a simpler backup plan. The shuttle was laden with equipment, supplies—all that he would need.

Sergei ordered the shuttle's doors to open and he stepped outside, onto the sand of the coppery-colored desert.

And there he stood, the last demonic male on Earth, quietly surveying the horizon. The air felt fresh in his lungs, clean, unpolluted. His bravado began to return and he grinned, his mind already making new plans. And then he coughed…

Acknowledgements and Identifying Notations

• When Isa quotes to Yoshi:

"Nowhere in all space or on a thousand worlds will there be men to share our loneliness. There may be wisdom; there may be power: somewhere across space, great instruments... may stare vainly at our floating cloud rack, their owners yearning as we yearn. Nevertheless, in the nature of life and in the principles of evolution we have our answer. Of men elsewhere, and beyond, there will be none forever..."

Isa is quoting the sentiments of anthropologist Loren Eiseley, as presented in his 1957 book *The Immense Journey*.

• The ideas and philosophy expressed by the Man were derived from two works in particular:

1) *Dark Nature: A Natural History of Evil*, by Lyall Watson, published 1996;

2) *Demonic Males: Apes and the Origins of Human Violence*, by Dale Peterson and Richard Wrangham, published 1996.

A Note from the Author

This author hopes the reader found Yoshi's journey into outer space and toward intellectual maturity interestingly different, appreciating Yoshi's conscious mind finding ways to give him comfort.

Yoshi deciphering the alien manuscript while in a fever pays homage, of course, to explorer, anthropologist, and biologist Alfred Russel Wallace, who while in bed with a fever independently thought up the idea of natural selection. (Wallace and Charles Darwin later published a joint paper in 1858 arguing the theory of evolution and natural selection. Darwin published his seminal book *On the Origin of Species* a year later.)

Regarding the Minoan language: When "Day of the Women" was written the purported decipherment of Linear A by French accountant Hubert La Marle remained unconfirmed by academia and rejected by specific scholars. Scholars today continue to work on the decipherment of Linear A. This author thus presented Linear A in this story as having yet to be successfully deciphered.

On a scientific note: This story presents the biological phenomenon of sexual reproduction, involving a male and female of a species, as being a widespread phenomenon in the universe in regard to intelligent life, from the Man's perception. This may not necessarily be the case, however. Here on Earth we have examples of asexual species (like starfish) as well as examples of multisexuality—species that are biologically quadrisexuals (fungi), and even examples of life with between five and ten sexes (e.g., the paramecium, a unicellular protozoa).

For further reading on this interesting topic, this author suggests the book *Xenology: An Introduction to the Scientific Study of Extraterrestrial Life, Intelligence, and Civilization*, by Robert A. Freitas Jr., © 1975-1979, 2008. Chapter 12, "Alien Sex."

As for the question of Sergei's fate, if there were to be a sequel to this short story, it would be titled "The Last Demonic Male on Earth."

Lastly, this story was crafted for thought-provoking entertainment purposes. This author is not by any means advocating the elimination of the male from the human species. Especially as he is one (a male).

Niko Zinovii
Santa Monica, California
10 January 2015

Addendum:

This author has discovered that a Japanese science-fiction film titled *Warning from Space* (U.S. title), *Uchûjin Tokyo Ni Arawaru/Space Men Appear in Tokyo* (Japanese title), which was released in 1956, featured cyclopean human-sized aliens of starfish shape. This author has not yet seen *Warning from Space*, but he has viewed images of the film on the Internet and can confirm that the film's extraterrestrials are very similar to what he had independently imagined for the starfish aliens in "Day of the Women."

Niko Zinovii
Santa Monica, California
19 March 2015

Niko Zinovii

Painting Penelope

The music presented itself within Stefan's mind as he swam. It was not an act of conscious creation, the soft notes, the romantic lyrics; they just came, mysteriously, as if from out of the ether. It was always like this when the creative moment descended upon him. It just happened. There was no predicting it. No preparing for it.

Stefan prompted the emerging melody to repeat itself, over and over, so that he could commit it to memory. For he still had a half-mile further to swim, to make it back to his small seaside villa. Too many times in the past he had lost forever fragments of unique poems, songs, and musical compositions, all born at inopportune times, moments when he was unable to write them down. Like now, during his ritual evening swim.

Yet he did not rush. A hypnotic yet strangely alert calm descended upon him, and he intuitively knew that these self-assembling dulcet tones would play in his mind long into the night. That his unusual mental state of heightened creativity was only now just at its beginning.

And so, as he swam on, he actually slowed his pace, lifting and holding his face above the waves. His blond good looks contrasted strikingly with his solemn expression and deep, soulful eyes. Keeping his lungs full of air for added buoyancy, and taking short, calm breaths, he stroked evenly, fluidly, rhythmically, with his arms beneath the surface.

Quietly he turned his gaze away from the glory of the setting sun as it gently dropped into the Sea of Crete and focused instead on the craggy beauty of the rugged island of Karpathos, on its wild, untamed mountains lit by the magnificent colors of the sunset. The cloud-wrapped villages high up above, the turquois coves down below, soaked by the ancient sea… Stefan could not help but appreciate once again how this island was touched not only by this evening's waning light, but by Aegean magic as well. For it was a place where the allure of the classical past overpowered the present.

~

Hours later, at his piano, Stefan played his song as if in a trance. The melody was now completely composed, scribbled out in pen on the few music sheets spread out before him.

A sensitive man, Stefan this night wore the expression of a distant, troubled romantic suffering from profound disillusionment. As he sang the lyrics, he did so softly, with gentle, heartfelt emotion. It was not a long song, but it was nevertheless an emotional strain on him, so genuinely did he feel and mean the loving words. When he finished, he sat silent for the longest moment, reviewing the piece in his mind, asking himself if it was worthy.

Completely satisfied, he smiled, bowed tiredly to his piano, put a kiss on his fingertips, and then placed it upon the sheets of music. Rising, he crossed the antique-accented room, feeling the subtle comfort of its art, of its Persian rugs, lilac walls, and mahogany furnishings. Aching for the deeper comfort of his huge bed, he stretched and then froze as he noticed the man standing silently within his open front door, standing beside the huge, man-high pottery jars that sat there near the entrance.

"Well, well, well," Stefan said with a rising smile of recognition, surprised but pleased to see his dear friend.

"Dr. Walter Maynard. And what strange dreams did you have? That you flew to Karpathos, drove all the way out here, so late at night?"

Walter stepped forward with a twinkle of subversive humor in his eyes, holding out two boxes. "Octopus in ouzo," he replied. "And spinialo."

"Spinialo?" Stefan asked.

"Devilfish and urchins in seawater. Direct from Kalymnos."

"Ah," replied Stefan, "then I should open a bottle of retsina, from Rhodes, to start us off. But what is the occasion?"

"Stefan," Walter mildly rebuked him, "it's your birthday."

"My..." Stefan had completely forgotten. "Yes... yes, it is. Forty-seven, I think."

"You say it like you're old," Walter replied in his cultured tone. "Wait until you're my age."

They both laughed and Stefan went to pour the wine.

"Shouldn't you be on Kos," Stefan asked, "digging?"

"We retired anthropologists—archeologists," Walter responded, correcting himself, "we don't go digging in the dirt all the time." He picked up a book lying open. "You're reading Persian poetry now? I didn't know you spoke Farsi."

"There are many things you don't know about me." Stefan handed Walter a glass of retsina.

"True," Walter acknowledged. "But I do know when I have a friend in need."

"How long were you standing there?" Stefan asked. "Did you hear my playing? My singing?"

Walter nodded, saying nothing more. They both sipped their white wine, and Stefan paced off.

"... Yes, I'm not myself lately," Stefan admitted in a low tone. "More of a walking emptiness..."

"Holding out for the ideal," Walter replied cautiously, "can do that to any man."

And Stefan just stood there silently.

"I thought you'd be back in Sorrento by now," Walter commented before asking: "Why are you still here, Stefan? On Karpathos?"

"It's quiet," Stefan answered rather solemnly, thinking it out, "remote. It's vibrantly Greek. An authentic Greek island. I appreciate that, in the depths of my soul. Yes, something, I think, something in all of us inclines us to be Greek. In our hearts. In our minds."

Stefan shook his head, and Walter brought a hand to his chin and stared at his friend with a mischievous, wry grin.

"What?" Stefan smiled back.

"I'm just trying to imagine you as a hardy sponge diver or a nut-brown fisherman, mending nets, scaling fish. Biting octopus. Drinking ouzo, or retsina, endlessly gazing out to sea..."

And they both stood there, quiet for a moment.

"Yes..." Stefan finally broke the silence. "And perhaps I should try to imagine you as that sunburnt archaeologist you pretend to be, finding fulfillment and acceptance digging up and categorizing old pottery..."

And Walter's mood dropped, although he tried his best to maintain his sociable, clubbable Londoner appearance. "Well Stefan," he said, "unfortunately tonight is not about me, it's about you. The birthday boy."

"Well then," Stefan responded, "shall we step into my studio?"

"Yes, let's," Walter answered, following his friend into an achingly elegant art studio overlooking the Aegean, the dark sea outside lit by a moon waxing toward fullness. The room's half-dozen double French doors were all open wide, allowing the sweet rose fragrance of pink oleander and the ancient smell of the calm, cool beauty of the night, delivered by Arabian jasmine, to waft into the chamber and imbue it with a scent most lovely.

"At night," Stefan sighed, closing his eyes, allowing his mind to be carried off by the redolent fragrance, "it smells like her. It's the only time I paint her. At night."

Walter merely nodded as he paced forward, concerned, silently looking over the many completed paintings standing against the back and side walls. They were all of the same woman: a woman of intoxicating beauty, of inaccessible romantic glamor, a stunning woman with the face of an exotic angel and the body of an elegant goddess.

Stefan removed the drop cloth from a new painting, one resting upon a heavy wooden easel in the center of the studio. The canvas revealed an unfinished portrait of the same woman. The high cheekbones, the sensual lips, the alluring eyes… Her beauty was fascinating, bewitching.

Walter took a sip of wine as he approached the new painting, expressionlessly scrutinizing it.

"Have you given her a name?" Walter asked, his voice deadpan.

"Penelope."

"Penelope?"

"Yes, Penelope."

"Why?"

"I don't know," Stefan answered, his soulful eyes growing solemn, his mind turning inward. "It sounds right. Feels right."

"Stefan…" Walter started in a tone that caused his friend to turn about and face him.

"She's waiting for me," Stefan said gently. "Somewhere. Patiently. I know it."

"You really are the hopeless romantic," Walter responded, frustrated. "Stefan, she doesn't exist. You made her up. Created her, here in this studio. Your imagined, ideal woman. How can you hope to find what doesn't exist? Obsessing on this vision of yours, it's not healthy. How many hours, days, these past months have you spent painting this imaginary woman of yours? This Penelope?"

Stefan silently picked up his palette, preparing to paint.

"That song you composed," Walter went on. "It was for her?"

Stefan forced a nod. Then slowly, as he began to paint, he untensed, he relaxed, allowing himself to feel the soft sea breeze that was wafting into the room, to feel the magic of the night. "I do appreciate your concern, Walter, I do. But... I'm most satisfied when immersed in painting her. I don't know why. I just am. But I'm not falling in love with a painting. You don't need to worry about insanity. No, I'm only temporarily choosing to live a loveless life. To wait."

And Walter listened, waiting for more.

"You see..." Stefan continued, struggling to make sense of it himself, touching lightly with his brush the object of his hopes, "my paintings of her... they represent the personification of the woman who can make me complete. Whole. Penelope, she's the embodiment of what I'm willing to wait for. Forever, if necessary.

"The past women in my life... they all left me lonely, so empty. Longing for some imagined love. Someone whose wonderful eyes and heart and mind I could swim in..."

And he turned to his friend, whom he saw soften.

"Artists..." Walter finally shrugged and half-smiled, completely defeated, abandoning driving further any point to be made, instead embracing fully the unconditional friendship and love that he felt for Stefan. "I'll bring in another bottle of wine. And the octopus. And the spinialo."

~

After Walter had finally left, Stefan found himself down on the beach, alone, sprawled out, staring up at the stars, an empty bottle of retsina in hand. Listening to the rhythmic waves, he thought of how time and the tides had been caressing this small island for all man's history, and longer still. Transient man... The eternal sea...

Peering up into the heavens, he quivered as he felt the orderly harmony of the god of Spinoza and Einstein. But the moon, so huge and high above the sea, it only made him feel lonely...

A flash from a shooting star, and Stefan made a lonely wish. Sitting up, he then tossed his bottle out into the Aegean, as if sending out an SOS... And he watched the tide take it out.

He was about to lie back down when webs of lightning lit up the darkness, thunder rumbling somewhere out there where the sea invisibly curved off the Earth. A storm was approaching. It looked like a bad one. A few stray raindrops heralding what was to come struck Stefan on the head, on the hand, thudding upon his loose shirt, over his troubled heart.

"Damn," Stefan muttered and rose, retreating to his villa to plummet into a comfortable, quiet darkness filled with weary dreams.

~

It was daylight when Stefan awoke to distant calls for help. "Help... Help me..."

Was he imagining this? No, he heard the call again.

Stefan followed the woman's voice down to the beach, quickly navigating his way through the felled tree branches and palm fronds that were scattered about everywhere, remnants of last night's storm.

"Help..."

At the beach, the tide was in, the water brilliantly blue. What appeared to be the lost cargo of a small boat was floating in the surf and washed up along the shoreline, scattered about. Contraband goods—replicas of brand-name purses, belts, hats, shoes, sunglasses, watches—cigarettes, tobacco, alcohol, all black market items of a smuggling operation apparently gone wrong, the boat likely now at the bottom of the Karpathian Sea.

Amongst the flotsam, bobbing about in the clear turquoise waves, was a large prefabricated crate, its top damaged, split open on one side.

"Help me, please," the voice called out from within the crate.

Stefan found himself approaching with caution, so odd and unexpected was the situation. As he stepped into the sea, he turned the crate, the tide assisting his effort. The man-sized box tilted and sunk a bit into the sand as it spun its cracked-open side to face Stefan, exhibiting its interior to him. And Stefan leaped back, in shock.

"Help me," spoke a young woman's face and head, which were securely fitted within a wall of foamy, close-fitting packing material. "Let me out."

It took Stefan a few stunned seconds before he was able to make sense of the uncanny moment. "My god..." he mumbled aloud. "You—you're a Comfort Woman. Aren't you?"

"You look nice," she responded, her voice pleasant, soft and calm, paradoxically innocent yet fascinatingly seductive. "Put me together. Please."

It was only then that Stefan noticed her separated limbs, all four packed there about her talking head and torso, all her pieces snug within the formfitting foam.

"Attach my arms and legs," she asked. "I'll do whatever you like in return."

Still quite dumbfounded, Stefan pulled from its protective plastic sleeve the "Catalogue of Comfort Women," an owner's manual that was packed there amongst her parts.

"Model number five, universal," Stefan read aloud. "Highly personalizable, employing the latest Morph technology. Select any hair color, style, eye color, skin tone… Obedient, attentive, willing to please…"

Stefan looked back in at the attractive face staring out at him. He had heard of these forbidden, ultra-expensive sex dolls, of how they were now, with the use of advancing robotics, much more than mere dolls, but he had never imagined that these… androids… were so incredibly lifelike. It was absolutely uncanny. He felt as if he were looking at a real person… a real woman. Only with her arms and legs detached for practical packing and shipping purposes.

"You would like me to put you together?" Stefan asked, utterly unsure how to respond to her.

"After the ship sank," she replied softly, sadly, reliving the experience, "I floated all night. Stuck in this box. Dolphins kept visiting me, all through the storm, asking me questions I couldn't understand. I don't know who switched me on, or why. Perhaps it was by accident. I was so frightened, so lonely… Won't you please help me?"

My God, Stefan heard his own thoughts race, *they've ventured beyond mere robotics… she seems almost human. But… sentient artificial intelligence doesn't exist yet. Can this all be just programing?*

~

Stefan had dragged the crate up from the beach and into his art studio, where he had unpacked the Comfort Woman, model No. 5. He had found assembling her quite easy; it was really just a matter of snapping into place the arms and legs, and then some inner mechanism had whirred and automatically tightened the limbs securely to the torso. The Comfort Woman had been clothed in a platinum-colored bikini, which offered no obstacle to the assembling process.

Most amazing was how the seams at her shoulders and hips had self-sealed almost imperceptibly, leaving behind only the slightest of traces, only noticeable after up-close, concentrated visual scrutiny. The texture of her skin, it was so incredibly lifelike… So real.

And so she now stood there before Stefan, fully assembled and seemingly alive.

Stefan watched her as she noticed a peacock's tail feathers standing fanned out, displayed in a nearby antique Greek vase. She moved to the feathers, drawn to their beauty. Walking on her long, attractive legs, she looked so very much like a real living, breathing woman. It was amazing.

"Eyes that never sleep," she commented softly, reaching out to gently touch the feathers. "Like my eyes. Always awake."

"No dreams?" Stefan wondered.

She smiled at him, her introspective mood disappearing completely. "What are dreams?"

Stefan smiled back, more out of his own sudden realization that he was talking to a doll, an android, and not a real woman.

"No." He said it more to himself than to her. "I don't suppose you do dream."

And Stefan smiled yet again, this time as he caught himself looking over her marvelously feminine and attractive body.

"Ah," he said, shaking his head, finding the entire situation pleasantly amusing yet a bit uncomfortable. "Excuse me, I'll be right back. I'd like to get one of my robes, for you to put on. I think it would be better that way."

"Okay." She smiled widely and naively as he left her alone in the studio.

She stood there motionless for a moment before curiosity moved her to the unfinished painting on the easel in the center of the room. Hesitantly, she pulled away the protective drop cloth, revealing the painted face of Stefan's imagined woman.

"Oh," she said, startled. And she stared at the painting until her face began to glow.

Stefan re-entered the room, and when she turned to him, she was transformed: her face now an exact replica of Stefan's idealized woman. With a Mona Lisa smile, she slowly and seductively moved up close to him.

"Is it okay?" she asked him, her feminine voice low and sensual.

"Yes," Stefan muttered, astonished, scrutinizing her new face. "Perfect. It's perfect. You're perfect..."

She looked back at the painting, contemplatively. "I look like your painting now, and yet, I'm not like her at all... although she's what I'd like to be."

"What's your name?" Stefan found himself asking her.

"Anything you want it to be." She smiled innocently.

"Penelope," he insisted.

"Penelope?"

"Yes, Penelope."

"Hi, my name is Penelope," she introduced herself rather stiffly, as if some courtesy programing had temporarily kicked in. "It's nice to meet you. What's your name?"

"Stefan..." he answered. "Stefan Schumann."

"Stefan Schumann," she repeated it, leaning into him, pressing herself against him. She gently ran a feminine hand into his shirt, across his chest.

Stefan felt himself pull back slightly, disturbed at how real her touch felt. At how good it felt... At how much he welcomed it.

"What's this?" She lifted the ancient coin that hung about his neck on a thin leather cord.

"Oh," Stefan answered, staring transfixed into her lovely eyes, "just an old coin, from Itanos... a fantastic place of old ruins, on the east of Crete..."

"I can feel your heart beating, Stefan Schumann."

And he just looked at her, realizing once again that he was talking to a doll, an android, and not to an actual person. And more, he realized that he could never hope to feel her own heart beating, for she had no heart. A power cell probably lay hidden there in its place. She was hardware. She was not real... But... she was. She was real. Penelope was now real... He could not help but follow her outside.

~

Stefan caught up to Penelope in the garden, where she stood with gentle beauty, just looking at the pink oleander and flowering hibiscus.

He stared at her, thinking of how he had felt intrigued by her earlier. And how now, after her transformation, he felt utterly mesmerized by her presence. He had imagined his Penelope in his mind, and in his heart, and now here she was, standing before him. Alive. The woman of his dreams. All he could think of was making love to her.

He watched her as she reached out and touched the planted lavender and jasmine. *Can she smell?* he wondered... *The sweet and alluring scents...*

"Nothing is more beautiful than the sound of the rain," she whispered, "and flowers..."

Stefan stepped up behind her, taking her slim shoulders in his hands. She felt so real. He remained silent as he watched her look up at the sun, directly at the sun, unblinking.

"There are little black dots on the sun," she remarked, puzzled.

And Stefan felt himself loosen his grip as he realized once again how utterly different they were. How inhuman she really was. Yet she was his Penelope. *How can all of this have come to be?*

Together, in silence, they watched a bird give chase to a butterfly. No matter how hard the bird tried, he could not catch the fluttering, brightly colored, winged beauty. The chase was poetic, a beautiful dance across the sky.

Penelope laughed softly, femininely, appreciating the butterfly's uncapturable grace. Stefan found his tensions leaving him as he too became absorbed into the magical moment offered by nature. Parts of a poem he had once read came to his mind, and he recited the lines aloud, they seemed so fitting:

> I am not what I was yesterday,
> No one knows my name.
> I am made in a smooth and beautiful way,
> And full of flame.
> I dance above the tawny grass
> In the sunny air,
> So tantalized to have to pass
> Love everywhere
> O Earth, O Sky, you are mine to roam
> In liberty.
> I am a soul and I have no home,
> Take care of me...

"... If I could be anything," Penelope thought aloud, her face as innocent as a flower, "aside from what I really am, I'd be a butterfly."

"Why?"

"So that no one could catch me. Box me up again." And she smiled and ran off, playfully.

They ran together through the garden, he chasing her, like the bird and the butterfly, he unable to catch her. When she finally let him, they fell into the grass together, laughing. She looked up at his handsome face, framed by the sky, and suddenly, in that moment, something began to change in her.

"You make me feel important..." Penelope said, a bit startled, as if realizing her sense of self-worth, of value, for the very first time. "You make me feel beautiful..."

"Yes," Stefan responded. "Because you are beautiful." And he kissed her lovingly, passionately. She kept her eyes open and she found the butterfly again, flapping about in the sunlight.

Stefan wondered what he was doing and he sat up, looking at her. At his Penelope. She looked perfect, eternal, like the love he felt for her. Eternal like the garden's decorative rocks behind them... While he was as ephemeral as the nearby singing sparrow.

"You look at me with such questions in your eyes..." she said, her eyes searching his.

Rising, Stefan stood above her, still looking down at her. He sensed stirring within him the unwearying strength of male lust, and it suddenly felt as if he would never again need to sleep. He felt an urge to tether her to the nearby olive tree with his belt, to make her his property, his and his alone, to keep her from ever leaving.

"You look like a giant." She smiled. But then her smiled turned to concern as she sensed his mood, although she did not understand it. "You're staring at me with a hundred eyes... Like your feathers. But the beauty, it's gone from your eyes now... Why do people make love?"

Her comment and question broke the spell on Stefan. He felt the surge of his carnal passions subside and the more worthy emotions of his heart rise. "Because it feels good," he answered, his mind almost completely elsewhere. "And... it's sometimes an escape."

"From what?"

"From the real world. From facing our mortality. In those moments, we try to live a lifetime, love a lifetime."

He could tell by the expression on her face and the look in her eyes that she did not understand, but wanted to.

He felt the oceans of difference between them. He had no idea what would happen next. Or how long this could last. He only knew that he wanted to swim in her heart and mind, artificial or not. And he momentarily lost himself, gazing into her eyes, which seemed more real to him at that moment than life itself.

But he then forced himself to look away. She was an expensive piece of hardware, he reminded himself. The owners would come looking for her soon. She was their property.

"Will you swim with me?" he found himself asking her, wanting at least to share that experience with her. Before contemplating anything further...

~

Together, they swam out into the Sea of Crete, all the while looking back at the dramatic splendor of Karpathos, allowing the island's unspoiled primal beauty to captivate their senses, to fill their minds and hearts.

They swam seemingly forever in the shadow of rugged, vertical cliffs, holding hands until feeling the sunlight again. Stefan then pulled his Penelope close to him, and they slowly spun counterclockwise, treading water so gracefully it all began to seem like a dream. If it was a dream, he wanted to sleep until the end of his life...

Stefan then remembered that Prometheus of myth hailed from Karpathos. And he felt as if he were a modern reincarnation of this Titan, giving to an artificial woman, to his Penelope, the gift of his chaste love. A love that burnt within him as brightly as the torch that Prometheus had stolen from the sun.

He looked at her intoxicatingly beautiful face. At the face of his idealized woman. At the woman he had painted over and over these past months of seclusion and loneliness. Without a doubt, he loved her. Suddenly, reflected in her eyes, she seemed to become just as human as he, even more so.

"I love you," she whispered. And she kissed him.

A seagull flapped by overhead, and Penelope gently yet forcefully pushed away from Stefan.

"Thank you," she said.

"Penelope?"

"I'm alive now," she answered, having realized it for the first time. "And I need to find my own way now..." And she swam off, following the gull out to sea.

Stefan remained in that spot, treading water, watching her until she disappeared over the distant horizon. He wondered if there were other Comfort Women in the world, perhaps kept secretly in the closets of certain wealthy elites, robotic women who might also turn on, to become sentient beings, if given genuine love. Was this how sentient artificial intelligence was to rise? From the sex doll industry? From something so unplanned, so unanticipated? From something that just happened? By chance? Because of love?

He did not know the answers. All he knew was that he felt a tormenting sadness sweep over him. A punishment suitable for a modern Prometheus.

Acknowledgements and Identifying Notations

• The few poem stanzas Stefan recites are taken from "The Butterfly," by American poet Alice Archer Sewall James, 1870-1955. The stanzas were modified only slightly to fit the story.

A Note from the Author

This author was inspired to write "Painting Penelope" by his personal emotional reaction to the sound (not the lyrics) of the Iranian love song "Mitooni Moshte Mano Va Bekoni," as sung in Farsi by Persian recording artist Ramesh Namaz.

Another source of influence was the ancient Greek myth of Pygmalion, about a sculptor who fell in love with the statue he had carved, a statue that the goddess Aphrodite later miraculously brought to life.

Abyss Creations of San Marcos, California, manufactures life-size, anatomically correct, lifelike sex dolls (the RealDoll) with PVC skeletons, stainless-steel joints, and silicone flesh. This author imagined that in the future such products might continue to evolve, incorporating the technologies of robotics and artificial intelligence, and that this might be a likely path to the birth of the android of science fiction. (This author became aware of Abyss Creations' product after having by happenstance seen the 2007 critically acclaimed film *Lars and the Real Girl*, which is about a socially inept man who attempts a romance with a modern sex doll, a RealDoll.)

The term "comfort women" was borrowed from history, being the translation of the Japanese *ianfu*, a euphemism used to describe the women and girls forced into military prostitution and sexual slavery by the Imperial Japanese Army before and during World War II.

The character of Walter Maynard in this story is the same Walter Maynard from this author's 2012 novel *The God Antenna*. Chronologically, "Painting Penelope" takes place before the events depicted in *The God Antenna*. To learn why Walter is in Greece, dabbling in archeology, this author refers readers to *The God Antenna*.

On robotic women:

The National Institute of Advanced Industrial Science and Technology (AIST), a Japanese research facility, displayed their HRP-4C feminine-looking humanoid robot at Tsukuba City, Japan. In 2011 upgrades were made to the HRP-4C's human-like walking ability.

In 2003, Japan's Osaka University displayed Actroid, a human appearing female robot, at that year's International Robot Exhibition. Actroid was designed to mimic lifelike blinking, breathing, and speaking. The robot was manufactured by Kokoro Company Ltd. A number of additional models have been developed since, the latest released in 2011.

Niko Zinovii
Santa Monica, California
11 March 2015

Addendum:

In September of 2015, it was reported that cosmetic company L'Oreal started working with bio-engineering start-up Organovo to 3D print skin, potentially making even more lifelike androids possible.

Niko Zinovii
Santa Monica, California
21 October 2015

Niko Zinovii

Great and Mighty Things

~ 1 ~

Michael, slim, fortyish, displaying the staid countenance of a dour, humorless accountant, drew no attention as he entered the lavish exhibition hall. No one in the gathering crowd noticed the troubled look in his eyes... In fact, no one noticed him at all. Michael was quite worthy of notice, however, for he was a most peculiar man: a man who suffered from a rare genetic disorder, one that made him incapable of feeling fear.

This lack of fear extended even down into his subconscious, for an old and deeply rooted part of his brain had long ago wasted away. Deep within his temporal lobes, there were now only two little hollows where his amygdalae had once been. What was required for triggering states of fear in vertebrates was wholly absent in him.

Michael's IQ, however, was high; his memory was good; his lifespan was expected to be of normal length. But his disorder, this Urbach-Wiethe disease, it had afflicted him with a complete immunity to fear. He considered this a curse, because it made it impossible for him to recognize danger, to react appropriately to threatening situations or stimuli. It was not even possible for him to recognize the expression of fear in the faces of others...

Worse still, Michael often found himself feeling overcome by curiosity when confronted by perils that any normal man would have immediately fled from. As a result, he routinely stepped into unpleasant and painful incidents, unintentionally, over and over again, without ever being able to learn any better from experience. He had given up on doctors, and for years now he had sought out unorthodox remedies to his situation. It was this that had brought him on a moment's-notice flight from New York to Rome, and here to the hotel hosting this year's annual Italian Chess Championship.

Michael was not a fan of chess. In fact, he had never even played the game. He had no interest in the tournament itself. But this trip would be worth every penny to him—and it was a considerable expense—if he could just learn one thing… For some time, he had been following the rumored extracurricular exploits of the European chess grand master and former world chess champion known simply as Massimo. Retired from chess since the age of thirty, and having been absent from competition for the past decade, Massimo was to make a rare personal appearance here today, to play a single game, for exhibition purposes, against the CPA, the American Chess-Playing Android, colloquially dubbed the mechanical man.

Michael was desperately interested in seeing Massimo. In learning more about this rather mysterious man, in meeting him if possible. Rumors about Massimo portrayed him as a world traveler and a daring hunter of large, dangerous game. Furthermore, unsubstantiated anecdotes painted Massimo as absolutely fearless, displaying unheard-of daring and unsurpassed equanimity during the hunt. Michael suspected that Massimo also suffered from Urbach-Wiethe disease… that Massimo was also a man without fear. But where Michael floundered through life, this Massimo strode, successful and undaunted. Michael wanted to learn his secret.

~ 2 ~

As Michael moved farther into the palatial hall, he found himself taking furtive glances at faces in the crowd, trying to imagine what the countenance of fear might look like. But it was beyond his mental grasp. And so he soon gave up. It was then that he noticed up ahead, seated on display before an elaborate chess table, the mechanical man, the CPA. Michael had never seen it before. It was man-sized, a humanoid robot. But this Chess-Playing Android, it really had no strong visual human likeness. It surprised Michael that no effort had been made to make the mechanical man appear more like a man. Instead, it was completely robotic. It assailed the senses as an automaton, a mechanical device, one with ingeniously designed robotic arms, intricate hands of great dexterity, and rather slender legs with large feet. Michael guessed that the large feet were for balance.

What Michael was most drawn to was the mechanical man's huge, bulbous head. It was quite impressive, with all its sparkling innards on display beneath its transparent brain case. It was like something one might see at a world's fair. Only it suddenly made Michael think about the inner workings of his own mind, and his brain's missing pieces, which had handicapped him. And he felt a momentary, detached sadness creep over him.

The mechanical man turned to look at Michael and made eye contact with him, with its two huge glass eyes, which were pupilless and sedate. Michael saw deep intelligence and even hints of creativity in the machine's stare. Yet the thing appeared somehow incomplete. *Something is missing from him too*, Michael surmised, feeling the coldness of its inhuman gaze.

Michael suddenly felt more curious about the robot, about its brain, and he immediately wondered if he might perhaps be misinterpreting some potential danger. A stealthy, calm glance about the room satisfied him that those nearby seemed to be acting normally... So most likely there was nothing to be concerned about?

He now found himself feeling a bit foolish. But he had made so many mistakes in the past, being completely unable to detect danger. That stranger on the subway last week... The zoo recently, when he felt himself inexplicably drawn toward the escaped snake, overcome with curiosity, wondering what it might be like to hold the serpent. He had to be warned off by a guard, told not to poke the death adder. All his past regrettable incidents, they apparently now had him guessing, to try to avoid potentially unpleasant happenings, for, as always, his normal state of mind was completely at ease with the outside world, devoid of fear or caution.

Michael snapped back to the present when he noticed someone rather striking standing nearby, tall and regal, dressed in tribal red, with brown ancestral bracelets dangling from his thickly boned ebony wrists. Michael had read descriptions of this Tanzanian bodyguard of Massimo's. His name was Kapalei, He was a Maasai warrior, from the region of the African Great Lakes. It was rumored that Massimo had saved Kapalei's life during a lion hunt and that Kapalei had dedicated himself to serving Massimo faithfully thereafter, for life.

Michael watched, open-mouthed, while Kapalei's long hair, woven into braided strands, swung across his broad shoulders as he turned to the entrance from which his master Massimo was now entering the hall, unannounced.

Massimo strode in with a calm, confident walk, moving as if the world were his, as if he stood at the center of all maps and everything and everyone simply moved about him.

To Michael, Massimo appeared the mightiest, most charismatic man he had ever laid eyes on. The former chess champion's short, raven-black hair, broad sideburns, thick moustache, and minimal goatee framed a handsome face overpowered by unbridled maleness. His smile radiated confidence. His composure was absolute, his presence captivating and commanding. Nearly as tall as Kapalei, Massimo was wider than his bodyguard across the shoulders and chest. With his narrow waistline, he looked more like a bullfighter than a chess grand master—sleek and full of power, coordination, vitality, and vigor.

Oblivious to the applause and even to the presence of the crowd, Massimo immediately sat himself across from the CPA and at once activated the game clock and moved his king's pawn forward, tapping again upon the timer. The mechanical man with equal speed countered with the Sicilian Defense, and the match was set in motion.

The initial moves occurred somewhat rapidly, the exhibition more resembling a game of speed chess. Michael did not understand the moves, but he was impressed by the central thrust made by Massimo. And when Massimo moved his queen out, the mechanical man surprisingly slipped into a motionless, Rodin-the-Thinker pose, finally reacting with a passive move, using its own queen to defend a pawn. And the game slowed, although the ambient intensity rose. It was electric. The entire crowd stood on edge, breathing hushed breaths.

With each successive move, Massimo appeared more vigorous, bolder, while the mechanical man seemed to waver, discontented with its position, especially after it was forced to move the same piece twice. The machine appeared to spend more time analyzing than Massimo, who seemed to play by sheer instinct coupled to raw intellectual force, driven by an indomitable will to win.

It puzzled Michael that the CPA was not doing better. Michael had an education in mathematics, and although he did not understand chess, he did appreciate the sheer computational power of computers and of the world's new machines of artificial intelligence. This mechanical man must have been able to evaluate hundreds of millions of moves per second. Surely brute-force computing power belonged to the CPA.

It was then that Michael noticed how Massimo stared intently into the mechanical man's artificial eyes with each move. And how the robot seemed to be avoiding eye contact with the human. *Is it intimidated by Massimo?* Michael wondered.

Everyone suddenly *oohed* and *aahed* as a number of pieces were exchanged. Something was building. Michael wished he understood the game, to be able to follow it. He sensed that something eminently graceful and beautiful was now unfolding.

And then came the surprise. Movement stopped. Both players sat motionless for a silent moment, eyeing the board. Massimo then lifted a hand, and with a thick finger he pushed his own king over, conceding defeat.

Michael noticed Massimo look briefly at his robotic opponent. And, surprisingly, Michael could have sworn that he saw a hint of a smile momentarily lift and drop within Massimo's eyes.

Massimo nodded formally to the mechanical man, and then he rose amid the utter silence. He said something in Swahili to Kapalei, and the two men left together, followed by the gawking stares of the crowd.

It was only then that Michael realized the cultural impact the defeat was having upon those around him. To them it registered as a human defeat, for it was not just a computer that had beaten a chess champion, but a thinking robot, a mechanical man. It was also not just any chess champion who had been defeated, but Massimo, their hero.

Michael looked back at the mechanical man, who sat there sedately, rather aristocratically, as its human handlers slowly appeared upon the scene, tending to it. It was as if the thing's very presence now announced the end of the age of man and heralded an unsettling new age to come.

~ 3 ~

Michael walked the streets and alleys of Rome late into the night, wandering aimlessly, unable to sleep. So stunned had he been at the mechanical man's victory he had missed his opportunity to approach Massimo... And so he walked with utter abandon. Why not? After all, it seemed he was cursed to forevermore remain the man without fear.

As he roamed, ignoring completely the splendor of the historic buildings, the artistic grandeur of the eternal city, his mind kept bringing him back to that chess match: to the inexplicable, haunting glint of delight that had appeared momentarily in the eyes of Massimo after his defeat; to the seductive view of the inner workings of the mechanical man's incredible artificial brain...

Michael soon found himself pondering a novel thought. What if he could be repaired? Like a machine would be repaired. What if, in the future, artificial amygdalae could be inserted down into his brain, into both his left and right hemispheres? To enable him to feel fear, anxiety, stress—to correct his impairment. To make him wholly human, complete, for there were other things, also, aside from the fearlessness. Smaller things. He had never felt aggression. And socially, he routinely found himself struggling to make accurate judgments of others' faces. Often it was difficult for him to be aware of his own emotions, let alone others'. Although he hid it well, he really felt himself an outcast, existing nearer the fringe of humanity. Disconnected from it.

Looking up, Michael was surprised to find that he had unintentionally walked out to the Colosseum, and that he now stood there in the piazza near its entrance. At this late hour— it must have been after 1 a.m.—the archaic monument, although lit by the warm glow of spotlights from within, was of course closed to the public. But was it? The high entrance gate, behind the barrier, appeared ajar... And a pair of carabinieri, in their distinguished dark-blue uniforms, stood nearby, smoking, chatting, with their backs to the Colosseum. Michael had noticed pairs of Italy's military police elsewhere, patrolling the city on foot, likely to deter crime, so he gave their presence here little thought. Lured forward by a tourist's curiosity, Michael silently slipped behind the two men, through the open gate, and into the Colosseum.

Walking softly, Michael moved deeper into the amphitheater, eyeing its timeworn walls, its dark, ancient archways, its moss-stained brick and stone... Slowly, he made his way around the inner circumference of the monument, toward its opposite end, where lay at its epicenter its partially reconstructed arena floor, covered by a gritty white sand.

It was not until Michael stepped out onto this arena that he noticed the man who was already standing there, in silence, looking out at the huge, elliptical amphitheater that engulfed them.

With no sense of urgency or desperation, but rather with an insouciant calm born from the acceptance of a miracle, Michael walked up to and stood alongside Massimo.

"I've been standing here," Massimo said, close to a whisper, without bothering to look at Michael, "attempting to sense if any of the long-ago barbarity had somehow lingered on, echoing itself into our present."

Michael just stood there quietly, listening to the man whom he had traveled across the Atlantic in hopes of meeting, to the man to whom fate had amazingly delivered him this night. As Massimo spoke, Michael could not help but feel captivated by the man's personal charisma, his charm, his magnetism, the overwhelming power of his personality.

"But as I opened my senses," Massimo went on philosophically, "here under the quiet moonlight, I only felt the night's soft breeze... I only heard the tired barking of a distant dog... the lazy, low rumble of the occasional car passing on Via Celio Vibenna... the incessant talking of my two solicitous escorts...

"The men who died here—all the magnificent animals that died here... the lions, tigers, the elephants, rhinoceroses, hippopotamuses, the bears, the panthers, the leopards, the thousands upon thousands of mighty and beautiful animals that were slaughtered in their perverse, staged hunts... I can sense none of it. Time has washed it all clean. The bloodshed, it's all been swallowed by the past."

Massimo then movingly recited a poem, his voice echoing ever so slightly within the silent amphitheater:

"For ever we shall be no more but the World will still be,

No name, no trace of us will remain.

Before we were, nothing was lacking,

After we are no more, nothing will change."

And Massimo turned to look at Michael for the first time, scrutinizing him, recognizing him. "You were at the tournament."

"Yes," Michael admitted, diffidently. "To see you."

Massimo looked at Michael in a searching yet genuine and personal manner, one that made Michael suddenly feel authentically connected, physically, emotionally, spiritually. The eye contact felt good.

"Then come with me," Massimo said as he walked off. "To see more."

~ 4 ~

Michael had not imagined that he would ever again be peering into the inner workings of the mechanical man's huge, shining head, yet here he now stood, once again staring transfixed at the CPA's artificial brain. At the mind that had been clever enough to beat Massimo in their first game of chess.

But this would now be their second game, the artificial man now set to play white, Massimo, the defeated, to play black. Massimo, like before, resembled more a matador come to do battle, every fiber tensed, held ready, his focus and composure absolute, his manly confidence radiant and supreme.

Kapalei's tribal bracelets jangled as he placed a large earthen cup, steaming with the fragrance of exotic jungle herbs, on the table beside Massimo. Stepping back, the Maasai warrior then tended to a worn oil-burning Iranian samovar, crafted from German silver, for the heating and boiling of water for additional tea.

Michael found himself glancing back across the empty tournament hall to its distant entrance, where stood Massimo's escorts from earlier, the two carabinieri. The men were chatting away, paying no attention to the privately arranged rematch about to take place.

Kapalei offered Michael a cup of tea, and Michael accepted it graciously. He sipped the brew. It was powerful and bitter, tasting of the undiscovered wild. The heavy scent reminded Michael of the rumors that Massimo ritually consumed rare jungle herbs, roots, and even the bark of certain trees as a means of heightening his senses for the hunt, sharpening his reflexes, increasing his strength, stamina, and agility.

Michael wondered if Massimo might also use these herbs and things to stimulate his mental acuity when facing intellectual challenges, like the one now confronting him...

Michael then eyed the lean, bearded man who stood poised to start the chess clock, wondering who he was. Then he heard Kapalei call him by name: Poulad. And Michael immediately recalled reading that Massimo had a private pilot and gun handler named Poulad: Persian, ex-air force, from Shiraz. Although fully gray, the man appeared contemporary in age with Massimo. By the way Massimo looked at Poulad, Michael sensed that Massimo was quite fond this man's companionship.

Michael recalled that there was a fourth man in the group that composed the grand master's entourage, a Swiss-German named Gunnar who handled all the logistics of Massimo's travels and hunts. Michael wondered why this Gunnar was not present...

Taking another sip of tea, Michael silently stepped forward, to stand himself alongside towering Kapalei, to witness the rematch up close.

Massimo looked into Poulad's eyes and unexpectedly recited a poem, its depth of meaning and style like the verse that he had recited in the Colosseum:

"We are puppets and Heaven the puppeteer,
May this be said as a truth and not a metaphor.
While we play on the stage of Existence,
We fall, one by one, into the chest of Non-Existence."
Poulad nodded, in appreciation, and responded as if by ritual:
"Those who are old and those who are young,
Each runs a little while to fulfill his desires...
This old world does not last for anyone.
They have gone, we will go, others will come and go."
And Poulad started the game clock. As the match commenced, the Iranian sat down leisurely upon the floor nearby and began to play melodiously upon a classic Persian *setar*, the instrument of choice across Greater Iran and Central Asia.

The opening poetry, the old Iranian music, the herbal tea, the intensity and beauty of the movement of the chess pieces, the life of the game, everything became enhanced in Michael's mind as the night went on. And there was more and more tea, and the continuous flow of the hauntingly ancient-sounding music. Michael's head soon began to swim in a new reality. One that was timeless yet firmly rooted to the earth. For this was the sound of man, and this was the long night of a challenge taken: ancient mortal man against the rising eternal machine.

The second game ended in a draw. And then the tide turned. The third game went to Massimo. And the fourth. As did the fifth. And the sixth, which the CPA conceded, defeatedly, several moves before the pending checkmate.

As Poulad continued his hypnotic playing, Massimo rose, like an indomitable giant, his eyes focused on the mechanical man, which stared back at the human champion with what Michael perceived as a sadness in its great glass eyes. For it was still the age of man. The time of the automaton had not yet come… Massimo had proven it here, this night. Man was still supreme. At least, one man was: Massimo.

"To yield," Massimo said to the machine with unexpected compassion, "is not to lose. It's to find our place."

The machine slowly nodded, working this out and then accepting it completely, all the while remaining locked in intimate eye contact with Massimo.

"Your place," Massimo then announced, "is now with me."

Again the machine understood and nodded, in willing acceptance. Massimo was now its alpha. And it was absolutely comfortable with this. For it had found its place this night. Thanks to Massimo. Michael thought how the machine must have felt so very good…

"And now…" Massimo turned to Michael.

Michael wobbled unsteadily on his feet, the long night of tea and of music and of Massimo all having cast a dreamlike spell over him. Still, he found his voice and told his story. And then he waited for Massimo's reaction.

"You, the man without fear," Massimo responded with a smile rising in his eyes. "And I, the man driven by fear. How ironic. It seems that fate has delivered you to me."

"I don't understand," Michael groaned. "You don't suffer from Urbach-Wiethe disease?"

Massimo shook his head. "You have no family?" he asked Michael, visually appraising him.

"What?"

"Family," Massimo snapped gruffly, not liking to have to repeat himself. "Do you have any family?"

"No," Michael answered solemnly. "No family."

"Neither do we." Massimo motioned, sympathetically, to Kapalei and Poulad.

"We recently lost one of our own," Massimo went on after a poignant pause. "A man named Gunnar Heidegger, a good man. An accident in Botswana... I'd like you to take his place. Work for me. I will treat you well. I believe your unusual alignment makes you... uniquely suitable for the job."

Once again Michael felt an unusual calm sweep over him, born from immediate and complete acceptance, a surrender to fate. For intuitively he realized that he had found his place. And he accepted this wholeheartedly.

"When do I start?" was his response.

"Now," Massimo stated authoritatively. "It's time for us leave."

"But"—Michael realized certain consequences—"nobody knows. No one knows what happened here, that you beat the mechanical man. That you won. That humanity won..."

And Massimo stopped and turned to Michael, like a father might to a child, disappointed but patient. "Life is so much bigger than that. Each challenge leads to a new and higher peak. All encounters are a continuing introduction, to ourselves, and also to the very cosmos itself. —What I do, I do for myself. Hang the world of men!"

Massimo was one who did what he wished. Went where he wanted. Arrived when he pleased. Defeated his challengers. Left when he desired, and cared not about the affairs or opinions of men. The world was his stage to stride upon. He was a man whom any other would follow, if they would only allow their instincts to reign.

As these men did, who now followed Massimo off: Kapalei, Poulad, Michael, and the mechanical man. A new team assembled. A pack of three men and a unique machine, all following their alpha leader… But to what new ends?

~ 5 ~

Michael, half asleep, sank deeply into a seat in the back of Massimo's private Consolidated PBY Catalina, completely unaware that the aircraft type had been the most widely utilized and versatile model of seaplanes of World War II. And that presently, this upgraded amphibious craft, with its range of over 4,000 miles, capable of patrol, search and rescue, cargo transport, etc., served as the ideal expedition vehicle for Massimo and his team.

Michael glanced briefly at the mechanical man, seated nearby, and momentarily wondered how Massimo could afford to purchase such an expensive piece of new technology. But then he remembered that, beyond Massimo's personal success, Massimo descended from aristocracy, from old money. And lots of it.

Michael felt someone sit beside him: Massimo. With the late hour, the darkness outside, the dull humming of the twin propeller engines, the fatigue of all on board, Michael sensed correctly that this was to be a quiet, intimate conversation, one held despite weariness and exhaustion.

"I have something for you," Massimo said softly, unwrapping a cloth containing a dagger-like fossil. He handed it to Michael. "A gift. From the cellar of dead time."

Michael did not know what to make of it.

"It's a fossilized canine tooth," Massimo added, "from the Late Pleistocene."

Michael ran a tired hand over the eight-inch-long, saber-shaped tooth, from its blade-like point down its serrated length to the leather cord wrapped about its base—so that it could be worn as a necklace.

"It's from the most magnificent and massive of the saber-toothed tigers," Massimo went on rather quietly. "*Smilodon populator*. Twice as heavy as an African lion. Extinct now for over ten thousand years..."

Massimo unbuttoned his shirt and displayed his own fossilized tooth, hanging there about his neck. "We wear them when we go into the wild."

"Why?" Michael asked innocently, in a late-night state of mental dullness.

"To remind us that we're ephemeral," Massimo answered, his face becoming grim. He then turned away from Michael, gazing off into nowhere, seeing with his imagination alone.

"Imagine what it must have been like," Massimo went on, quietly yet passionately, "the last Ice Age, in North America, when men were so few and the continent was teaming with great and mighty megafauna: mammoths, mastodons. Wild horses, llamas, camels. Giant sloths bigger than African bush elephants. The short-faced bear. *Dire wolves*. Enormous stag-moose, giant bison. The American cheetah, the American

169

lion—*really a giant jaguar.* The saber-toothed cats… In Eurasia: the cave bear, the cave lion, the cave hyena! The Irish elk, giant polar bears, woolly rhinoceroses…"

And Massimo's words ran out, momentarily.

"Life…" Massimo finally added, quite drained, still staring off into nowhere. "There is no perfect ending. You can't leave a footprint behind. Time eventually buries everything. In the end, the only thing of importance, the only thing that matters, is what one has experienced."

Michael felt utterly intrigued by Massimo and the strange forces at work within this great, unusual man.

As they sat there together, about to slumber, Massimo slowly recited:

"… No one has pierced the mysteries of Eternity,
No one has taken a step outside of Being.
As I observe from novice to master, I note:
'Everyone born into this world is but powerless…'"

~ 6 ~

Michael stumbled out of his tent and visually surveyed the arid landscape, the died-down grass, the sparse, open bush, the bleached calcrete soil. It was only dawn, yet it was already hot. There was not a cloud in the sky, not even a whisper of moisture, only the presence of the almighty rising sun. For this was northern Namibia, late in the dry season.

They had flown in late yesterday, at sunset, Poulad skillfully landing their expeditionary aircraft on an ancient salt pan. They had tented down nearby, alongside a dried-up riverbed. The clear night sky had been perfect for stargazing, but Michael, Kapalei, and Poulad, all bone tired, had retired early. Even the mechanical man had powered down to conserve its energy for what was to come. Only Massimo had stayed up late into the night, drinking copious amounts of something distilled from various roots and tree bark.

As Michael stood there in the early-morning light, he recalled how he had been told by Poulad that their camp was set on the fringe of the Place of Mirages, of the Land of Dry Water, and he thought how aptly the land was named. Yet in the distance, Michael could see a surprising array of wildlife, gathering in concentrated numbers around the region's scattered and shrinking waterholes. He could see elephants, giraffes, zebras, and other herbivores whose names he had heard Kapalei mention: blue wildebeests, elands, impala, kudus, and steenboks. He thought of the predators that probably lay in hiding, invisible to his eye—the lion, the cheetah, and the leopard—and he could not help but smile at the comfort that his disability now afforded him, for he felt completely calm, as always, feeling absolutely no concern, no fear. Yes, Massimo was right, he was uniquely suited for this new job.

Touched by Namibia's rugged beauty, Michael momentarily felt himself surreally attuned to the land, so much so that he believed he somehow sensed an all-powerful expectation in the morning air. It was as if life itself seemed to be just waiting, waiting spellbound for the arrival of summer's dramatic thunderstorms. But rain was still months away…

Drawn forward by the unusual shining whiteness of the evaporated lake, where sat their plane, Michael leisurely strolled away from camp. Walking out upon the natural depression, he heard and felt the salt and gypsum crunch underfoot. Nearing their aircraft, he slowed his pace and then stopped and stood there silently beside Massimo.

"I like you," Massimo said without bothering to look at Michael. "I don't mind telling you this, because it's true. Already you follow the rhythm of the animals, rising at dawn to watch them feed in the coolness of the morning."

"Coolness?" Michael almost stammered.

"Wait until the midday heat." Massimo half smiled, turning to face Michael. "We'll rest then. I'll not start out until late afternoon."

Michael nodded, once again feeling comfort in direct eye contact with Massimo. He knew his place with Massimo. It was as a subordinate, and he was accepting of and comfortable with this. It felt natural and good. It felt right. And more, he felt indebted to this man who had provided him a feeling of belonging.

"Everything lives only once," Massimo went on, looking back out across the Land of Dry Water. "In the end, everything ends up down in those cellars of dead time. But if you truly live…"

Michael felt captivated by Massimo. "Back in Rome…" Michael heard himself comment. "You said that you were 'the man driven by fear'…"

"Everything that we need is on the other side of fear," Massimo responded cryptically, as his attention slowly turned back to focus on Michael. "You need to be careful walking off from camp. There are big cats nearby. Elephants, black rhinos. But you know that, don't you?"

Michael nodded.

"And yet you still walked out here alone, unarmed?"

Michael nodded again, feeling slightly weakened by the power of Massimo's penetrating gaze. And Michael sensed the irony: here Massimo was trying to understand him, yet he did not even fully understand himself.

"Later in the afternoon," Michael asked, hoping to distract Massimo's scrutinizing stare, "what will you hunt?"

"I don't hunt!" Massimo snapped. "Don't ever accuse me of that."

"But the rifles," Michael responded deferentially. "I don't understand…"

"The rifles are for Poulad and Kapalei," Massimo growled, "and for self-protection only. I've never hunted down and put a cowardly bullet in any animal."

Massimo then placed a fatherly hand on Michael's shoulder as he went on, having a genuine interest in the welfare of his new man. "The .416 Rigby," he explained patiently, "is Poulad's; he favors Mauser craftsmanship, and the extra firepower. Kapalei the Holland and Holland .700, for its thousand-grain bullets. The Jeffery double, it belonged to Gunnar…

"But for you"—Massimo handed Michael the belted single holster that had been slung over his shoulder—"a snub-nose .500 Magnum revolver, Smith and Wesson's bear gun. You don't need to be skilled; it's for close range. Just point and pull the trigger."

Michael withdrew the revolver from the holster and grimaced at the weight and size of the piece.

"But remember," Massimo warned him sternly, "it's for self-preservation only, and only as a last possible resort."

Michael nodded, but his mind was elsewhere, still struggling to understand the unforeseen turn of events. "But, if you don't hunt, what are we doing here?"

Massimo put his arm fully around Michael and turned them both to look out over the desolate salt pan, out toward the dawn. He then recited aloud:

"I cannot cover up the sun with clay,

I cannot pierce the mysteries of Time.

From the oceans of my meditation, clear-sightedness has drawn!

A pearl, which I greatly fear to reveal…"

And Massimo turned and started back toward camp.

Michael saw Massimo look back for a second, and there was that glimmer of a smile lifting momentarily in his eyes.

~ 7 ~

Late afternoon: The temperature dropped to 104 degrees…

And Massimo emerged from his tent, in garb most unusual. He wore a battered leather collar about his neck rimmed by badger fur… and a worn, muscled Roman cuirass, made of bronze, the torso armor sculpted to mimic an idealized human physique. Complete with realistic nipples and even a navel—as had been worn by gods and emperors—it projected a startling portrait of heroic bare-chestedness.

Massimo's forearms and calves were similarly adorned, protected by beat-up chainmail armor sleeves, the mesh of the small metal rings dancing resplendently in the brutal African sunlight.

Michael arose, speechless, abandoning completely his introductory game of chess with the mechanical man.

Kapalei pulled a long spear from the camp's fire. The Tanzanian had earlier pointed the pole's end by rubbing it against a rock. Having slowly polished it in the flames, lightly charring it, drawing the moisture from the wood, he had transformed the tip into a hardened glaze of wood, pitch, and carbon, making it harder than copper—a technology developed by humans 400,000 years ago. He handed the fire-hardened spear to Massimo, who took it in hand.

From Massimo's waist hung a belted short sword with a curved blade, an "honor weapon," a tactical *wakizashi*, something used by Japanese samurai since the 15th century for close-quarters fighting—small enough to be wielded with one hand, yet large enough to be held by two if need be.

"He hand-forged and tempered the weapon himself," Poulad said to Michael in a low tone, having noticed their new recruit eyeing the 20-inch blade. "That and the spear are all he ever takes with him."

"With him?" Michael asked. "With him where?"

"Out there," Poulad answered, looking off into the open bush. "There are two young male lions not far from here. Brothers. They've staked a claim on a territory around an ancient waterhole. Massimo aims to take part of that territory from them."

Massimo said something in Swahili to Kapalei, and the two men walked over to the others, prepared to leave. Massimo looked deep into Poulad's eyes and recited:

"It was a drop of water, merged in the sea.

It was a speck of dust, united with the earth.

What about our entering and leaving this world?

A fly appeared and disappeared."

Poulad answered:

"On this Earth, I see sleeping men,

Under the earth, I see entombed men.

When I look at the desert of Non-Existence,

I see those who have departed and those to come..."

And Massimo headed off, Kapalei following, both men walking out into the died-down grass, into the open bush. Into the Place of Mirages.

"No," Poulad said to Michael, restraining Michael from following with a firm hand across the chest. "Only Kapalei can follow. Only Kapalei."

Michael noticed that Kapalei was carrying a large and heavy big-game rifle: his powerful Holland and Holland. "Kapalei will protect him?" Michael questioned.

Poulad shook his head. "Technically, that's not allowed."

This time, it was the mechanical man's large glass eyes that prompted Poulad to explain. Although without a voice, the mechanical man communicated surprisingly well with its eyes alone. And, if one was inclined to read, in printed digital messages on the wide screen that ran across its metallic chest.

"You see," Poulad responded, "it's about territoriality. It's about dominance, and honor. It's Massimo's way, his code. Despite what you may have read in the media, Massimo's not a big-game hunter. He never has been. He's a dominator of great and mighty things. He doesn't hunt, he challenges the territory of predators, the personal space of large dangerous game, in order to force the animals to accept his claim of dominance.

"For example, with these two male lions out there, Massimo will enter their territory and mark off part of it as his own, with his scent, urinating on brush, rocks. Rubbing his perspiration on trees. If the lions enter his claimed territory, he'll give them warning, allow them the chance to retreat. Any animal that retreats, Massimo lets it go its way, and the victory is his."

"And if the lions don't retreat?" Michael asked, awestruck by what he was hearing.

"Then Massimo defends his territory," Poulad answered. "Not with a gun, but with that fire-hardened spear, with his short sword. With his fists, feet, knees, teeth…"

"If he fails?" The question silently typed itself across the chest of the mechanical man.

"Then we're to leave his bones to the earth, for eternity."

"And Kapalei?" Michael asked, dumbfounded. "He won't use his rifle?"

Poulad shook his head. "Massimo trusts that he won't. He knows I probably would. So only Kapalei can accompany him, watch from a distance."

"Why?" Michael asked

"So that we know the outcome."

"Why?" the typed word came from the mechanical man.

"I just—" But then Poulad stopped, understanding the look in the CPA's huge, sedate glass eyes. "Oh, you mean why does he do it?"

The mechanical man patiently awaited an answer, but Poulad had none.

Michael looked at the CPA and felt its inhuman, artificial, computing mind struggling to understand. He then considered his own odd mind, with its missing parts, and his resulting peculiar behavior... He then thought of how Massimo went through life apparently seeking out one challenge after another, one conquest after another, his life an exercise in the expression of man and the male spirit.

"It's his programming," Michael provided his own answer, an insight that completely satisfied the mechanical man. "He can't escape it."

~ 8 ~

The Namibian night was surprisingly cool, in the low seventies.

Their camp's great fire lit up much of the surrounding area. Near the fire, Michael tended the oil-burning samovar that Poulad had set up earlier, its silver reflecting the dancing flames in a silent yet chaotic and restless manner.

As Michael refilled Poulad's cup, he could not help but notice the Iranian's restlessness.

"Anything?" Poulad asked the mechanical man, who sat amongst them, tending to their camp's stationary two-way radio. The CPA shook its head negative.

"You've been with Massimo long?" Michael asked Poulad.

Poulad nodded and slowly sat back. "I've seen things you wouldn't believe. Massimo confronting hyenas, angry Cape buffalo, even a hippo. African wild dogs, a fifteen-hundred-pound Kodiak bear... A tiger in the snow. The most beautiful jaguar... Massimo exerted his will, his dominance over all of them, and so many more.

"I once watched as Massimo gained the respect of a pack of timber wolves. Big, gray, so handsome... When Massimo left, the wolves, they all howled, they howled their hearts out for their departing alpha… And he looked back at them, as if in his own heart he yearned only to run off with them… to be a thing of the wild, forever.

"This wildness in Massimo… If he survives tonight, and tomorrow, and the next day… I fear that he'll soon have nothing left to conquer. He's done everything these past ten years… And what will become of Massimo then, without a challenge? I think then he will surely, finally die. I believe he senses this is coming. Fears that the time is almost upon him…"

As Michael pondered these words, he noticed the robot suddenly looking up with its huge glass eyes, up into the pitch-dark sky above.

"What?" Michael asked.

"A shooting star?" The words slowly typed themselves across the robot's chest.

Before Michael could look up, the radio crackled, and over it came Massimo's confident voice. As the device operated in half-duplex mode, they could not talk and listen simultaneously, so they listened first:

Massimo:

"O friend! Come, let us not think of tomorrow.

Let us enjoy this moment plundered from life.

Tomorrow, when we leave this old Temple,

We shall be equal with those of seven thousand years old."

Then crackling static.

Michael noticed Poulad smiling, ever so slightly, as he activated the transmitter with the push of a button and replied:

"Today you have no control of tomorrow.

Worrying about it will bring you but sorrow.

Spoil not the present moment, if your heart is not insane.

For the time you have left to live remains unknown…"

The radio then went silent on the other end.

It was only then that Michael noticed that the CPA was still looking up into the night sky, transfixed. Michael looked up. Like the night before, it was unusually dark, no moon, scintillating stars everywhere, with the splendor of the Milky Way Galaxy arcing across the heavens as a dim, white background glow. Michael could not see anything unusual, but he suddenly felt something quite odd. He felt... observed.

Michael lowered his eyes and looked out past the light of their fire, wondering if perhaps the two lions Poulad had spoken of were somewhere just outside the perimeter of their camp, stealthily watching them...

The radio crackled, and they heard Kapalei's voice, whispering something in Swahili. When the Tanzanian finished speaking, Poulad translated for them:

"He said the lions are moving in on Massimo..."

"Kapalei is with Massimo?" Michael asked.

Poulad shook his head. "No, he's at a safe distance, observing. Using a mobile radio, like Massimo."

Their stationary radio crackled again, and they heard lions roaring.

"Massimo," Poulad explained. "He's switched his set to transmit..."

The roars turned to growls, and the horrific sounds of man versus beast ensued. It was prehistoric, hair-raising.

Michael sat there stiff, for the first time in his life feeling... concerned. Not for himself, but for Massimo. It was compassion mixed with worry. Michael had never felt anything like it before.

The sounds of the clash reached a bloodcurdling height and then died down completely. In that lull came Massimo's voice over the radio, breathing heavily, sounding physically wounded yet spiritually unyielding:

"Oh, come with old Khayyám, and leave
the Wise
To talk; one thing is certain, that Life
flies;
One thing is certain; and the Rest is
Lies;
The Flower that had bloomed forever
dies..."

Lions roaring again! And the brutish, disturbing sounds of Massimo in combat, fighting for his life. Like before, the bone-chilling noises rose to a crescendo, this time climaxed by a primordial roar of death, followed by utter silence. And then Massimo, nearly out of breath:

"There was a Door to which I found no
Key:
There was a Veil past which I could not
See:
Some little Talk a while of Me and
Thee
There seemed—and then no more of Thee and Me..."

And Massimo's voice faded, as if dying.

A crackle of static, and Kapalei spoke in his language. Poulad translated after each sentence:

"Massimo had to kill one of the lions... Drove the other off... Massimo is the victor... I'll bring him back... He's injured... Meet us halfway... He's bleeding badly..."

~ 9 ~

Kapalei walked alongside Massimo, attentively, although Massimo would not allow the Maasai warrior to assist him in any way. Whether this was out of pride or a spirit of self-reliance, or both, it mattered not; Massimo limped along, using his fire-hardened spear as a walking staff.

Speaking softly in Swahili and smiling occasionally, Massimo ignored the pain from his wounds and his loss of blood, still on a serene high born from victory. His self-assured voice and composed mood slowly calmed Kapalei, although the Tanzanian's countenance remained etched with concern. For the makeshift bandages wound about Massimo's left upper arm and forearm and one of his thighs grew more crimson with each step that they took.

Along their walk, Massimo paused to recite to Kapalei:

"Last night, I broke my jug on a stone.

I was drunk when I behaved so disrespectfully.

The broken jug seemed to tell me:

'Once I was like you, and you in turn will one day be like me.'"

Suddenly, Massimo froze and motioned Kapalei to remain silent. Ever so slowly he nodded toward the nearby brush, where a huge, solitary black rhino was feeding nocturnally, as was their habit, eating bushes and trees. Light gray in color, the creature stood out rather dramatically against the background of sheer blackness. The height of a tall man at its shoulders, the animal must have weighed close to two tons. With skin of dermal armor and the foremost of its two horns stretching outward nearly five feet in length, the creature's appearance was still very much that of the prehistoric beast of its fifty-million-year heritage.

For several moments Massimo and Kapalei stood there, still, for black rhinos had a keen sense of smell and sharp hearing. And more, they were fast, formidable, unpredictable, and dangerous—a challenge that Massimo, tonight, could not resist.

Waving Kapalei to remain in place, Massimo limped forward, slowly lowering his long spear until he held it horizontally, pointed at the black rhino.

"Hyah!" Massimo suddenly yelled, threatening the rhino with his spear, purposely invading the animal's personal space, step by step. Challenging the beast. The challenge accepted, the huge creature lowered its impressive head—its mighty forward horn still held higher than even tall Kapalei—and charged.

Had Massimo already run out of realistic new challenges, as Poulad feared? What else would instigate such madness? Why would Massimo, wounded and unprepared, be so willing to instantly hurl himself at such danger? Was he perhaps unconsciously fearing his own end and hastening himself toward it?

At the moment of impact, Massimo's spear snapped in two like a twig. Massimo careened off the shoulder of the massive creature, and he went sailing up into the air, then came crashing down upon the ground, lying there still, unmoving.

Kapalei ran to Massimo as the rhino continued onward, racing off, disappearing into the darkness…

It was at that moment that the African bush elephant appeared, having been spooked out of the brush by the rhino. Standing there before the two men, towering twelve feet above them, the old bull trumpeted loudly, threateningly, its enormous ears flared fully out, its tremendous ivory tusks menacingly curved upward.

For a moment Kapalei was too shocked to even think, let alone move, for he was intimately aware that the African elephant was far more dangerous than the rhino, even more deadly than the lion. It was one of the most dangerous animals on Earth, trampling to death hundreds of people every year. Sometimes aggressively goring to death its victims with its dangerously sharp tusks.

Gathering himself, Kapalei carefully stepped protectively in front of Massimo, who still lay there on the ground, although he was now regaining consciousness. Slowly raising his powerful

Holland and Holland rifle, Kapalei readied his finger on the weapon's double trigger, aiming for a brain shot.

~ 10 ~

Michael could not see much in the darkness as he followed Poulad, the mechanical man in turn following him. As they entered a clearing, Michael did spy, over Poulad's shoulder, Kapalei, standing there with his back to them... his rifle pointed up at... a bull elephant so large that it looked more like something out of a dream.

The elephant trumpeted as the trio stepped out of the bush behind Kapalei. Poulad stopped instantly, as did Michael and the CPA.

As Michael stared in wonder at the animal, he felt himself tremble as a wave of awe swept over him—so inspiring was the sheer size of the magnificent beast. But more, there was also a palpable presence of high intelligence and emotion emanating from the creature, something that surprised Michael even more so than the unexpected sight of the enraged elephant.

Frozen moments ticked by, but Kapalei's shot did not come. In fact, the Maasai warrior surprisingly did the opposite: he reverently lowered his rifle, it seemed in recognition of the elephant's magnificence being greater than his own humble existence...

Poulad quickly stepped forward, lifting his own rifle, but Massimo rose, still strong, still in command, and firmly pushed the barrel down. "No," Massimo ordered in a low tone, his voice racked with pain. "It would be a sin. You'd never forgive yourself..."

Massimo then turned about to face the elephant, with firm hands pushing his men behind him. "Perhaps this is my penance alone to pay, for the death of that brave lion. All of you... start backing away now, slowly. I'll... stand my ground. Unyielding. If this is to be my end... so be it."

183

But Poulad, Kapalei, Michael, and the mechanical man did not move. They stood there with him, for him. For they moved in his world, he was the center of their existence.

Michael stared at Massimo, who stood there tense, ready, still the bullfighter, but one who was wounded, and worse, seemingly resigned to facing his final, last challenge. For he had done it all. There were no more genuine challenges to win. Perhaps this was the most suitable end for such an extraordinary man as he.

Michael had never before felt such overwhelming loyalty and admiration. He found himself stepping up to Massimo's side, to stand there silently, beside him. Like he had done in the Roman Colosseum. As he had stood there beside Massimo on the desolate salt pan. It was where he felt most comfortable. Where he felt he most belonged.

"Michael," Massimo asked, in a low, warm, fatherly tone, not bothering to look at his new man, satisfied to merely feel his presence, "you feel no fear?"

"… Only curiosity," Michael answered, and he slowly and calmly walked right up to the elephant, finding himself irresistibly compelled to find out what it would be like to touch it.

Without apprehension, in a state of complete calm, Michael reached out and gently stroked the old bull upon its massive, sensitive trunk. It felt good. To touch the god of Africa. To look into its intelligent and emotional eyes.

Massimo, Poulad, Kapalei, and the mechanical man all stood there in absolute silence, watching the man without fear interacting with a living cousin of the extinct woolly mammoth of the last Ice Age, with the largest living land animal on Earth, with a truly great and mighty thing.

As they stood there, marveling at the moment, slowly the great beast grew tranquil in reaction to Michael's fearless and gentle touch. Unhurriedly, the elephant quietly and majestically turned away and walked off into the African darkness from whence it had come.

"It may be best in life..." Massimo commented aloud, appreciatively, yet sounding defeated—for his elected end had not come—"to surround yourself... with those on the same mission as you. Whether they know it or not."

The dim light of typed letters glowed from the display on the CPA's chest. The letters spelled out: "The shooting star? Again."

All eyes turned upward, and the men, and the mechanical man, witnessed what appeared to be a falling star—only it moved upward... It then dimmed and traveled laterally, very slowly, resembling in brightness a planet or a satellite. If one had not first seen its initial flashing, one would now find it quite difficult to notice. But then it grew abnormally bright and descended significantly in altitude, moving slowly, soundlessly, oddly, across the dark sky.

Once again, Michael suddenly felt the strange, inexplicable sensation of being... observed. This time, however, he intuitively understood that the source was not natural, and that it came from... above.

The bright light began to move erratically, growing larger and still brighter. It then abruptly dropped and vanished behind the distant tree line.

"... A plane?" Michael suggested, although he himself did not believe it.

Massimo shook his head, suspicious, and limped forward with heightened alertness.

"I've seen something like it before..." Poulad admitted, his voice near a whisper, full of unease. "Twenty years ago, over Tehran. I was flying an F-4 Phantom III jet... It was bright, like this. I approached to within a few miles.

"My jet, it lost all instrumentation and communications capabilities... Weapons systems completely shut down... I broke off the intercept. Systems all resumed functioning... The sighting was confirmed by ground radar. A military spy satellite also recorded the UFO..."

The acronym *UFO* reverberated through Michael's mind, and his perception of reality, of the Namibian night, seemed to tilt and sway off kilter. *A UFO?*

As Massimo's team stood there, waiting, a huge, bright light slowly rose up out of the trees only a hundred yards distant. Soundless, it changed from white to luminous yellow, the shift occurring in a fluid, eerie, threatening manner.

Within moments, the UFO, disc-shaped, was hovering directly above them, perhaps fifty to eighty feet overhead. It was then that the apparition sent down a menacing tube of light, which engulfed them all.

As Michael experienced within himself an intense feeling of coming apart, he looked to Massimo who, like himself and the others, was floating up into the sky. Massimo was smiling broadly, embracing the abduction, completely re-energized to take on life once again, fully accepting this new, unimaginable challenge. He was the matador, his focus and composure absolute, his manly confidence radiant and supreme. And despite his injuries, full of power, coordination, and vitality, every muscle in his fatigued and injured body tensed, held ready to do battle anew.

Michael calmly looked up at the UFO at zenith that was supernaturally sucking them toward it. He felt not a tinge of fear or even concern, only curiosity—and more: a wry sense of the ironic.

"Oh," Michael whispered aloud, with a mischievous smile creeping across his face, speaking rhetorically to whomever or whatever controlled the glowing aerial craft, "you're making a terrible mistake."

And then Michael, in an instant, without warning, fell completely unconscious.

~ 11 ~

Michael awoke abruptly to find himself lying flat upon his back, calm but quite disorientated. He attempted to lift his head, but found that he could not. Looking forward with his eyes alone, he noticed his bare feet, in the forefront of his vision, as his eyes slowly focused. He thought how odd this was, that his feet were bare. What had happened to his shoes? Where were his socks?

But Michael then noticed and realized that he was stark naked. And he immediately felt himself flush with embarrassment and awkwardness, becoming painfully self-conscious.

He attempted to get up, but found himself paralyzed, unable to move anything but his eyes. And his discomfort grew. He felt absolutely no fear regarding the extraordinary situation he found himself in, but he did feel mortified. Lying there stripped, undressed, exposed. He did not like it. Not at all. But his curiosity began to grow…

Moving his eyes to his left, Michael saw that Poulad and Kapalei were similarly lying unclothed upon what appeared to be small, individual examination tables. Unlike himself, however, both men were still unconscious. Michael rather quickly averted his eyes, surprised and uncomfortable at seeing his new associates in the nude.

Michael next turned his eyes to his right. And there lay Massimo, naked and unconscious: a magnificent human specimen of sturdy bone and sculpted muscle. Michael was quite surprised to see how hairy Massimo was, the man's chest and stomach covered by a thick carpet of dark hair. Even his shoulders had hair upon them. Michael suspected his back did as well.

Michael saw that Massimo's wounds appeared to have been superficially treated and stained with some white dye. Like Poulad and Kapalei, Massimo lay there silent, unconscious.

Michael momentarily wondered why he alone had regained consciousness. Could it possibly have had something to do with his Urbach-Wiethe disease, which had caused the bilateral lesions in his temporal lobes? Had this caused him to awaken before the others?

Looking past Massimo, Michael saw that they were within a circular chamber, one with a peculiar hazy environment. The area directly in front of them, it was bright and constantly changing, doing something very strange. It seemed to be where the UFO's tube of light had emanated from.

Near this strange area, Michael noticed the mechanical man haphazardly propped up against the bulkhead, seated there on the floor amongst their clothing, boots, rifles, etc. The CPA made eye contact with Michael. It was conscious, all the lights within its brain sparkling. But its transparent brain case had been removed... and something dark and ugly, shaped like a miniature anvil, had been attached directly to its artificial mind. Looking into the robot's huge, dignified, and subdued eyes, Michael sensed its helplessness, for it too was held paralyzed. And humiliated.

As Michael thought of the indignity of their situation, a malevolent face appeared above him, looking straight down at him. The face—at first it reminded Michael of an insect, of a bug, as it had huge eyes like an ant but also because its unusually large head sat upon a neck no thicker than Michael's own wrist.

As Michael looked at this face, experiencing no fear, his curiosity climbed to such a height that he completely forgot about his uncomfortable nakedness. The face was so unlike anything that Michael had ever seen or even imagined. So different was it from that of a man. From a human. It was certainly, without a doubt, an alien creature from a far-off star.

Suddenly, Michael's small personal universe of perception expanded far beyond New York, Rome, and the Namibian north. Suddenly, there was much more. What was it that Massimo had said to him, in Rome? *"All encounters are a continuing introduction, to ourselves, and also to the very cosmos itself."*

Michael lowered his eyes and looked over the alien, the aliens—for a second alien now appeared above Michael, looking down at him—they were tall, almost as tall as himself. Their naked bodies were surprisingly anthropomorphic, although eerily exotic and elongated, lacking any apparent sex organs. Their skin was a dark gray in color, hairless and extremely smooth, seeming almost artificial, akin to something between rubber and plastic. Adding to this unnatural effect, their bodies lacked muscular definition, and there were no visible signs of an underlying skeletal structure. Their hands had two sets of two opposable fingers, and palms that could fold in half vertically. No need for a thumb.

As the two Grays leaned over Michael, examining him, Michael wondered how they breathed: their chests did not move, their faces lacked noses and nostrils, and their insignificant mouths, just barely perceptible slits, remained closed. They did not seem to be biologically alive, yet obviously they were. Michael wondered for a moment if they might be artificially constructed...

Michael stopped wondering about the Grays when one of them—there were now four of them standing over him— placed a cup-like device over his genitals while another of the Grays inserted something into his anus. Simultaneously, the remaining two began to peer into his ears and mouth and count his vertebrae with their long, probing fingers.

In awkward humiliation, Michael turned his eyes away, but only to become more mortified as he saw that Poulad and Kapalei, although still paralyzed, were now conscious and helplessly watching what was happening to him.

Michael turned his eyes away again, to find Massimo lying there silent but awake. He made eye contact with Massimo, wordlessly pleading for help. There, in Massimo's eyes, he saw something he had not previously seen in Massimo: rage.

As he maintained eye contact with Massimo, to his shock he saw Massimo's hands beginning to clench, his arms trembling, beginning to move. Michael calmed for a moment as he remembered the stories that he had read about Massimo, about how this reputed big-game hunter had routinely subjected himself to all types of venoms and poisons, in order to grant himself varying degrees of immunity against lethal snakebites and the stings and bites of tropical spiders and insects. Could Massimo's enhanced immunity allow him to break free from whatever the Grays had subjected them to that caused their paralysis?

Michael tried to move, but he could not. He looked back at Poulad and Kapalei. They too remained immobilized. He looked over to the mechanical man, but saw that the CPA was staring at Massimo.

Michael looked past the Grays, behind them, to Massimo, to witness Massimo rising like an indomitable giant, his enraged eyes focused on the Grays.

As one of the Grays pulled the cup-like device from Michael's genitals and Michael felt the shame of having a sperm sample stolen from him, he knew there was only one hope: Massimo.

The same Gray next looked at Michael with its huge, black, mesmerizing eyes, and Michael felt its eyes painfully pushing into his own eyes. Pressing into his brain. The pain was horrible. And worse, Michael suddenly found himself privy to this alien's unspoken intentions: after the physical examination, it intended to dissect them all—while they were still alive.

"Massimo!" Michael cried out, his voice racked with humiliation, pain, and helplessness.

And Massimo came forth like a jaguar.

Michael watched as the Grays turned to find Massimo launching himself upon them. Although their mask-like faces remained expressionless, Michael felt the utter shock and terror from the one who had been pushing into his mind. It was the first time that Michael had ever experienced what it was like to feel fear. It was absolutely, unforgettably terrifying...

Michael lay there, motionless, watching Massimo take vengeance on the Grays. They broke like twigs in the might of Massimo's angry bare hands.

As other Grays came rushing into the chamber, Michael looked on quietly, calmly, feeling fully avenged, all his confidence in Massimo. He watched as Massimo, having claimed the room as his territory, took possession of one of their big-game rifles, using it as a club. It was like watching Samson of the Hebrew Bible slaying an entire army with only the jawbone of an ass.

~ 12 ~

Clothed, Michael joined Massimo, Poulad, Kapalei, and the mechanical man on what appeared to be the bridge of the UFO—which was now theirs. The wall before them was somehow transparent, functioning as an enormous viewing portal from which they could see the African dawn and the Land of Dry Water below slowly awakening to the rising sun, life responding to the diurnal rhythms of the land.

As Massimo removed the anvil from the CPA's brain, Michael stood ready to help place the robot's brain case back on. Michael wanted very much to assist in doing this, to give the robot back its dignity.

"There are no controls anywhere..." Poulad stated, agitated, pacing back and forth. For he and Kapalei, having just completed an extensive examination of the craft, had been unable to recognize anything resembling engines for propulsion or to find any controls of any kind to enable the piloting of the saucer. "How did they fly the thing?"

"I can hear it thinking now." The words slowly typed across the robot's chest.

"What?" Massimo asked.

"The UFO," the answer typed itself out.

"... Is it a computer?" Massimo guessed.

"No."

"What is it?" Massimo demanded.

"It is," came the enigmatic answer, typed across the CPA's chest.

"It's *alive?*" Massimo asked.

"Wait..." the CPA typed.

And they waited, for some time. Finally, the mechanical man began to type again, and as it did so, they all read along silently to themselves:

"Yes, it is alive... It served to transport the biomechanical things that have been killed... But it was not created by them... Its original masters were the wardens of the thousands of discovered planets in this section of our galaxy...

"Planets for which these wardens assumed paternalistic responsibility... Planets abounding in life but containing no sentient life... And also a few rare planets of sentient life beneath or at Earth's present level of technology...

"All these planets were maintained for millions of years as reservations… The wardens allowed no visitations. No trespassing. No hunting… These protected reservations had been kept pristine… Earth is one of these reservations…

"The biomechanical aliens, although few in number, recently conquered these wardens. The biomechanicals are now slowly surveying the spoils of their victory: these reserves.

"This ship awaits your instructions. It is at your service."

And Massimo smiled, his voice vibrating with vitality:

"My mind has never been deprived of learning,
Rare are the mysteries that have remained unnoticed.
Day and night, for forty-two years I meditated,
To reach the certitude that nothing is certain!"

~ 13 ~

After returning to their camp at the dried-up riverbed alongside the ancient salt pan to load all of their supplies aboard their new exploratory vehicle, Massimo and his team flew to northwestern Namibia—in their thinking, self-piloting UFO— where they loaded up with additional supplies and purchased a dozen Himba women of the OvaHimba tribe, the last seminomadic people of Namibia.

The tribal headmen were very willing to sell a mere dozen of their women in exchange for the great wealth that Massimo bestowed upon them. No Himba woman was taken who did not willingly volunteer to go. The women only made one demand: that they be allowed to take with them a lifelong supply of *otjize* paste, their most highly desired beauty cosmetic, made from a mixture of butterfat and ochre pigment, perfumed with the aromatic resin of the omuzumba shrub.

Michael found the topless, calfskin-skirted, barefooted Himba women quite attractive, especially how they kept their skin and their one braided hair plait tinged orange-red by their *otjize* paste, which they completely covered themselves with. Michael wondered if the wilderness that dwelt within Massimo might be rubbing off on him.

As the OvaHimba were polygamous, Massimo took six of the women as wives, leaving the others for Michael, Poulad, and Kapalei to divide amongst themselves. Michael felt that this was fair, as Massimo's appetite for everything in life was clearly much larger than that of any ordinary man.

And they flew away from Earth, in their flying saucer, each man with his fossilized saber tooth hanging about his neck. Massimo had instructed the sentient craft to transport them to a reserve planet that contained no intelligent life, but one with great and mighty megafauna rivaling that of Earth's last Ice Age.

Michael walked up to the ship's huge, transparent viewing portal and stood there silently at Massimo's side, where he intended to forever remain.

He looked at Massimo, who was staring straight ahead, out into the starlit infinity of outer space, and he thought of how Massimo no longer needed to fear running out of the type of challenges that he sought. Of how the only thing Massimo now ever needed to fear was his own inevitable demise, something all men must eventually face. On this, Michael felt that Massimo had an old, insightful, and realistic attitude.

As they departed, Michael listened to Massimo reciting aloud yet another poem by the twelfth-century Persian philosopher and poet Omar Khayyám:

"Ah, my Beloved, fill the cup that clears
Today of past regrets and future
Fears—
Tomorrow? Why, Tomorrow I myself may be
With yesterday's Seven Thousand
Years."

A Note from the Author

This author hopes that the reader enjoyed this tale of UFO abduction and more.

The UFO abduction in this story was loosely based on both the Allagash Abduction, alleged to have occurred to a group of four men during a camping trip near Allagash, Maine, in 1976, and also on the earlier Barney and Betty Hill Abduction, an alleged extraterrestrial abduction of an American couple in New Hampshire in 1961. This author does not believe these cited abductions actually occurred, but he views the stories as interesting "What if?" pieces of fiction.

When the character Poulad refers to his UFO sighting when he was a pilot in the Iranian air force, this is based on the 1976 Tehran UFO incident, where an Iranian pilot had a visual sighting of an unidentified flying object (a UFO) over Tehran, the capital of Iran.

Earth being presented in this story as a reservation is based on the zoo hypothesis, which seeks to offer a possible explanation as to why there is no evidence of Earth ever having been visited by extraterrestrials despite the high statistical probability that alien civilizations may exist in abundance. This author first encountered this theoretical explanation in Isaac Asimov's 1962 book *Fact and Fancy*, in the chapter titled "Our Lonely Planet."

Urbach-Wiethe disease is a real rare genetic disorder. In recent years, a woman from Kentucky suffering from this brain disorder has garnered significant media attention and has been dubbed "the woman without fear."

The poetry in the story is that of this author's favorite poet: Omar Khayyám, the Persian mathematician, astronomer, philosopher, and poet who lived in Iran from 1048 to 1131.

This author strongly recommends that readers who are interested in Omar Khayyám acquire the *Rubáiyát of Omar Khayyám*.

A few more from the great Omar Khayyám which did not make it into this story, although the author would have liked to have found a place for them within the novelette:

"Dread not the trials and tribulations of Time,
They are not lasting, do not fear them.
Live this present moment full of joy,
Think not of the past and tremble not at the future."

"This lifetime, a few days long, went by fast like
Water down the brook and wind across the desert.
There are two days which have never worried me:
The day to come and the day that has gone."

And this author earlier utilized this very special poem by Omar Khayyám below in his sci-fi novel *The God Antenna*:

"Ah, make the most of what we may yet spend,
Before we too into the Dust descend;
Dust into Dust, and under Dust to lie,
Sans wine, sans song, sans singer,
and—sans End!"

Niko Zinovii
Phoenix, Arizona
12 May 2015

Great and Mighty Things

Niko Zinovii

Garden Metamorphosis

G ian stood there stiff, unmoving, his searching light-brown eyes peering out over his small rooftop garden, his vision focused on the midday full moon, hanging there ghostly between billowing cumulus clouds.

Gian's tousled hair, as much gray as it was black, along with his mature, serious countenance, made him look much older than his thirty-three years of age. The gray in his month's growth of ruffled, untrimmed beard added dramatically to this illusionary effect. The discontent in his eyes—he seemed a man born to be intellectually restless in this world, one to challenge everything, in his mind, silently, broodingly, indignantly, as if life had early on shown itself to him fully and wiped away his smile... Handsome yet unkempt, he more resembled a tormented, struggling artist than the priest he was: Father Gian Marie.

His eyes, reservoirs of deep philosophical thought and tormented discontent, slowly dropped from the moon, and his unfocused stare settled down upon his bare feet...

"Damn those students from Milan..." He muttered the curse, barely audible, his voice wavering.

When he finally looked up again, it was to notice his C-class robot, still standing at attention nearby. It was a slender thing of metal, cylindrical, multiple eyed, its many appendages hanging there relaxed at its sides. Gian sensed nothing spiritual in its intelligent gaze. For this reason he disapproved of it. He saw no beauty in it, unlike the beauty he intuitively perceived in his bountiful garden of miniature fruit trees and fragrant herbs. It was in nature that he saw God's handiwork. Yet it was from nature also that he drew his restless discontent.

The world was amazing, so full of beauty, but also of ugliness. From an early age, Gian had struggled, intellectually, to reconcile these extremes. Was God, the marvelous designer of butterflies and snowflakes, also the creator of cancer and volcanoes and famine? Does a benevolent, thoughtful, and loving creator act so sadistically? *So we blame Satan for everything that is bad?* But then did this not imply that God was not omnipotent?

It all made Gian wonder. And so he had, early on, studied biology, from which he had drawn a pearl which he greatly feared facing. For he could almost sense how complexity could arise from randomness over vast vistas of time... Yet in his mind, he simultaneously could not fathom existence without a divine creator. He intuitively saw and felt a perfect hand at work, touching and planning each living thing with a unique design and purpose. These extremes intellectually tore at Gian.

So he had entered the priesthood, praying for divine guidance...

Summoning up his inner strength, Gian forced himself to look past his garden, out over the surrounding red-tiled rooftops of historic Rome, to the high walls of Vatican City State, looming there hazily in the distance.

Perhaps if he had been there when it happened, at the Vatican... But he had been away, in Naples. And that was his personal torment. That he had been spared the fate of his brethren within the Holy See.

It was still difficult for Gian to believe that, for over a month now, the Vatican was no longer the center of the Catholic Church, but merely an abandoned relic of the past, soon to be turned into a museum.

How could it have gotten so out of control? his thoughts cried out. For the life of him he could not understand how the world was now changing, or why. He thought back, back to the arrival of Little Miracle... It was only less than a year ago when that biotech company from Singapore had developed its treatment for temporal-lobe epilepsy: a tiny white pill that altered various genes of the brain. It cured the neurological condition while unexpectedly dramatically improving memory and boosting intelligence. No wonder it was nicknamed Little Miracle. This pill, however, it also eliminated religiosity and the predisposition to believe in God...

The Vatican had urged people to rise up in protest against Little Miracle. Yet its use instead became widespread in record time. Many took it to attain an advantage over others, choosing an enhanced IQ over religiosity. Others took it as an experiment, especially the young, not bothering to consider that its effects were irreversible.

Nonbelievers worldwide, after they learned that Little Miracle could be dissolved in water without inhibiting its effects, tainted city and bottled water supplies, starting with Vatican City State... the subterfuge carried out by university students from Milan. And now... copycats were doing the same all over the world. Little Miracle had become a runaway snowball, a mad wave that was presently sweeping across the world. Sweeping it clean of religion, of believers...

"Damn science to hell." Gian muttered the curse, his heart aching, full of despair—and guilt. For if he had not been away, he too would have drunk the Vatican's tainted water...

But would he also have lost his faith? Like *all* his fellow priests had? This was the question that was tearing at him, tormenting him. This was the question.

The C-class robot sent a thought impulse into Gian's mind, notifying him that his visitor had arrived, that the front door had been automatically opened, the visitor instructed to come up to the roof.

Gian nodded, unconsciously, and turned to the small door that opened to his rooftop sanctuary. After several moments, a stranger stepped out onto the roof: a calm, dignified, middle-aged Englishman.

"Who are you?" Gian asked the man, rather gruffly. "Where's Rudolf?"

"I'm a friend of Rudy's," the man explained. "He couldn't make it. He asked me to deliver this to you."

And the man opened one of his hands to reveal a small pharmaceutical bottle containing a single white pill.

"My name is Walter," the man introduced himself. "Dr. Walter Maynard. Anthropologist, retired."

Walter took several steps forward and placed the bottle containing Little Miracle down upon a table. "You do know what this is?" he asked. "What it does?"

Gian slowly nodded. "Yes..." he answered, his voice dry, momentarily weak.

"And you still want it?" Walter asked in a concerned, cultured tone. "Perhaps we should talk about it?"

And Walter lifted his other hand, which held a bottle of white wine. "Do you have two glasses?"

Gian nodded to his thin robot, which rolled off and retrieved two wine glasses as both men sat at the table before them, Gian staring intently at the small white pill, at Little Miracle.

Walter pulled a corkscrew out of his pocket and proceeded to open the bottle, his Londoner appearance sociable, clubbable.

"You do know what happened at the Vatican?" Walter asked, keeping the tone of his voice even.

"Of course I do!" Gian snapped back.

"And you still asked Rudy to bring you this? Why?"

Gian just sat there, silent for a moment, and then: "Truth is truth…"

"A test of faith?" Walter asked as he poured the wine.

"Will I still believe?" Gian asked himself, his gaze still transfixed upon Little Miracle. "Or will I be left without hope? Believing only in the world. Feeling truly lost…"

"So," Walter asked, "you want to join your Vatican brothers. Why?"

"I don't know," Gian confessed. "It seems that I must. Otherwise, how will I ever truly know…?"

"Know what?" Walter asked.

"Why things are as they are…" Gian guessed.

Walter silently raised his glass, and they each took a sip of the wine.

"You live in Rome?" Gian asked.

Walter grew rather serious. "No," he answered, "just passing through. I'm on my way to Greece and her islands. Archeology beckons."

Gian sensed there was much more to it than that, but his own troubles dominated his mind. "Have you taken Little Miracle?" he asked Walter.

Walter shook his head. "No," he answered. "I never needed to."

"You're an atheist?"

"Let's say a non-theist," Walter responded. "It covers all religions, gods, superstitions."

"How do you make sense of the world?" Gian asked passionately and sincerely.

And Walter thought about it as he drank more wine.

Finally, he answered urbanely, "I don't try to."

And before Gian could respond, Walter added, "Perhaps you shouldn't either."

"But if you don't make sense of it…" Gian grasped for something.

"I accept it," Walter responded. "As it is. I believe in the world."

And both men sat there for a spell, silent, drinking their wine, Gian eyeing Walter.

Finally Gian grabbed the pharmaceutical bottle and opened it, pouring the single pill into his trembling hand.

Walter looked at Gian extremely seriously. "Its effects are irreversible."

"Don't you think I know that?" Gian growled as he popped the pill into his mouth. Taking a swig of wine, he swallowed it.

"Damn science to hell…" Gian uttered, turning his eyes up to the light of the midday sun, as if seeking divine guidance. None came. Slowly, he turned to face his guest.

"What will happen now?" he asked.

And Walter shrugged. "I have no idea. Perhaps we should finish the wine?"

And they did. After which Gian felt his mind swim into darkness, and he passed out.

~

Gian awoke to see Walter's cultured face staring down at him.

"How long?" Gian asked, feeling odd sensations in his mind, memories churning, surfacing and then sinking, interlinking, a persistent tingling in his forebrain. It was frightening but it felt good, strangely freeing…

"It's been three days," Walter answered, concerned, motioning to the IV bottle hanging nearby. "I had a doctor come by. He said your unresponsive state was due to a negative reaction to Little Miracle. He said to watch you, that you would awaken without any ill effects."

And Gian arose and tore himself free from the intravenous therapy. Stumbling forward, he made his way up toward his rooftop garden, Walter following behind him, solicitously.

Halfway up the steps to the roof, Gian encountered his robot. In fact, he collided with the slender thing of metal. In doing so, he came eye to eye with the robot's many eyes. In its eyes he saw intelligence, and the magic of consciousness—an incredible human achievement. This staggered Gian, for he had never previously felt this way about the artificials before. *My God*, Gian's thoughts rumbled, *has my mind been altered, changed?*

And Gian raced up the remaining steps. To the roof, he had to get to the roof, to his garden. Would he see it differently? Would its beauty be gone? Stolen from him by that damn white pill?

Gian stood there, unsteady on his feet, bathed in the early morning rays of dawn. Oddly, for the first time in his life, he felt no psychological need for a god... Reality and truth suddenly seemed so very clear to him. And more, as he stared at his garden, he felt privileged to understand the path of life's evolution. It was not something easily taken on board. But the effort of doing so was well worth it. For the truth was staggeringly exciting. All his studies, the knowledge offered by science—he suddenly understood what had previously intellectually eluded him. His knowledge of science and his heightened intellect made it possible, that and the absence of a proclivity to embrace the supernatural. It all made sense now.

And so there he stood, also seeing even himself anew on this new day. And it was a beautiful perception. He was the heir of 3.5 billion slow, gradual years of evolution, as was all humanity. *We are cousins to all living things.* Gian's heart lifted at the beauty of the thought. For when he put it against the measly, piddling, and diminishing idea of a divine creator with a perfect hand planning each and every living thing, there was just no comparing.

Walter took Gian by the shoulders to steady him. "Are you all right?"

And for the first time in his memory, Gian smiled, feeling like a man born blind and suddenly given the gift of sight.

Acknowledgements and Identifying Notations

• Wording near the very end of this story is based partly on a comment that evolutionary biologist Richard Dawkins once made when juxtaposing the reality of evolution and the biblical creation story of Genesis. A few sentences are reproduced in this short story verbatim.

A Note from the Author

"Garden Metamorphosis" is related to this author's 2012 science-fiction novel *The God Antenna* and also to this author's 2013 vignette "Little Miracle."

The character of Walter Maynard in this story is the same Walter Maynard from this author's 2012 novel *The God Antenna* and from this author's 2015 short story "Painting Penelope." Chronologically, "Garden Metamorphosis" takes place before the events depicted in both *The God Antenna* and "Painting Penelope." To learn why Walter is en route to Greece, to pursue study in archeology, this author refers readers to *The God Antenna*.

Niko Zinovii
Santa Monica, California
28 May 2015

Niko Zinovii

Fragile in the Sun

Isolation and the lure of the deep dive... they had ultimately led Jules Kreisler to latitude -20° 09' 00" S, longitude -175° 09' 00" W. To where he now floated in silent repose seventeen fathoms beneath the surface, immersed in the ocean realm that he had long ago lost all subjective fear of. It was where he felt most comfortable, pleasantly removed from the noise of the outside world. Hovering there some eighty-plus fathoms above the summit of the Feinga Seamount, he patiently endured another lengthy but necessary decompression stop, which he really did not mind. He loved spending time in the open sea. Also, he welcomed anything that would delay his eventual return to the ship awaiting him above. For this was his final contracted dive for the Harrington Corporation.

Framed by his wet blond hair and painted upon his intriguingly handsome face was a solemn, intelligent countenance, one that emanated even more powerfully from his blue, soulful eyes. He was an oceanaut by profession, a modern-day explorer, but also a man presently seeking seclusion, a man looking for a way to hide from the world, for a little while.

He had always perceived deep open-ocean diving to be exciting and even mysterious. But that was not why he had signed on for this tour of work. It was simply to get away.

The Feinga Seamount lay in the far-off South Pacific, lost somewhere in the backwater of the Kingdom of Tonga. He welcomed the remoteness. It would give him time to sort things out in his mind and heart. For he had yet to come to terms with the recent death of his mentor, Yves Séverin, luminary of marine science.

Jules had come to see Séverin as the father he had never had. And more, he had believed in the wide-ranging, reflective mind of this slim, long-legged man, whose calm, ascetic face had the habit of unexpectedly breaking into a devastating grin, one which openly displayed his lively and optimistic soul.

The death of this great man had a sobering and devastating effect on Jules. Not only did he feel that he had lost a father, he also felt that he lost his future. He had been so fully committed to following Séverin, to participating in what the scientist had advocated in terms of colonizing the sea…

Lowering his head in hazy contemplation, Jules peered down into the depths. During these past weeks of introspection, he had successfully carried out over two dozen dives to the summit of the Feinga Seamount, where he had completed a variety of challenging underwater equipment-assembly exercises. The Harrington Corporation was studying the feasibility of utilizing the summits of seamounts as undersea platforms for deeper-seafloor mining operations. Thousands of square miles of the Pacific floor lay covered by a virtual treasure trove of metal-bearing nodules containing manganese, nickel, cobalt, and copper. Harrington aimed to be the first to find a practical way to gather up this wealth of the deep.

Was this as close as Jules would now come to his past dreams?

As Jules lit another undersea torch to brighten the underwater gloom, he allowed the grander visions haunting his mind to surface. He imagined a future Earth of sea farming, where vast plankton plantations floated out there in the swell of the oceans—producing enough food to eliminate starvation, hunger, and malnutrition in all the poor countries of the world. He envisioned the cattlization of whales, immense pods bred for their prodigious output of milk. And undersea cities, too... why not? Everything that had been accomplished on the surface could one day be done under the sea. Could it not? It would simply be the conquest of the next logical frontier, even if it were a whole new realm. The Aqua-Lung had been only the very first step...

... But this was not his vision. It was the prophecy preached by Yves Séverin, which Jules had been a disciple of. Jules thought back to the day when he had first heard Séverin speak. It was over a decade ago, at the World Congress on Underwater Activities held in Paris. In his mind's eye, Jules could still see Séverin, slender and with the appearance of careful frailty—for he had decades earlier been seriously injured in an automobile accident—step up upon the stage and position himself behind the podium to face the awaiting audience of oceanographers, biologists, geologists, divers, and oceanographic technicians.

"A new species of human being is evolving," Yves Séverin had said with a smile. "*Homo aquaticus*, who will live in the depths of the sea. Aquatic man will dwell among his kind in undersea cities and swim about on his daily labors in the open depths."

Jules remembered all too well the uncomfortable murmurs that had at once started among the delegates. As an esteemed scientist, Yves Séverin had an unassailable reputation. This man was also the president of the World Underwater Federation, the director of the Musée océanographique de Monaco, a recipient of the world's highest honors and distinctions. Yet he opened the conference proclaiming a vision of *Homo aquaticus*?

"It will happen," Séverin had continued, undisturbed. "Surgery will affix a set of artificial gills to man's circulatory system, right here at the neck, which will permit him to breathe oxygen from the water like a fish. The lungs will be bypassed, and he will be able to live and breathe in the deep for any amount of time without harm. Do you realize what this will mean? He will be able to observe, train, cultivate, and exploit the sea first hand. Maybe the first aquatic man will be an undersea farmer, or miner, or rancher, maybe just a scientist. At any rate, there will be no depth-time barrier, we know that. When his duties are done, he will be rehabilitated to air breathing by more surgery. It will happen, I promise you.

"I think it will be a conscious and deliberate evolution, *Homo aquaticus*, spurred by human intelligence rather than the slow, blind, natural adaptation of the species. We are now moving toward an alteration of human anatomy to give man almost unlimited underwater freedom.

"Of course, an even better way to produce *Homo aquaticus* will be to make a real man-fish. He would inhale water instead of air, just as a fish does. He would be able to swim to a depth of about a mile, instead of the hundred or so fathoms of present-day divers. *Homo aquaticus* won't be able to go beyond a mile, because when we reach that stratum, the external pressure will be about 170 atmospheres.

"This race of *Homo aquaticus*, future generations will be born under the sea, adapting to the environment so that no surgery will be necessary to permit them to live and breathe underwater. It is then that we will have created the man-fish.

"To me, the coming undersea life will be inspiring. I don't mean spiritual or religious, but life full of daily inspiration like that to which man has risen as a result of creative developments in his past—the Greek concept of ethos, the High Renaissance, the 18th century revolutions. Their echoes form the best in our lives today. I think undersea man will have the purest of this series of adventures."

Jules remembered the absolute silence that had followed. Although he and a few other young, idealistic men had been deeply inspired by the speech, the audience as a whole flatly dismissed the forecast as fantasy.

Was it fantasy? Jules asked himself as he floated there quiescently in the deep, decompressing. Could men really one day soon be surgically or genetically altered? Be given gills, to enable them to live under the sea? To become true masters of the deep. To inhabit the sea bottom, becoming underwater farmers growing algae or undersea cattlemen herding seafood. Was it reasonable to believe in Homo aquaticus, a fish-man able to obtain his oxygen directly from the water, as fish did?

And Jules shivered as he unexpectedly realized what had been unconsciously tearing at his heart and soul. He had lost faith. Even before the death of Yves Séverin. Sometime over the past few years, he had stopped truly believing in the vision of Séverin. Although he had still clung to it, stubbornly, with more hope than actual devotion... And now the prophet too was gone. Jules suddenly wanted very much to get out of the sea.

He looked up. He could clearly see the lead diver floating less than ten fathoms above him. It was his diving partner on this assignment, an Australian named Scobie who was built like a rugby forward.

Very soon Scobie would be hauled aboard the *Southern Surveyor*. And Jules would move up to Scobie's present depth, for his final decompression stop.

~

The last one remaining in the sea, Jules floated there beneath their ship, impatiently monitoring his wristwatch. Time—he could not see it or hear it, yet it held him hostage there under the waves.

What was that? Jules suddenly asked himself. It felt like a pressure wave… There it was again, another one, this time stronger. And a third—he now had to hold on tightly to the dive line that ran from the ship above down to the Feinga summit below.

What's happening? An undersea earthquake?

He looked up to see bright colors reflected upon the ocean's surface—a tumultuous, dancing pattern of refulgent red, yellow, and orange.

He then thought, for a just second, that he noticed lights moving about… below him? But then, a moment later, after he had positioned himself to peer downward, there was nothing but murky darkness below. Was it a reflection? An optical illusion? *What the hell's going on?*

Then came the noise from above, the sound of splashes, the near-deafening hail of a torrent of splashes. Jules looked up to witness small, irregular shapes raining down upon the surface of the sea. The objects looked light in color, and they floated. Most of them did.

Jules pushed away from the dive line to avoid a few of the things as they plummeted past him. They had a frothy, vesicular texture. And Jules understood—gas bubbles, trapped in rock, igneous rock, during the rapid cooling of gas-rich magma. Somewhere nearby, there must have been a violent volcanic eruption.

Suddenly there were a number of tremendous splashes and very loud, disturbing noises from the ship above. A large block of pumice—the size of a house—twirled as it sank past Jules, almost sucking him down in its wake.

Jules kicked madly and swam back to the dive line, which he grabbed hold of and held onto tightly.

He looked up and gasped as he noticed a number of jagged holes in the hull of the *Southern Surveyor*... The ship groaned as it listed to starboard.

Again, there was a flash of colorful light from somewhere beneath him. No... there was nothing there... It must have been an illusion brought on by his troubled senses. He knew full well that there was no latitude on reality. Yet every sound now seized upon his imagination, and upon his fear. If he had been in the depths, he would have attributed the sight to an alteration of his consciousness due to nitrogen narcosis. But he was only ten fathoms deep.

He looked at his dive watch. He could not surface yet. Doing so would risk decompression sickness. Diving protocol dictated that he must wait. And so wait he did. Lying there, floating horizontally, looking upward, transfixed by the haphazard rhythm of the torrential splashing above, every splash pounding on his psyche.

Eventually, the rain of pumice slowed, and then stopped completely. It was time for him to surface. And he did.

Jules broke the surface in the midst of what looked like snowfall—only it was not snow, but volcanic ash. Like the pumice, the ash was low enough in density to float upon the sea, which was quickly turning gray all the way to the horizon. To Jules, it was surreal, even hypnotic—despite the distant, continuous gas blasts that assaulted his nerves and altered his auditory perception with their powerfully loud crackling and booming eruptions.

Time seemed to stop for Jules… But then he noticed the state of the *Southern Surveyor*. She was on fire, disabled, sinking aft-end down—there was no way to board her. The ship's bridge was squashed flat beneath a tremendous block of pumice. Several other large blocks were sunk into the deck. There was no sign of life. Likely all of the small crew, including Scobie, had been on the bridge when it had been hit… Jules was utterly alone, the sole survivor of this ill-fated expedition.

He pulled his diving mask off, and just let it sink into the sea… Kicking near lifelessly, in a daze, he slowly spun himself about to face due north. And there on the horizon, just twenty nautical miles distant, rose a tremendous eruption cloud of gas and tephra, rumbling straight up into the stratosphere, where it then spread out laterally across the sky like an ominous umbrella. It was the cloud of a catastrophic Plinian eruption…

Slowly, Jules' eyes dropped down from the cloud to its source, the stratovolcano of Tofua Island. The island was beyond the limit of his vision from sea level, but he found himself imagining its steep-sided composite cone blackened, fissured, and covered by lava flows. He suddenly remembered the geologist of their expedition, Frank Willouby, having one night mentioned Tofua, and how the volcano had erupted numerous times, mildly, during man's history, even as recently as a few years ago. Willouby had noted in a chastising tone that the Tongans reported eruptions but did nothing to monitor any of their active volcanoes…

A swell gently lifted and dropped Jules as it rolled over him, traveling westward. Jules wondered if that gentle caress would end up a devastating tsunami a few thousand miles distant…

Kicking again, Jules slowly pirouetted, looking to every horizon. He was completely alone. The sparsely populated, low-lying atolls of Tonga's Ha-apai islands lay to the east, across over twenty nautical miles of open sea and against the prevailing currents. And Tonga's main island of Tongatapu lay three times that distance to the south…

Perhaps if he could stay afloat in situ long enough, he might be rescued? Jules stripped down, tossing off his garb and gear until he was naked, except for his flippers; he kept these on. They would allow him to tread water more easily, remain afloat longer.

He felt so vulnerable as he bobbed there, naked in the sea—especially as he witnessed the *Southern Surveyor* slip completely beneath the surface, leaving him utterly abandoned. And as he sensed the frightening loneliness of being a lost human being on Earth, he suddenly jolted alert as he saw something peculiar a mere fifty yards distant: colorful, mesmerizing lights swirling just beneath the waves… He watched breathlessly as the lights rose and broke the surface. It was some type of metallic craft, approximately sixty feet across. It looked extraordinarily like a… flying saucer. But it had come from beneath the sea…

Is it—could this be a USO? Jules asked himself. During his time in the French navy, Jules had heard stories about "unidentified submerged objects"—the maritime analog of UFOs (unidentified flying objects)—but he had never paid any mind to the accounts, dismissing them as hoaxes or poorly observed natural phenomena.

Jules unconsciously dipped himself lower into the sea as he witnessed beings coming out of the floating saucer, spreading out upon its smooth, featureless surface to observe the incredible eruption of Tofua Island.

To Jules, the creatures… they appeared protean, epicene, phlegmatic, with the features of deep-sea fish—giant eyes… forward-facing light organs… blue-and-red bioluminescence…

photophores producing unique displays of light… And more, these beings, they seemed so… fragile in the sun, creatures terrified of the universe that existed outside the depths of the sea.

Jules found himself beginning to swim toward the USO. He did not understand why he did so. He just did so. And one of the beings saw him. Then the others did as well. They quickly disappeared down into their silvery craft. The saucer then rose straight up out of the sea. Wobbling slightly in a rocking motion, tipping starboard and then port, like a boat anchored on the water, the saucer then glided toward Jules, an airborne UFO.

Jules squinted as a bright light flashed in front of him, akin to a dangling fishing lure used by deep-sea fish to attract curious prey.

~

The next thing Jules knew, he awakened to find himself alone, lying supine upon a deserted white-sand beach, beneath the swaying shadows of lofty palm trees dramatically leaning out toward the sea.

He sat up, and his vision focused in time for him to witness the multicolored saucer tilting to a 45 degree angle and plunging into the ocean, vanishing beneath the waves. Apparently he had been saved, plucked from the sea and transported here, to this atoll. Why? He did not know, or care.

"Thank you," Jules whispered, dumbfounded, "my friends from the deep…"

To the northwest, on the horizon, he saw the spectacular eruption cloud of Tofua Island, and he knew that he was now somewhere in the scattered Ha'apai atolls.

He looked back to the spot in the sea where the UFO/USO had disappeared, and he thought of the strange beings that he had seen. Who were they? What were they?

218

Where were they from? Were they from this Earth? Was it possible, could they be intelligent life that had evolved here in depths of this planet's oceans?

And Jules thought about it. No, he did not think they were from Earth. He did not believe that sentient life, even if it could arise in an underwater environment, could ever develop technology without first discovering and taming fire— something impossible under the sea. Perhaps he was wrong? But his guess was that these were extraterrestrial beings from some far-off, distant world. Beings that had originally evolved on land, as man of Earth had evolved on land, but unlike man, these creatures must have returned to the sea, like dolphins had, but these beings had taken their technology with them. Perhaps, faced with an overpopulated world, these aliens had sought out additional living space in the oceans of their own planet, and later they had spread to the oceans of other worlds. Or maybe they were a race that had simply chosen to return to the sea because they could. Maybe they were a race that dared to dream.

And Jules arose, his heart pounding with realization. These beings were Yves Séverin's imagination brought to life. They were living proof of what intelligence coupled with imagination could accomplish. Jules heard Séverin's voice from the past: *"It will happen, I promise you."*

Standing there alone and naked, lost to the world, Jules smiled. His mentor had been right. It had happened. Only it had not happened here on Earth. Not to man.

Not yet.

A Note from the Author

The fictional character of Yves Séverin in this tale is based entirely on famed French underwater explorer and scientist Jacques-Yves Cousteau. All the dialogue of Yves Séverin is nearly verbatim selected spoken words of Jacques Cousteau who, in 1963, introduced his vision of *Homo aquaticus* to the World Congress on Underwater Activities held in London. His prophecy did not meet unanimous approval. In fact, one official dismissed Cousteau's forecast as "science fiction." Cousteau's response to this was:

"What's wrong with science fiction as a presentiment of reality? Ever since Jules Verne, and lots of people before him, the informed human imagination has projected what is to come. Actually, I was trying to be conservative in talking about the underwater future in London. Why, there were people there who wanted to talk about milking whales in regular underwater dairies."

Those interested in learning more of Jacques Cousteau's prophecy of *Homo aquaticus* might start by reading the April 21, 1963, *New York Times* article "Portrait of *Homo Aquaticus*," by James Dugan.

An alternate version of the above mentioned article was later published by Dell Publishing Co., Inc. in a 1966 paperback titled *Edge of Awareness 25 contemporary essays*. James Dugan's essay in the book is titled "Portrait of *Homo Aquaticus*."

A note of minor interest: The Feinga Seamount was selected as the setting for this tale due to its proximity to volcanically active Tofua Island and because this seamount's summit-depth lies a magical 679 feet beneath the surface, which is a mere nineteen feet deeper than the limit for light penetration sufficient for plant growth, permitting the protagonist of this story to have visibility even at the bottom of his dive, albeit minimal.

On USOs: Like UFOs (unidentified flying objects) there have been thousands of reported sightings of USOs (unidentified submerged objects.) As many of the sightings were of USOs emerging from the water to become UFOs, some view USOs as a subset of UFOs.

The reader might ask himself: What best explains most USO or UFO reported sightings? Are they hoaxes? Hallucinations? Optical illusions? Poorly observed manmade objects? Poorly observed natural phenomena, known or unknown? Extraterrestrial spacecraft? Or are these unidentified objects something else entirely?

This author would like to end by thanking Claire, who unknowingly provided the title "Fragile in the Sun."

Niko Zinovii
Santa Monica, California
15 June 2015

Niko Zinovii

Winged Men of the Lost Planet

~1~

Jon Laban found himself lost in contemplation as he secured his rope to a bolt anchored into the rock face of the Hörnli Ridge, which rose between the east and north faces of the Matterhorn—Switzerland's pyramidal colossus of a mountain.

Pulling himself up upon a small ledge of rock and ice and snow, Jon rose to stand tall and distinguished in bearing, as was his nature. At six foot four, he was quite a striking figure, stately, handsome. Blond. Deeply bronzed. His eyes were the most captivating gray-blue in color... There was also a great confidence about him, as well as a sense of calm intelligence. In many ways, he appeared rather heroic.

The climb, in terms of difficulty, was not extreme, and at an athletic thirty-seven years of age, Jon was endowed with far more strength, endurance, and coordination than necessary to ascend this steep, exposed approach to the summit. Yet the efficiency of his movements was off—he was not climbing quickly and surely, not as he should have been—and his attention to technique was lacking. For his thoughts were still fully on the man with whom he had met privately a day ago in Strasbourg.

Since his youth, Jon had always been intrigued by ideas that ran contrary to mainstream beliefs. He attributed this to his lifelong search for truth, which he found himself pursuing to envision a better future, one that he could welcome.

The common misperception of the future had been that it would be wondrous to behold, a hypertechnological age, a techno-utopia of unprecedented advancement. A few historians and Austrian School economists had known better, however, and they had ultimately been proven correct.

The nature of the dim future that now awaited man produced a sense of foreboding in Jon's mind and heart. Yet despite what the world had become, he still expected something of the future. Something different. Something better. And this was his silent torment, for he felt powerless to alter the present sad fate of man.

This was also the primary reason why he had arranged a personal meeting with his boyhood hero, Frédéric Oran, famed oceanographer, marine explorer, and defender of the oceans—and more importantly, Jon felt, an iconoclastic wise man from an earlier generation.

Oran, lean and gray, had greeted Jon with a large smile on his thin lips, his countenance like that of an amiable but wary old eagle. "So," Oran had asked Jon, "you would like to talk to me? About what?"

"Everything," Jon had answered.

Oran's eyes had sparkled at this, radiating his famed relentless inner energy and insatiable curiosity. "The happiness of the bee and the dolphin is to exist," Oran had begun affably, with compelling charm. "For man, it is to know that, and to wonder at it."

Jon inhaled the mountain air as he stood there alone against the rugged rock and magical light of the day. The air was invigorating, cold and pristine, as if from the mythical lamasery of Shangri-La. But rather than his mind conjuring up imagery of a gentle, isolated utopia of near immortals, Jon instead heard echoing in his thoughts the chilling words spoken to him a day ago by Frédéric Oran:

"What should we do to eliminate suffering and disease? It's a wonderful idea but perhaps not altogether a beneficial one in the long run. If we try to implement it, we may jeopardize the future of our species. It's terrible to say this. World population must be stabilized, and to do that, we must eliminate 350,000 people per day. This is so horrible to contemplate that we shouldn't even say it. But the general situation in which we are involved is lamentable."

~2~

Stepping out of his chauffeured luxury sedan, Jon crossed the sidewalk and ascended the steps of one of the oldest surviving private banks in Lausanne, Switzerland. It was an institution that specialized in asset management for its affluent clients. Jon was the bank's youngest client, and its wealthiest. Jon's grandfather had invested in fine wines, valuable works of art, and precious metals just before the world finally crashed under the crushing weight of fiscal and monetary mismanagement. The result was global economic depression followed by interminable stagnation, as well as the rise of new elites, new aristocrats, such as Jon's grandfather, then his father, and now in turn Jon himself.

As Jon entered the bank, he stepped firmly back into the reality of the current world at large. Everyone present had a small metallic disc, two and a half inches in diameter, attached to the partially shaven left side of the head, above the ear. The last great technological achievement before the world had slipped into its state of economic and technological torpor. The Plug was its colloquial moniker. It was a surgically attached brain-to-computer interface mechanism. It allowed its wearer to wirelessly "plug in" to the Global Brain. And access information ad infinitum.

Jon smiled ever so subtly as he noticed the confusion on the faces of those around him. They were unable to ID him. They were all using their Plugs to search the Global Brain, attempting to learn who he was. For Jon was Plugless, and a Plugless man was a rare site. A curiosity. Jon valued his privacy, however, and some years ago he had utilized the power provided by his vast wealth to have his presence wiped from the Global Brain's database. So he was a complete stranger to those around him, a walking enigma.

Jon glanced back at them critically. He understood man's rise and decline, and the factors to blame—democratic government, socialism—yet he placed most of the blame for man's continued stagnation on the Plug itself. For men of previous generations had always been inventive, technologically finding ways to increase productivity. If fusion power had been developed, for example, it would have forestalled the global crash. But man no longer invented....

Looking over those plugged in, Jon considered what he perceived to be the fundamental flaws of the Plug: Its inventors had believed that everyone would draw the same conclusions from the same facts, if these facts were simply made available to all. That worldwide peace would result from humankind plugging in. It had not. These men had not understood that it was scarcity that generated conflict, not a lack of facts. And they had wrongly assumed that people would interpret facts the same way if given the same data. They had not. And society itself had also overlooked that with such an extreme ease of acquiring limitless information, man would eventually opt not to think...

"Account number?" the banker asked a client, to access her account.

In a whisper, the woman rattled off the twenty-plus-digit number with ease, reading it in her mind, courtesy of her Plug.

"Name on the account?" the banker asked.

The lights in the building flickered off and a second later came back on.

"Your name?" the banker repeated the question.

"Wait…" the woman responded, suddenly confused. "The system's down…"

Jon reacted: "You don't know your own name?"

She became more confused, unsuccessfully trying to pull information from her mind without the aid of the Plug.

Jon shook his head disapprovingly and turned to face all who were present, his voice level yet severe, his frustrations and private torment surfacing. "Is this what the future holds?"

"Nancy," the woman interrupted, struggling with it. "My name… it's Nancy. —I know my name!" She shouted the last part of it, angry, embarrassed.

Jon paused, considering how to phrase what he was about to say. When he spoke, he did so with passion but also with compassion and intelligence. "Yes, you know your name. But drawing out information, accessing facts, it's only part of it. Much more critical is the interpretation of facts and the defining of their relevance. This is always what creates the real difference. With the Plug, you develop laziness about conceptions, because you can always pull up the facts, and so easily. So you don't worry about the interconnectedness of facts. What does this particular fact mean? In relation to what other set of facts? It relates to what objective that is relevant?

"Profound thinking only occurs when people take a body of facts and challenge it, and develop other theories about it. The danger is when you are so good at collecting facts… you freeze things."

227

And Jon stopped. He knew it was one thing to say something was a problem, but quite another to have an answer to it. But it was at that moment that a Randian, Galt-esque thought came to him, and he spoke it aloud as he perceived it.

"I'm going to turn off the world," he proclaimed solemnly, "and awaken the minds of men."

He looked at everyone staring at him. Not one of them appreciated or truly understood a word he had said. "I'll stop there. Saying only that."

Tugging on his gloves, in a gesture of finality, he turned to leave. Halfway to the door, he collapsed, unconscious.

~3~

When Jon awoke in the hospital, he was told that he had a rare, incurable cancer. And that he had six months to live.

~4~

With each step that Jon took, the majestic island of Ikaria presented itself to him with dramatic contrasts of scenery: stunning mountains, the wild beauty of bare cliffs, green slopes, rugged rocks, hills of rare flowers, forests of ancient oaks, gushing waterfalls, high mountain streams, canyons, gorges, caves... abandoned stone houses shadowed by pines, breathtaking views of the sparkling Aegean Sea...

Pausing where great trees leaned over him, their susurrating leaves echoing nature's great living presence, Jon closed his eyes to listen to the wind. He loved being alone in nature, to contemplate amongst its quietness.

There are not many better places in the world to die, Jon found himself thinking.

A small herd of goats suddenly made their presence known by the jingling of the bells dangling about their necks. As the animals passed by, freely pursuing their desires, Jon noticed that they smelled with the freshness of flowers and dried grass.

A wild falcon, soaring up high, caught Jon's attention next. He watched the bird for a time. And then a sudden chill came over him as he realized even more deeply how he would very soon no longer be playing upon life's stage. The thought broadened his perception of life, and struck at his ego. For he had always felt that his life was of singular importance. That he mattered, as if mythical gods had ordained this to be so.

"What will the world do without me?" he asked aloud, sincerely and rather softly.

Strangely, although he was deeply aware of his fate, he found that within him there remained an unshakable belief in himself. As if he was still bound to all that he might have been, all that he might have accomplished. This he did not understand.

As he took in the stunningly beautiful Ikaria, thinking the old island akin to an Aegean Garden of Eden, he was surprised to hear the voice of Frédéric Oran interrupt the peace of his inner thoughts:

"To manage nature, a certain amount of wisdom is needed. Perhaps one day, taking long-term factors into account, we shall succeed in managing nature as we now do when we create a pretty garden."

They were words Oran had spoken to Jon during Jon's visit. And Jon sat himself upon a rock, his mind releasing from memory other words of Frédéric Oran:

"We should ask ourselves how many animals and people our planet can continue to support before the quality of life deteriorates, before all Earth's beauties fade… Years ago, when I was in the United States, I tried to construct a mathematical model to find out how many people our planet could support with income, purchasing power, and amenities enjoyed by the average American at that time. With the parameters I had at my disposal, I came up with the figure of 700 million."

And Jon thought of the world's present population: over 9 billion.

~5~

As Jon descended the mountain trail, approaching his new and final home, he thought of why he had chosen the island of Ikaria as the setting for his death. First and foremost, it was a Plugless population, by choice, one of the very few in the world.

It was also an anomaly in the world, geographically and temporally set apart from the march of modernity. Ikaria, having achieved independence from Greece, was a communal unit that represented a political consensus. It was a place that was not in any way a factor in world politics, yet its people felt that they existed at the center of the world.

The Ikarians were a resilient people, hardened by the many sufferings they had endured over time. They were reputed to be stubborn and wise, with a single-minded disposition to hold freedom dear. Different, peculiar, unique, lovely... The Ikarians were a people of solitude, living in a place far away from other men.

A place immersed in legend, an island uniquely touched by the sun. For it was Icarus of myth who was the first man to fly, doing so on wings made of feather and wax. Feeling that he could be as mighty as the gods, he attempted to fly as high as they. His wings, melted by the sun, plunged Icarus to his death in the deep sea off Ikaria...

Jon turned to catch a glimpse of the Icarian Sea; it lay there flat and tranquil, timeless.

As Jon neared his new home, which he could now clearly see ahead of him, he smiled at its austere, aging elegance, at its old slate roof, at its whitewashed stone exterior, at its two acres of neglected vineyards. He had already selected the spot where he wished to be buried; it was there, shaded by the oaks that overlooked the sea. And Jon stopped in his tracks, staring at that calm spot. Moments passed. Finally, he recited aloud something he had recently read, embracing fully the reality of life:

"Whatever else a man may be, he is a mammal and mortal like the rest. His bones lie scattered and buried across the Earth."

It was at that moment that Jon wondered if he had also unconsciously chosen Ikaria because it was often referred to as 'the island where people forget to die,' due to there being more centenarians alive on Ikaria than anywhere else in the world. Perhaps as he was so near death, Jon felt it comforting, in some small way, to be around others, around centenarians, who were also closer to their ends?

~6~

Jon arrived in the small town of Agios Kirykos, Ikaria's capital, just in time for the uncrating of his gift to the island. His gift had arrived in two crates, each over fifty feet in height, each weighing over two tons. It had taken a team of men using heavy lifting trucks and equipment a full week to move the twin crates up from the port to the town's new center, where they now rested, side by side, facing out toward the open sea.

Each day during that week, the curiosity of the Ikarians had grown and grown. The town now seemed to contain every Ikarian who lived on the island—all 10,000 of them—all gathered there today for the unveiling.

Jon found that he had to seat himself, as he felt fatigued, weak, due to his illness. He excused himself from the small stage, and sat off to the side, allowing the president of Ikaria and the island's Grand Council to preside over the unveiling.

The crates were removed to reveal two huge bronzes—sitting winged figures wearing the look of eagles. The two nude bronzes were identical, heroic and mythical, with upthrust wings rising thirty feet in height. Were they angels? Or winged human beings of the far future? Or something more: a magnificent symbolism in human form?

As Jon looked at the figures, which had been weathered to a green patina, burnished in spots to a soft gold, a feminine voice interrupted his thoughts.

"*The Winged Figures of the Republic?*" the voice correctly identified the bronzes.

Jon turned to the woman who had apparently come up to stand behind him. There was a great dignity and a deep and unusual beauty to her, a dark, timeless beauty that embodied the magnificence of the Aegean and reflected the valiant strength of its enduring people.

"Yes," Jon answered her, surprised.

"Why?"

Jon responded intelligently, with discreet passion and a clear awareness: "To evoke in you and your fellow citizens a realization of man… and to make that realization imperishable against the oblivion of time… To convey the potential nobility, the very best that lies within reach of the aspirations and endowments of the human race."

"Why?"

Jon thought for a second or two and then answered openly, honestly, emotionally. "My parting gift. To a people whom I believe in."

~7~

After spending several days in bed without sleep, Jon summoned up his waning energy. Night had fallen and he wanted to step outside, to breathe the cool air coming down from the mountains, to hear the sea, to see the stars. As he stepped outside he was surprised to see over a dozen Ikarians making their way to his home. Farmers, sailors, fishermen, beekeepers, store clerks, even a few council members. With them they carried food and drink—a local dry black wine, *Pramnios*.

Ikarian hospitality was legendary, but Jon had never expected such genuine interest in a stranger. They stayed for hours, talking late into the night, asking intelligent, probing questions, and listening, really listening to what he had to say.

"Is education the answer?" one old man asked Jon.

"To what?" Jon asked.

"To the problems of the world."

And Jon found himself forced to think, and to think deeply. He found it invigorating. "Education, intelligence, knowledge, all directing good will, and charity," he replied, thinking it out. "They're all necessary, in order to actualize the greatest number of our potentialities, to make the best of our human promise."

~8~

Over the following weeks, Ikarians visited Jon daily, every afternoon and often in the late evening. During the day they would bring herbal teas and lunch, at night fish, chicken, or lamb and always their local dark wine—bottles and bottles of their wine. At first Jon found himself apprehensive of drinking as much as they poured, but after a few glasses he found himself thinking, ...*I might as well die happy.*

One night, the young woman from Agios Kirykos, the one who had identified the winged bronzes, showed up in the company of others. Jon learned that her name was Eiríni. And that she was a teacher in their capital.

"I walk past the bronzes, your winged men," Eiríni started, "each day, on my way to the school..."

233

"Yes?" Jon prompted her to go on.

"Is it true of sculpture," she asked slowly, with careful reasoning, "that it gives meaning to man's other works? By interpreting man to other men, in terms of man himself?"

It was a deep thought, one that Jon respected, even admired. "Yes," he said slowly, nodding soberly, looking at her with deep-felt appreciation.

"We are not rich in Ikaria," Eiríni admitted solemnly, "but we have time for family and friends. We share our happiness and our hardships, and our love. But... how can we achieve more? What would we need to change?"

Jon went silent, and then thought long and hard, drawing upon past knowledge and over a decade of contemplation, for he had studied economics as a young man. And since then, he had spent considerable time intellectually exploring what he had learned, developing his own thoughts on the subject.

Jon outlined and explained three basic starting principles that he encouraged Eiríni and the others to bring to their Grand Council:

1. Participation and integration in the division of labor
2. Capital accumulation
3. Population control

Jon took his time in explaining to the Ikarians that nature, in her wisdom, had imbued in men physical and mental differences, just as there existed differences in the land, in terms of natural resources. And how this engendered a situation of what economists called absolute and comparative advantage. He demystified these terms, clarifying why it was advantageous to specialize in what one was particularly good at, or where one's disadvantage was comparatively smaller. And how doing so would increase Ikaria's overall production, making Ikarians wealthier.

Jon felt everyone's eyes on him as he spoke, and it instilled in him a sense of purpose, one that no dying man had the right to lay claim to. He went on to describe the importance of increasing the quantities of machines, equipment, and other tools and devices that businesses used in production. He pointed out that Ikarians needed to sacrifice, to save more, so that their savings would be available in their banks for the entrepreneur, and that to accomplish this their society needed to alter its collective time preference. They needed to become more future oriented, more forward thinking.

On population control, Jon revealed that it was crucial to establish and maintain an optimal population size, due to what economists called the law of diminishing returns. He described to them, quite sensibly, that for any combination of two or more production factors there existed an optimal combination. For workers and capital, that point defined the optimal population size. Go beyond it, and income per individual would fall... Drop beneath it, and income per individual would remain less than optimally possible.

Jon estimated that Ikaria needed to immediately increase its population by 10%. He offered to provide a starter list of names of high-quality individuals who, if invited, would likely be willing to relocate to Ikaria, adopting its culture as their own.

In conclusion, Jon pointed out that these three basic economic keys would also contribute to bringing about technological innovations, which in turn would increase individual production capacity and thus increase wealth still further.

The Ikarians asked many questions, until the sun set out over the sea. Jon responded genuinely and thoughtfully until he was too fatigued to continue. He slept deeply and peacefully that night.

~9~

The next day, Eiríni and her compatriots took Jon's three principles to their Grand Council, which examined them with enthusiasm and afterward began implementing them.

In response, Jon liquidated his great wealth held abroad, changing his holdings into gold. He placed the sum of that gold into the Ikarian banks—after the Ikarian president pledged that his government would not attempt to manipulate interest rates, but instead allow these rates to function as the accurate price of Ikarian money. Jon had extracted this promise because he wanted the Ikarians to have a fair opportunity to achieve prosperity. And he knew that for this to occur, government interference needed to be mitigated.

~10~

In the early mornings, Jon began to soak his fatigued body in the island's therapeutic hot mineral springs—steaming wells laden with large concentrations of radon, reputed to be among the most radioactive springs in all the world.

Soothed by the thermal waters, Jon began to plant vegetables in the abandoned garden behind his house. He did not expect to live to see the harvest, but for those few hours each day he enjoyed being in the warm sunlight, breathing in the salted ocean air, working the dirt while drinking hot teas brought to him by his neighbors, beautiful teas composed of wild mountain herbs and rare Ikarian flowers.

~11~

Over the ensuing months, something strange happened. Jon started feeling stronger.

Feeling ambitious, one afternoon he made his way back up into the mountains, to that spot where the forest's trees had leaned over him, their susurrating leaves echoing nature's great living presence. He sat there upon the large rock shadowed by the greenery. He sat there and thought. He found that he had never before had such an opportunity to explore his own thoughts so clearly, so peacefully, with no expectations about the future.

~12~

Jon began to make his way up the mountain each afternoon, to sit on that rock and think. One day, while sitting there, he saw Eiríni approaching him. She must have followed him, unseen, up the mountain.

"Why are you spending all your time up here?" she asked. "Your neighbors are worried. They know of your... condition."

Jon nodded; he was wondering what had prompted her to follow him. He smiled politely and humbly, and then answered her slowly, discovering the reason himself as he spoke. "Outside of books, I suspect there's a kind of wisdom that slowly comes to a man through passive contemplation. By allowing the world to simply come to him, absent of any imposed frames of reference. Unmodified by the conceptualizing mind within. Some things... come through, to the deeper mind. Providing insight. Wisdom. Truth. That's worth pursuing, isn't it? No matter what one's *condition* is."

Eiríni just looked at him for the longest moment, appreciating him.

"In the past," she finally commented, "it's been only the most artistic of thinkers who have exhibited sensitivity for ideas in the process of being born."

Jon took his turn, looking at her for the longest moment, appreciating her.

Eiríni then asked him, "Some of us are gathering at your winged men tonight. Would you accompany me there?"

Jon nodded yes.

~13~

Jon had not been back to Ikaria's capital, Agios Kirykos, since he had dedicated *The Winged Figures of the Republic* to the island and its people. He had almost forgotten how overwhelming the thirty-foot-tall bronzes were in appearance. How daring the winged men seemed, the two of them sitting there, wearing the look of eagles, their wings thrust upward in a single all-powerful, aspirational gesture. Seeing the bronzes freely for the first time, without any imposed frame of reference, Jon suddenly understood why the Americans had had no objection to selling him the figures, even though they were associated with one of their historical landmarks: the bronzes unconsciously impressed upon the mind as being works of some race entirely alien in mind and body to man's own... It was as if the winged men silently beckoned from some impossible future, asking man to accept the challenge to become truly great—a challenge that was not for the faint of heart.

Several dozen Ikarian citizens were gathered before the winged bronzes. After greeting Jon, the Ikarians asked him if he had any other recommendations. Recommendations that could help to make Ikaria great, like Jon's winged men.

Jon looked the Ikarians over. They were young, idealistic. Jon perceived in them a difference in interpretation, perception, and vision. It was such minorities that usually caused things to change, to evolve.

Pacing off, Jon thought deeply. Standing between the winged bronzes, he seemed to draw strength from them, daring from them, and he turned to those gathered and presented to them the winged imagination of his thoughts taken flight, announcing three new principles to implement:

1. The supremacy of and the subordination of everyone under one law

2. The absence of any law-making authority

3. The lack of any legal monopoly of judgment and conflict arbitration

Jon made it clear that he was suggesting a society without government, one based on ancient private property rights. It was a vision of a society of stateless capitalism, with order provided by private security, insurance, and arbitration.

Jon explained that such a society would allow for the rise of a natural aristocracy, of nobles, of individuals in positions of natural authority. Natural elites who would come to feel an obligation that extended beyond themselves and their families, a sense of personal responsibility for society at large.

As Jon stood there, between the giant winged men, he realized that life was about one's heart, and whom it beat for. And he discovered that his heart now beat for the Plugless people of Ikaria.

Jon went on and explained in detail, on through the night, the progress and decline of man. Telling of man's rise from the origin of private property and family, through the Neolithic Revolution, through the Malthusian Trap to the Industrial Revolution… And then of man's decline concomitant with society's transition from aristocracy to monarchy to democracy—pointing out the reasons why monarchy was better than democracy, and why aristocracy was better still. Jon spoke passionately and with complete abandon, for as a dying man he felt free of restraint.

~14~

Six months came and went. Jon did not die. Instead, he harvested his garden and, feeling emboldened, he put his vineyard in order. He also visited a doctor in Agios Kirykos, who ran a number of tests on him. Why had he lived longer than the six months allotted him? How much longer could he expect to survive? Did he have another month bestowed upon him? Perhaps two?

Days later, still awaiting the lab results, Jon found himself soaking in one of Ikaria's saline thermal springs. As he floated quiescently in the pool, submerged to his neck, he closed his eyes. When he did so, he heard replayed in his mind bits and pieces of his past conversation with Frédéric Oran. He heard the wisdom of Oran, and also the poetic charm of the man:

"From birth, man carries the weight of gravity on his shoulders. He is bolted to earth. But man has only to sink beneath the surface and he is free. Buoyed by water, he can fly in any direction—up, down, sideways—by merely flipping his hand. Underwater, man becomes an archangel."

And Jon held in a breath and slipped beneath the steaming water, to escape the reality of earth, to become an archangel.

Floating back to the surface, to reality, he rose and exited the pool. He stood there nude, the sunlight sparkling off the water glistening on his body. He had lost much of his musculature due to his illness, but he still appeared heroic, noble in his bearing. So much so that it did not seem necessary to clothe his bronze frame in any of the trappings which the weak were prone to wear in order to seem great.

As he reached for a nearby robe, Jon noticed Eiríni standing nearby in silence, looking at him as if he were not naked, but mighty of body and clean of soul.

"Dr. Glaredes," she said softly, "asked me to bring this to you." And she showed him a sealed envelope.

"Open it," Jon requested.

She did.

"Read it," he asked. "Please."

She read silently for several moments, and then, with trembling hands, she lowered the paper. "There's no more cancer in your body…" she said, staggered.

Jon stood there speechless, his mind working to adjust itself to the astounding news. For a moment it felt to him as if the daytime moon, and sun, and clouds had suddenly swirled about him before returning him to reality. The first coherent thought that his mind finally released to him was the sound of his own voice from six months ago:

"I'm going to turn off the world, and awaken the minds of men."

And Jon sat down, overwhelmed. Suddenly there was so much to do.

~15~

Forty years later:

Jon, silver haired at seventy-seven years old, stood tall and distinguished on the balcony of his city home in Agios Kirykos. The sea below danced with moonlight blended into the mirrored, shimmering lights of the town, reflecting the bold new architecture that had arisen over the past four decades. It was still Agios Kirykos, in spirit, but it was also much more. For it echoed the achieved prosperity of the Ikarians, and the promise of man.

In the sea, not far from the town's port, rested a Russian Borei-class submarine, floating high in the water, long and flat, its rectangular conning tower silhouetted against the full moon.

Jon eyed the submarine and thought of what was to come tomorrow. He thought of retreating to the comfort of his library, to sit there secure in its atmosphere of wisdom, but instead he looked up at the scintillating stars and made a wish.

"The moon affects the mind," his wife's feminine voice interrupted his thoughts.

Jon turned to find Eiríni stepping up beside him, affectionately taking his hand. Her face, still beautiful, although touched by time, was etched with concern.

"It's something I must do," Jon said to her softly.

"I know…" Eiríni responded, her eyes filled with loving understanding. "I know."

And she stood there with him, staring out at the foreign submarine.

Jon thought of how far Ikaria had come since he had first arrived on its shores. For nearly forty years now, there had been no governmental drag on the island's economy or on its people. Natural elites had arisen, men and women and families of character, virtue, wisdom, dignity, and taste. Aristocracy had proven itself the instrument of expansion necessary to bring into being a new and unique civilization. One that now flourished as nearly all the rest of the world still floundered in its torpid, frozen state of stagnation.

Jon thought of how ideas for successfully meeting society's challenges now came from the island's creative minority of nobles, and how these ideas were imitated, symbiotically adopted, and implemented by the majority. Of how Ikaria's natural aristocracy was respected for the wisdom and rightness of their solutions, solutions that never infringed upon individual liberty.

But Jon also considered how most men, even Ikaria's nobles, had a set way of perceiving things, an unconscious conformity invisibly imposed upon them by society. A conformity that changed only as society evolved. He reflected on how this societal mind-lock could limit future thinking, on how it might prevent new intellectual contributions from being born or from being understood and accepted by the majority—who were often maintainers by nature, usually wanting to keep things from changing. He thought of how after he had introduced certain basic concepts with complete abandon, he had then proceeded more carefully, courting the majority, wisely guiding Ikaria over the decades, presenting new ideas with care as Ikarian society evolved, aware of the risk of presenting too quickly what might seem too inconsistent with most people's perceptions.

And yet he had so much more to contribute to Ikaria. He understood that the course of history was ultimately determined by ideas, and by men inspired by and acting upon those ideas. There were still unspoken ideas that Jon held close to his heart, ideas that he did not want to see disappear with him...

"There are also things I must say tomorrow," Jon told his wife. "Before I go... Things that might not be readily accepted, not immediately. But in time..."

She looked at him lovingly; she understood. "Any self-actualizing human being," she whispered, "is always one who breaks out of his culture. All great seers have always broken out of their cultures."

Jon held his wife and looked out toward the horizon, thinking of how outside of Ikaria, and a few other Plugless societies, democracy and the Plug had swept man along, dimming his awareness, creating a new type of man, a non-thinking man, an undifferentiated mass man who fell so very short of his human potential. If nothing were done... it seemed that man and his promise would be forever lost.

Jon then thought of a better future, and in his mind he heard the guiding voice of the late Frédéric Oran:

"Regressive evolution is seldom a success; the system perpetuates those who move ahead. This is an alarming consideration. Man has stopped his own evolution! Instead of selecting the most fit to survive, we select the environment to suit our needs. Our medical sciences heal the sick, allowing them to reproduce and pass on inborn deficiencies to their offspring. We consider ourselves humane but we cannot supplement the forces of evolution by selecting the best of our species. In fact, our intellect may have rendered us incapable of even judging what is good or beneficial for our species. However, it is our understanding of the basic principles of evolution and that same medical science which will permit us to play sorcerer's apprentice and cure the ills of mankind. Through genetic manipulation, we can and will revitalize ourselves physically, and if our intelligence is a positive attribute, we will learn to use our mind and increase its capacities to make life pleasant and worthwhile for everyone."

~16~

At midday, with the sun at zenith, Jon rose to stand tall and alone upon the black diorite podium between *The Winged Figures of the Republic*. Agios Kirykos was filled with people, and cameras were broadcasting the event live to the island's 200,000-plus citizens living outside the capital.

As Jon stood there, waiting for the crowd to become silent, he appeared very much like the great winged figures flanking him. For his very stance and presence seemed to announce the immutable calm of intellectual resolution. Also, although nearly eighty, Jon appeared to still possess the impressive power of trained physical strength, mirroring the enormous might symbolized in the winged men. Jon was one of them. He was truly their brother, personified in mortal, human flesh. He only lacked the great wings…

The crowd became silent, the people giving Jon their full attention, respect, and admiration. Like the enthroned bronzes, Jon too was enthroned, in the minds of the Ikarians.

For as the head of the most noble of noble families, he was their undeclared king. Having him as their natural leader made people want to reach up and touch the sky, to stand as tall as they could.

"What I am compelled to do…" Jon announced, "it is likely that I will not return…"

And Jon looked over the concerned and proud faces in the crowd. He recognized so many of them. He looked for his wife, Eiríni, and found her loving eyes. Next to her stood his adult son and daughter, and his grandchildren.

"I was going to say many things," he continued. "But… instead I'll leave most things unsaid."

The crowd remained silent as he explained:

"Ikaria needs time to acquire a future discipline, in order to embrace certain new ideas… Culture permits us to be fully human, but it also limits our human potential by confining our thinking. So we are both the beneficiaries and the prisoners of our culture… This is something Ikaria will need to acquire the discipline to break free of, completely, in order to further empower our new and unique civilization.

"I'll leave you with this one parting idea, with this vision. Man is unlike all Earth's other life, which lives safely locked within its particular endowed natures, unaware. Only man can redefine himself, his humanity, his own conception of himself. In this ability to take the shape of our own dreams, man extends beyond visible nature. We are protean. We can do what we wish. We can give wings to the human spirit to reshape ourselves."

As the crowd applauded, Jon stepped off the podium, kissed his wife, said goodbye to his family, and then allowed himself to be escorted away by several Russian naval officers.

~17~

At the port, Jon entered a small boat, and he and the Russians motored out to the waiting submarine.

~18~

As Jon climbed up upon the long, flat deck of the huge nuclear-powered submarine, the K-560 *Vladimir Putin*, he looked back at Agios Kirykos, drawing courage from the town's towering winged figures, which could be seen clearly from the submarine, their wings aglow in the bright afternoon sunlight.

Russian submariners approached Jon and assisted him in slipping into a desert-tan, full-body g-suit. Donning a silver altitude helmet, Jon stood there in vibrant contrast to the dull black submarine, appearing much more mythic than a mere man.

Next, a number of Russians walked Jon to mid-deck, to the single, open ballistic-missile hatch. A hand signal was made, motors whined below deck, and a giant R-30 (RSM-56) Bulava SLBM slowly rose up out of its silo, exposing one third of its three-stage, forty-foot length. The missile's 1.15-ton payload of ten nuclear warheads had been removed and all its stages had been modified, the ICBM having been converted into a launch vehicle.

An entry hatch on the exposed upper stage was opened, and Jon was assisted into the ballistic missile.

Inside, as Jon sat and strapped himself in, he noticed that the missile's interior, with an inner diameter of over six feet, was roomier than the simulator he had trained in these past months. Still, when the entry hatch was shut, it would have seemed just as claustrophobic if it were not for the viewing portals that encircled him.

The crowd that had moved to the capital's port watched on in silence as the missile slowly descended back below deck.

The silo's hatch remained open. The Russians all withdrew into the submarine, which lay stationary, floating there in the calm of the Icarian Sea.

Jon found himself surprised at how tense he suddenly felt sitting there alone, in the darkness, aware of what was to come at any moment...

After a long silence, there was a deafening roar and an explosive red flash, and the forty-foot Bulava missile abruptly blasted up from the submarine and rocketed skyward.

Inside the missile, the vibrations were bone jarring, much more so than Jon had anticipated. It was a brutal, physical ride of constant acceleration. After a mere thirty seconds, he was traveling faster than the speed of sound, and accelerating.

Hurtling up through the atmosphere, the hypersonic missile disappeared into the clouds. The soul of man had been given wings...

~19~

In less than five minutes, the first stage disengaged, exploding off and dropping Earthward as the second stage rocketed the missile toward space, pushing it faster and faster.

Inside the upper stage of the Bulava, Jon felt himself being pinned heavier and heavier and heavier into his seat. It felt as if he were being crushed. It was becoming harder and harder to breathe. Jon found himself fighting for every breath.

I'm going to do... what I said I would do... No matter what!

~20~

Jon felt the engine abruptly shut off, having run out of fuel, and with an explosion the second stage separated. Suddenly Jon was weightless. Looking out the portals, he saw the stars of outer space... The space launch from the *Vladimir Putin* had been successful. He was now within the ionosphere, at an altitude of approximately 250 miles, between the atmosphere and the Van Allen radiation belt, within Earth's magnetosphere.

Jon heard the Bulava's cooling system kick in. Although he was within the safety of the space environment of low Earth orbit, protected from the sun's fierce and hostile solar activity by the ionosphere, Jon's modified Bulava was in direct sunlight. The metal of the craft would soon be heated to over 250°F.

And the clock was now ticking. Jon's missile was in a suborbital flight; it would not complete a full orbital revolution. He had less than twenty-five minutes to complete his mission. Jon turned a key and pushed down a heavy switch, and twin lightweight wings unfolded into space from tightly packed canisters on opposite sides of the Bulava. The wings were each thirty feet in length, containing small thruster units to provide maneuverable propulsion.

And Jon, now a winged man of a lost planet, finally found himself in position to carry out his promise to turn off the world.

Jon increased the Bulava's speed, and the onboard computer maneuvered his winged missile toward his target, one of four identical satellites launched into orbit years earlier by his Ikarian company InterOrbital Satellites.

There was a soft thud as Jon docked with the first satellite. Inner mechanisms whirred as Jon's Bulava delivered to the satellite the vital mechanism that would make it complete. In itself, the mechanism was unidentifiable. Merged with the satellite, the symbiosis produced a device unlike anything man had ever conceived.

Jon manually entered a security code known only to him, and he waited impatiently as the introduced mechanism automatically cycled through its activation mode. It was soon completed, and Jon undocked. With the aid of the computer, he set off toward the next satellite. He would need to deliver identical mechanisms to all four satellites, which were equidistant apart, strung about the planet in low Earth orbit.

As Jon flew on man-made wings, he looked toward the center of the solar system, at the distant sun. And for the first time in his life, he felt fear. Did man have the right to tamper with such power? Did man have the right to touch the sun?

~21~

Disengaging from the fourth and final satellite, Jon allowed the computer to descend the winged Bulava toward the atmosphere for re-entry. Despite the Bulava's heating system, Jon felt cold, icy cold, for in the darkness of the nighttime side of the planet, the exterior of his missile was now -275°F.

Entering the atmosphere, Jon experienced the discomfort of the Bulava accelerating. As the missile shook, he witnessed the atmospheric re-entry burning off his wings... Would his parachute deploy? Or would he simply plunge into the depths of the sea and die, like Icarus of myth? Had his own extreme pride made him careless? Had he flown too close to the sun?

And Jon lost consciousness.

~22~

Jon awoke to the explosion of the canopy blowing off the top of the missile, exposing his improvised cockpit to the elements. A sea breeze buffeted the Bulava as it floated there in the ocean, bobbing up and down. The parachute had deployed, as had the missile's inflatable floatation system, although all the instruments in the Bulava now suddenly went dead, powerless.

Still seated, Jon looked up at the early morning sun. In his mind's eye, he imagined the solar probe that InterOrbital had launched over two years ago. Sometime during his re-entry,

249

it had come close enough to reach out and touch the sun. And it had. Artificially inducing the eruption of a high-speed stream of solar wind.

The shock wave would strike Earth in minutes, the increased wind pressure compressing Earth's magnetosphere, allowing the solar wind's magnetic field to interact with Earth's, transferring tremendously increased energy into the magnetosphere and in doing so generating a powerful geomagnetic storm.

Jon's InterOrbital satellites would act to accentuate this storm, supersizing it, triggering a series of electromagnetic pluses. The resultant intense magnetic fields would in turn generate surging ground currents strong enough to burn out all the power lines and major electrical equipment on the planet.

Suddenly, as Jon sat there, the sky erupted. The southern aurora australis had surged northward and ignited the heavens with its brilliantly colored, dancing show of light. It was dramatic, entrancing, magical—fascinating to behold.

And Jon knew that the catastrophic event had commenced. Cities around the world were darkening. Man's world was going powerless, being taken off the grid. The Global Brain was being electrocuted. Humankind was being unplugged.

As the Plug device ran on modest electrical power, those wearing the implant would survive without injury. But their Plugs would be functionless and dead. People would have to start to think.

Jon was turning off the world. And the heavens appeared to be celebrating the promise of man renewed.

Ikaria had prepared, of course. All electrical equipment had been turned off, disconnected. The Ikarians had also stockpiled large transformers and installed powerful dampers functioning akin to lightning rods that would dump surges harmlessly into the ground. The island would be spared the devastating effects of the massive electromagnetic pluses.

Bathed in magical aurora light, Jon rose to stand tall, surveying his surroundings. He had landed in the South Pacific, within the territorial waters of the little-known Cook Islands, waters on which a group of Ikarian corporations had a decade ago taken out a hundred-year renewable lease—a lease on an exclusive economic zone of 690,000 square miles of ocean.

As far as the eye could see, in every direction, the ocean was brilliant green with an algae bloom. Jon had landed in the middle of one of Ikaria's free-floating algae farms. The exceptional sea-born algae had been engineered to be hardy, prolific, harmless to the environment, and of exceptionally broad nutritional value. These vast farms would soon come to the aid of and feed the needy, collapsed, devastated, unplugged world.

Also engineered into the algae was a unique inhibitor. Those consuming the algae would experience significantly suppressed fertility. World population reduction and control would be accomplished by way of charity. Diminishing the human population in this manner would address the need stated by Frédéric Oran. It would also allow the implementation of Jon's third basic starting principle of population control, only this time instead of operating insularly, it would be imposed on a global basis.

As Jon stood there, aglow with surreal, heavenly light, waiting for help to arrive, he thought of what was next. He questioned if a system of stateless capitalism, of anarcho-capitalism, was sufficient to meet the future objectives that he had in mind… He did not believe it was. He saw education and the media as controlling propaganda instruments currently being wielded by the powerful to promote their own interests.

He had grown concerned over the militia power held by enlarging private security firms. He realized that Ikaria would soon need a military, now that it was stepping into world affairs. Money would need to be raised for this. Infrastructure developed solely by capitalistic market forces left room for significant improvements...

Jon was also deeply concerned about Ikarian interests, for although there was free collective bargaining, the results were limited to being either some compromise or a case of zero-sum gain where businesses or workers achieved a more favorable deal. There was no mechanism to secure what was in the best interest for Ikaria, first as a civilization and secondly as a fundamental unit of human organization. Jon saw a role for a limited state here, and also for providing soft authoritarian leadership. He foresaw a small, limited government seated at the head of the table to ensure outcomes that would always be in the best interest of the Ikarian civilization and nation.

Jon concluded that he needed to assemble brilliant minds. Men devoted to the truth as the highest principle, truth and nothing but the truth, men with knowledge, but also with real-world experience. Such men could examine and discuss these issues, and others, and plan out Ikaria's next steps. For the planet had been saved. Mankind could now accept the challenge silently issued by *The Winged Figures of the Republic* of becoming truly great by reaching out for a seemingly impossible future.

A future that Jon now planned to see, having survived the space launch and splashdown, for as an Ikarian he planned to live well over a hundred years, and possibly even forget to die.

And Jon's memory released into his foremost thoughts the inspirational words spoken to him long ago by Frédéric Oran:

"After the dangers of the bomb and starvation in the Third World have come to pass, finally by gene manipulation, we achieve the eternal. People don't age. They die by accident. Then what should they do? They create evolution from the beginning! They create a superzoo with every possible mutation as part of a favorable environment, and we get back to where we are now! Finally, they communicate with other civilizations that are developing, and they all end up eternal. Then they decide not to fight anymore, no more star wars. There's a big meeting, and it's like Olympus because they're all gods and you're back to the original Greek concept of the gods of Olympus ruling the world! So that's how I see the future of the universe."

Niko Zinovii

Recommendations

• For those curious about the economics and politics of monarchy, democracy, and natural order, Hans-Hermann Hoppe's 2001 book *Democracy: The God that Failed* and his 2015 book *A Short History of Man: Progress and Decline* are recommended as a starting point, along with the 2005 pamphlet by Hans-Hermann Hoppe titled "Natural Elites, Intellectuals, and the State." All can be purchased from the Ludwig von Mises Institute. Hans-Hermann Hoppe is a German-born American political philosopher and Austrian School economist.

• *The UNESCO Courier*, the November 1991 issue, page 8–13, an "Interview with Jacques-Yves Cousteau"

• "With the Look of Eagles," by Oskar J. W. Hansen, a chapter published within the pamphlet *Sculptures at Hoover Dam*, by the U.S. Department of the Interior, 1976

Acknowledgements and Identifying Notations

- Algae that reduces human fertility is the idea of Hungarian-American physicist Leó Szilárd, presented in his magnificent 1961 science-fiction short story "The Voice of the Dolphins."
- The dialogue of Frédéric Oran—with the exception of Oran's opening question—consists of verbatim statements originally made by renowned undersea explorer and oceanographer Jacques-Yves Cousteau. The fictional character of Frédéric Oran is based on Jacques Cousteau.
- The twin bronzes in the story are *The Winged Figures of the Republic*, sculptures on display at Hoover Dam, created in 1935 by sculptor Oskar J. W. Hansen.
- When the character Jon speaks of the danger associated with focusing so intently on accessing gathered facts, he is loosely paraphrasing American political scientist and diplomat Henry Kissinger as spoken by Mr. Kissinger on April 17, 2015, during the "Dr. Henry Kissinger Fireside Chat with Eric Schmidt" presented by Talks at Google.
- Small parts of Jon's dialogue and narrative were derived from thoughts originally presented in various interviews by English writer and philosopher Aldous Huxley. The author of "Winged Men of the Lost Planet" wrote this story featuring a fictional protagonist who was familiar with the thoughts of Aldous Huxley.
- The economic principles and initial political recommendations introduced by Jon are based directly on the content of Hans-Hermann Hoppe's book *A Short History of Man: Progress and Decline*.

• Some wording used to describe *The Winged Figures of the Republic* is based on the sculptor's descriptions of his own work as presented in "With the Look of Eagles," by Oskar J. W. Hansen. Similarly, some wording used to describe the protagonist is also based on these descriptions provided by Mr. Hanson of his bronzes.

• When Jon recites "Whatever else a man may be, he is a mammal and mortal like the rest. His bones lie scattered and buried across the Earth," Jon is reciting the written words of American anthropologist Loren Eiseley.

A Note from the Author

This author hopes the reader appreciated this heroic and ideological utopian tale. It was inspired by *The Winged Figures of the Republic* sculptures at Hoover Dam, created by sculptor Oskar J. W. Hansen.

The objective of this tale was not to preach economic or political ideology but to stimulate thinking and to entertain. Thus the writing, although cerebral at times, touches only lightly on the economic and philosophical ideas presented.

Although this author presented a utopia of stateless capitalism, this author is not himself an anarcho-capitalist.

Regarding global usage of the Plug, this is in accordance with what is often observed with technological products. Upon initial release, such products do not work perfectly and are very expensive. Over time, the product is perfected. The price also tends to drop. At some point, the product functions almost flawlessly and is affordable to practically everyone.

Notes of interest:

The protagonist's miraculous recovery from cancer while living on Ikaria was based on the real-life recovery of Stamatis Moraitis who, in 1976, when he was in his mid-60s, was diagnosed with lung cancer—a diagnosis confirmed by a number of doctors—and given nine months to live. Instead of seeking treatment, Mr. Moraitis relocated from Florida to Ikaria, where he lived until his death in 2013. He died at the age of 102 years, cancer free.

In 2012, a number of media outlets reported that the island of Ikaria had expressed wishes to secede from Greece and be annexed by Austria. Although in a poll taken at that time 83% of Austrians surveyed were in favor of Ikaria leaving Greece to join their country, this did not occur.

The protagonist's launch into space via a Russian ICBM from a submarine was based on the Planetary Society's successful launch of an unmanned solar sail spacecraft, *Cosmos 1*, on June 21, 2005, from the Russian submarine K-496 *Borisoglebsk* in the Barents Sea.

Regarding a manned ICBM launch:

To this author's knowledge, this is the first science-fiction story in which a man launches into space from a submarine, riding inside a modified ICBM. This author's back-of-the-envelope calculations in regard to acceleration and g-force appear to display that a man could endure such a launch.

Given:
Average acceleration = (change in velocity)/(time elapsed)
(change in velocity)/(time elapsed) = Delta V/Delta t
Delta V = Final velocity - Initial velocity
Delta t = Final time - Initial time
To convert to Earth gravity = Acceleration/g
g = 9.80665 m/s^2

So, with an initial ICBM speed of 0 mi/s and a burnout final speed of 2.5mi/s, over 300 seconds, the acceleration would be 13.4112 m/s^2, and as 1 g = 9.80665 m/s^2, this scenario would generate 1.3675 g's over the trip from launch to burnout speed.

The solar sail launched by the Planetary Society was reportedly rocketed into space at 3.9772 mi/s. This scenario would generate 2.1756 g's from launch to burnout.

Assuming that the modified ICBM in this story reached the speed of sound within, say, the first 30 seconds, the g-force experienced by a pilot at that moment would be approximately 1.15 g's.

Astronauts launched into space normally experience a maximum g-force of around 3 g's during a rocket launch. The space shuttle takes 510 seconds to reach space, accelerating from 0 mi/s to 4.8611 mi/s, astronauts experiencing 1.56 g's over that trip.

Regarding re-entry: If using the standard ICBM re-entry speed of 4.3 mi/s over 120 seconds, the g-force would be 5.88 g's. In this story, however, re-entry would be much slower and slowed dramatically by parachutes near the end as opposed to missile impact speed. Modern pilots can typically handle a sustained 9 g's, and a typical person can handle about 5 g's. At approximately 9 g's, most humans black out.

Niko Zinovii
Santa Monica, California
5 August 2015

Niko Zinovii

Ending Note from the Author

I hope readers enjoyed or appreciated these tales in some way. I wrote the stories employing informed imagination, philosophical thought, and a bit of daydreaming. I consider my writing to be nonstandard, sci-fi.

My personal favorites from this collection are:

"Box of the Supermen"
"Fragile in the Sun"
"Painting Penelope"

In that order.

Niko Zinovii
Santa Monica, California
20 August 2015

niko@zinoviiartstudio.com

www.zinoviiartstudio.com

www.ingramcontent.com/pod-product-compliance
Lightning Source LLC
Chambersburg PA
CBHW030530030726
47495CB00004B/932